# JOSEPHINE'S
# GUEST HOUSE
# QUILT

# JOSEPHINE'S GUEST HOUSE QUILT

## Ann Hazelwood

Publishing

PADUCAH, KENTUCKY

Publishing

American Quilter's Society
5801 Kentucky Dam Rd,
Paducah, Kentucky 42003

**Library of Congress Cataloging-in-Publication Data**
Names: Hazelwood, Ann Watkins, author.
Title: Josephine's guest house quilt / by Ann Hazelwood.
Description: Paducah, KY : American Quilter's Society, [2016] | Series: East Perry County series ; 2
Identifiers: LCCN 2016024949 (print) | LCCN 2016031051 (ebook) | ISBN 9781604603910 (softcover) | ISBN 9781604604276 (e-book)
Subjects: LCSH: Quilts--Fiction. | Paranormal fiction. | GSAFD: Mystery fiction.
Classification: LCC PS3608.A98846 J67 2016 (print) | LCC PS3608.A98846 (ebook) | DDC 813/.6--dc23
LC record available at https://lccn.loc.gov/2016024949

EDITOR: ADRIANA FITCH
BOOK AND COVER DESIGNER: CHRIS GILBERT
PROOFREADER: CHRYSTAL ABHALTER
PRODUCTION MANAGER: SARAH BOZONE
DIRECTOR OF PUBLICATIONS: KIMBERLY HOLLAND TETREV

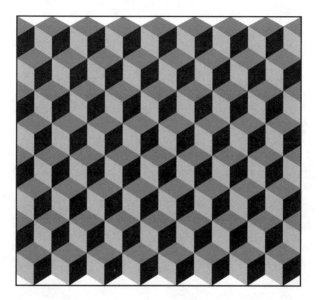

TUMBLING BLOCK

# THANK YOU

My love for family, writing, business, and quilts were instilled in me from my parents, Esther (Bachman) Meyer and G.L. (Fritz) Meyer. I feel they have been with me on this journey through East Perry County where we all grew up.

My success in these endeavors I owe to my immediate family, close friends, and my dedicated readership. I will be forever grateful to you all!

Love, Ann

# CHAPTER 1

"How about a little more to the left," I instructed. "No, that's a little too much. I think a little more to the right." I paused. "It could be a little higher, I think. Now don't go too high! Just keep your eye on the center, Cotton." I stepped further back from the house. "I think we're close! Hold it a bit longer. Ellie, what do you think?"

She slowly nodded.

"I think this is it!"

"Are you sure now, Miss Kate?" Cotton asked as he and his friend struggled to keep the sign in place. I stepped even further back to make sure. "Okay!" I shouted to Cotton and Ellie. "It's perfect!" Ellie clapped her hands as she cheered.

Cotton and his helper looked relieved as they secured the sign at the top of the porch of 6229 Main Street.

"Josephine's Guest House," Ellie announced as she gave me a little squeeze. "Congratulations!"

"I can't believe it!" I said, feeling overwhelmed. "Isn't Clark's sign beautiful? It's not too much, is it?"

"It's perfect, just like you said," Ellie said grinning. "I wish he were here to see it right now."

"I do, too," I added. "He won't be back till next week. He was certainly right about where to hang this.

"He'll be pleased, Kate," reassured Ellie.

"Thanks so much, guys," I said as the two young men came down from the ladders.

"I wasn't gonna give you much longer, Miss Kate," Cotton teased with his country accent. "Yup, it looks right nice!" He and his friend both looked up to admire their handiwork.

"How about you all come in for some of my homemade lemonade and chocolate chip cookies?" I offered.

"We'll take ours to go, if you don't mind, Miss Kate," Cotton suggested. "Susie's expectin' me and I'm already, late."

"That's fine, but how about you, Ellie?" I interrupted as she still gazed up at the sign.

"Count me in!" she said grinning.

We all went into the back sunporch where cookies and lemonade were waiting on my new wicker round table. I went to get paper cups of ice for the guys and Ellie helped herself.

"Here's a big bag of cookies to take with you, Cotton," I said handing him a plastic bag full. "Be sure you share them with Susie and Amy Sue."

He nodded and smiled. The two young men both left like happy little boys just given a treat for being good.

As I sat down next to Ellie, she said, "Well, you can't back out now, girlfriend. The sign is up and the word is out. Borna has a guest house, open for business!"

"Hold on there a minute," I warned. "I told you, no one is getting booked here till after my open house next week. I have some finishing touches to do and besides, I kind of like having this pretty big house to myself right now."

"Enjoy it while you can because I think you're going to have lots of guests," Ellie expressed. "Are you sure you don't want to come to the winery tonight? Kelly's been doing barbecue all day today. Remember how much you like his ribs?"

"It's tempting, Ellie," I acknowledged. "I want to get a few more flowers planted before the rain shower they're predicting. I'm also expecting Imy from the antique shop to make a delivery later today. She cut down a darling table for me, so I could use it as a coffee table up in the attic suite. I can't wait to see it."

"Man, I bet that girl has doubled her income since you came to town," Ellie teased. We both laughed at the truth of it.

"She's been a huge help," I noted. "She has a great eye for things and I wouldn't have been able to purchase Mrs. Bachmann's dining room furniture without her connections. I love it!"

"It is gorgeous! So who will be the first dinner guest to enjoy it?" Ellie asked with some hidden agenda.

"I think it'll be when Maggie and Carla visit from South Haven for my open house," I revealed. "It will be so special to have them here! I wish my son, Jack, could also be here. He said he may even bring his girlfriend. "

"So the two are still together?" Ellie wondered.

"I think they're pretty solid, now," I shared. "They've had some adjustments to make, but I think this may be the real deal for Jack. I sure hope so. She has made a huge difference in helping Jack adjust to his father's death."

"Does he ever talk about Clay's accident?" Ellie poured herself more lemonade.

"No, and I'm the same, I'm afraid," I admitted. "Clay's death from excessive drinking and his infidelity had to be put aside or I couldn't have gone on with my new life here in Borna. To think I first came here to put this property on the market and now it is my new home." It was all amazing to me.

"Your neighbor buddy helped," Ellie reminded with a smirk on her face. I chuckled at the memory.

"Yes, you did!" I said, almost choking on my lemonade. "You took me in, clothed and fed me. How could I ever leave you?" We both got the giggles. Ellie's generous offer for me to stay with her the first night I arrived here was most generous, since I was a total stranger to Borna. Thank goodness she lived right next door.

"Yeah, I think I surprised myself at the offer, but I guess I'm so used to talking and helping strangers at the winery, it came pretty easy," she explained. Ellie owned the Red Creek Winery, some miles from Borna. "I have to admit, when you went home for Christmas, I really thought you would decide to stay in South Haven. It certainly has more to offer than our little East Perry County."

"You are mistaken, my dear," I corrected. "Okay, no Borna beach." I snickered. "Jack has a life in New York, so besides my best friend, Maggie, and my housekeeper, Carla, there isn't anyone to keep me there. The Beach Quilters are dear to me, but Borna has quilters, too. It has the Friendship Circle you so graciously let me join. The house had such potential and the rolling hillsides here are like no other. There is nothing not to like!"

"You'll make quite the hostess and tour guide for your guest house, Kate," Ellie bragged.

"I hope so," I concurred. "Sometimes it takes fresh eyes to appreciate what's in front of you."

After Ellie left, I proceeded to plant more annuals here and there to fill in for some color in the new landscape. As I dug in the dirt, I felt so in touch with myself. This was something I was trying to recapture since I had become a widow. My mind drifted into the past.

It was surprisingly easy to leave the beach town of South

Haven where I grew up. Maggie and I had been friends since grade school. We didn't finish college because we both fell in love with guys who were anxious to marry us. Fortunately their careers took off, so we were privileged to be trophy wives and then, mothers. I had one son, Jack, and she had one daughter, Jill. We joked how in the future our Jack and Jill would be perfect together, just as in the storybook.

Maggie was truly shaken and sad when I told her I was moving to Borna. She knew Clay's death was hard on me, plus the unfortunate relationship I had developed with Clay's family was not pleasant. Clay had become the president of Meyr Lumber Company after his father died, years ago. Clay's brother James now became the head of the company after Clay's death. The friction developed when Clay left the property in Borna to me instead of his brother. When I kept the property instead of selling it, the situation became worse. It took me a while to realize, but getting a new start in Borna was just what I needed.

For the first time, I was experiencing some independence. Clay had made all the decisions and, despite my studies in interior design, he did not want me pursuing a career. I didn't realize till he was gone how many things in my life he decided. I watched Ellie with envy as she was living her dream with the winery. She made all her own decisions and was perfectly happy being single, as she participated in the Borna community. Her darling little house was next door to mine. It was a godsend, as I went back and forth with my house restoration. I would always owe her so much for being there for me physically as well as emotionally.

I got up from the grassy ground as I heard Imy pull in the drive with her pickup truck. She had her son with her, who frequently helped with the heavy lifting her job would sometimes require.

"You've met Jerry, haven't you, Kate?" Imy asked when she got out of the truck.

I nodded and smiled. "Nice of you to help, Jerry," I said, observing the covered table in the back of her truck.

"If you open the doors, Miss Meyr, we'll be able to get this table in the house," Jerry said politely.

"Oh sure," I said, jumping to the rescue. "Imy, did you tell Jerry we go to the attic with this?" Imy blushed with guilt and her son gave her a stern look.

We had to remove the legs of the table to get around the curved stairway, going up the attic. Everyone remained silent as we proceeded but once it was in place we all admired its location and beauty.

"I hope you'll be coming to the open house next week," I reminded Imy. "You are welcome as well, Jerry."

"I wouldn't miss it, Kate!" replied Imy. "I told both my boys they could come, but no takers, I'm afraid." Jerry smiled and went to the truck. "Thanks again, Kate. I'm glad you're happy with it."

The sun was going down, which was a favorite time of the day for me. The day's productivity gave me a sense of purpose. Little did I know I would not only be living in an old home in a new town, but also starting a business. I found myself becoming braver than I ever imagined!

While it was still light, I put the gardening tools away and walked back to the front of the house to admire the new sign. How did this happen? I had to trace the steps.

The idea of opening a guest house came from Clark McFadden, the local, famous woodcarver in Borna. I was fortunate to hire him for some custom cabinetry. His work was amazing, and we got to be good friends as he worked at my house throughout the winter. Clark was a simple, yet complicated man. He loved his artistic lifestyle living in a log cabin near Indian Creek. He was handsome like Sean Connery. He was single and had a dry sense of humor. We seemed to understand each other's lives without making us more than friends. He, like others, were concerned I would be leaving Borna once 6229 Main Street was restored. He started asking me what my future plans would be. First, he suggested I open a small bakery, because I loved to bake so much. I was the blueberry muffin queen from South Haven, but I didn't want it to be a career. South Haven was the blueberry capital of the world, which was where I learned to make such good blueberry muffins. My former husband, Clay had declared our home calorie free, so baking was not very well received.

I often complained to Ellie and Clark, there wasn't a place for folks to stay in Borna when they were visiting. I was surprised when I was in need of such a place and there was nothing available within twenty miles. So Clark suggested someone with a big house and sunporch, who enjoyed people, should consider opening a guest house. Of course, he was suggesting me. Sometimes it was hard to know when he was serious or teasing. This was not immediately well received, since I was just experiencing the independence of coming and going. He argued this business was perfect for someone who wanted to be in control of their schedule. I did listen and told him I would at least look into the idea.

So here I am, looking up at the fancy Josephine's Guest House sign.

I walked back to the sunporch and sat down near my guest list, which I had started for my open house. I had so many people to thank and so many folks were curious about the house now that the restoration was finished. In the short eight months since I arrived, I had met a lot of folks from the surrounding villages. They were teeny tiny and, with exception of Dresden, they were all under 300 people in their population count. These were all settlements that came from Germany in the early 1800s. Each community had its own history and namesake. Most of them were Protestant and the rest were Catholic. They financially supported their churches in ways I couldn't believe for so few people. There were some failed attempts to merge some of the villages together to save on services, but their independence prevailed.

East Perry's biggest employer was East Perry Lumber Company, located in Borna. They supplied and purchased lumber across the country. Their procurement range included southern Missouri, southern Illinois, western Kentucky, and northwest Tennessee. Having been married to a family in the lumber business, I knew this company to be enormous and successful! Yes, there WAS a relationship between Meyr Lumber and East Perry Lumber at one time.

Everyone I met here was very friendly except my potential realtor, Blade Schuessler. He was a shady character from day one and became nasty and belligerent when I decided to not list 6229 Main Street for sale. He did everything in his power to scare me into going back to South Haven. He had arranged a profitable deal with James Meyr to sell it to him as soon as I put it on the market. When I made a firm decision to move here permanently, he broke into my house on New Year's Eve. I don't know for sure what he had planned to do to me, because I awoke to the noise and came downstairs. We had words, I went for the light switch, we struggled, and he hit me and landed on top of me. It sucked the air right out of me. It was horrifying, but in the rage he didn't hear Clark come in the back door. When Clark saw the struggle in the window from the street, he knew there was trouble. Blade had a knife and pulled it out when he saw Clark approach him. Clark's dominant figure prevailed after a struggle. He quickly secured him and took him out to the car to lock him up until help arrived.

I hit my head hard when I fell to the floor in the struggle. I had cuts on my arms from the broken glass of a fallen picture. I was mentally shaken, but refused treatment when the sheriff's office arrived. Blade was taken away and to my satisfaction was sentenced to fifteen years behind bars. I didn't want to think about an early parole, but anything was possible. I was determined this one mean man was not going to define my experience in this loving community. I had to put this all aside and celebrate the good that was happening.

I began my list with my special guests from South Haven, Maggie and Carla. Now I could add the members of the Friendship Circle. Ellie made sure I met them, even before I decided to move here. They were all diverse in age and interests, which made it easy for me to fit in. Besides Ellie and me, four of them were single, which was nice. Some had moved back to East Perry because of aging parents or a divorce. They took turns meeting in their homes. I had not yet had the pleasure of entertaining them, so I was happy to have them attend my open house.

I had worker friends like Clark. He promised me he would return from his trip in time for my open house.

Cotton and his wife, Susie, had been a great help to me from day one. Cotton had been working for Blade, but I rescued him from the monster by giving him steady work. He was so appreciative and someone I desperately needed in my new environment and business venture.

Next on my list were folks I had done business with. Harold, from Harold's Hardware store was so friendly and helpful. He and his wife would have to be invited. There was Marv, from Marv's Grocery and Bar, just doors down from my place. His friendship and amazing food were great comforts to me. I couldn't forget Sharla Lee, the director of the Lutheran Heritage Museum, and her assistant, Gerard. She knew everyone and had a way of connecting folks where they needed to be. She was the happy, colorful face of the community. Her talents were many and I couldn't wait to get to know her better. Her helpers were so gracious in helping me research Doc Paulson and his wife, Josephine, the originators of my new home at 6229 Main Street. I wasn't sure the county knew how lucky they were to have this kind of resource.

I couldn't forget Ellie's employees at the Red Creek Winery. Trout, her bartender, and Kelly, her cook, were going to be catering my open house. Kelly could make anything I desired. I would have to go over my list with Ellie to make sure I wouldn't forget anyone. This was going to be an event like no other!

It was now pretty dark, so I reached to turn on the side lamp. I continued making notes about the food and little details. It had been a long time since I had entertained. I was a visual person and I wanted to picture it all in my mind.

As my mind wandered, I thought about Josephine, the secretive, former resident in this house. How would she receive the idea of all the town's people coming through her former home? How would her spirit handle complete strangers, once they started to book rooms at the guest house? She had such a private life in this house. They say when her husband saw patients in the little room on the first floor, Josephine was out of sight. Ellie and I knew she had to spend time somewhere, especially making quilts, so we determined it must have been up in the attic. It was sizable and had a great view of the street from a front window. We also assumed, if rumors were correct, Josephine was hiding from Doc when he was drinking.

I bonded to this woman, whom I never met, when I found a quilt hidden in an upstairs hall closet. It said many disturbing things. Biblical sayings in black thread were embroidered throughout the quilt, asking for forgiveness. There were also many references to death. I wondered if Josephine blamed herself for her husband's drinking and for them not having any children. I was married to an alcoholic, so I certainly could relate to that feeling. I would never know her actual thoughts, but it did help me with my own forgiveness. I didn't want to go through the rest of my life angry at Clay. He lost his life for his mistakes. There couldn't be any worse punishment. It certainly helped living here in Borna, away from the constant reminders of his work and family.

I sensed that Josephine knew I loved this house with all my heart. I kept her quilt hidden and only wanted to honor her, not expose her. Her spirit was here, no doubt. On the second floor, there was the frequent appearance of warm daylight in the middle of the night. When I would awake, thinking it was morning, I knew it was not a natural experience. What I couldn't explain was being able to go back to sleep with a warm, loving feeling. It was like someone was embracing me with love. Ellie was the only person I had shared this with. It was unfair for people to think the house was haunted, because I only felt love. I didn't know if anyone else had experienced what I had. It would remain our secret!

The excitement of Maggie and Carla actually coming to Borna was unbelievable. I wanted to show them everything around the county. It was such a beautiful time of the year. Blooms were popping and the shades of green in the landscaping looked like they came out of a painting. The open house would be a perfect way for them to meet all the folks I had talked about. Maggie and I always celebrated our birthdays together, since childhood. Mine June 17th and hers was June 19th. Even though it was only May, I wanted this to be our celebration together. She always teased me about being older than she was. I wanted us to christen my new set of antique dining room furniture. I would bake her favorite red velvet cake and perhaps Carla would be willing to make her delicious angel food cake, which we both enjoyed. My present to Maggie would be a crazy quilt, which I had purchased some months back from Imy's Antique Shop. I knew she would love it, even though she had several of them. I couldn't wait to catch up with all the South Haven gossip.

*What a grand time we'll have,* I thought.

As I wandered up to bed, my mind went to Jack. Oh how I wished I could share each day's experiences with him. He was so busy in his world. Visiting him in New York would be a challenge for me once I started receiving guests. Who would be my first guest, anyway? How will I feel with total strangers sleeping under my roof? Would I feel safe? How would I ever sleep with all the unknowns to this new decision?

# CHAPTER 2

The early morning light and the smell of my programmed coffeemaker had me arising earlier than usual. This morning Cotton was expected to come over and hang the guest quilt in the entryway. I had commissioned my Friendship Circle friend Ruth Ann to make me a signature quilt which guests could sign. I loved signature quilts and this would be a wonderful memory quilt as time went along. She made amazing quilts and had created a studio in her living quarters above the Lueder's Mercantile, just down the street. After much debate, she and I decided on a Tumbling Block pattern. The colors were burgundy, cream, and black to match the entry hall's Oriental rug. The cream piece would be perfect for the signatures. I felt somewhat guilty about having someone else make the quilt, but I had no time. Ruth Ann was delighted as she occasionally sold her quilts to make a little extra money.

I almost went down the stairs in my bathrobe, until I remembered this place was frequented by workmen at any time. I quickly put on jeans and a T-shirt and dashed down the stairs. I took my coffee outdoors, where the spring temperature was perfect. I was delighted at the early blooms of tulips and crocuses, plus buds on the lilac bushes which were ready to burst. I couldn't wait to find out if they were white or lilac. I wondered how many years ago they were planted and by whom. I was about to go back to the sunporch when Cotton pulled in the drive. I was surprised to see that Susie, his wife, was with him.

"I asked Susie to come along, in case we need some help," Cotton explained.

"That's great," I replied. "Where's Amy Sue this morning?" I asked as we all went in the house. "She is growing so quickly. I would love to have seen her."

"Oh, Miss Kate, she is such a handful now," Susie remarked. "She would be a terror in your house, plus her grandma didn't mind keepin' her for a while. I can't wait to see what all you've done to the house since I've been here last."

"How about having a cup of coffee before we get started?" I offered.

"No thanks," said Cotton rubbing his stomach. "Susie's mom done fixed us a big breakfast this mornin'. Do you have the rod and quilt ready?"

"Sure, but do you mind getting the ladder up from the basement?" I asked, looking helplessly at Cotton.

"Will do!" he nodded. "I ain't done nothin' like hangin' a quilt before, Miss Kate, but we'll get her done."

We did get the task of hanging the quilt accomplished, but not without a lot of adjustments and opinions. It had to be low enough for folks to sign, but not too low for everyone's hands to brush as they walked by. I stood back, hoping once again Josephine would approve of the guest quilt, just as I did for the sign above the front porch.

"Oh, Miss Kate, this is a mighty fine quilt," Susie admired as she stepped back. "The blocks look so real and yet I see stars. I can't believe someone made this. This pattern's mighty powerful."

I had to snicker in delight of her comment. Susie lived a

sheltered life, and I'm sure she couldn't believe a lot of things based on what Cotton reported to me.

"Thank you, Susie," I responded. "Please be sure to compliment Ruth Ann when you come for the open house. I'll get my phone to take a couple of photos."

"Well, if there's nothing else you need me to do, we need to rescue Amy Sue from her grandma," Cotton reminded.

"Thanks so much," I said following them to the back door. "Susie, I'll need you to help clean next week, don't forget!"

"Oh I haven't," she enthusiastically said. "It will be my pleasure.

Hanging the quilt was one of my final steps to being ready to open Josephine's Guest House. I stood back to imagine what it might look like when it would be filled with signatures. Ruth Ann gave me a special black, permanent marking pen for people to use when they signed the quilt, so the signatures would all be alike. The oblong piece of quilted art truly complemented the entryway as guests would come through the front door. My goal was to only have signatures from folks who actually stayed at my guest house, not the general public.

To the right, as guests entered, was the small reception office I had created for guests to check in and pay their bill. It was the same little room where Doc Paulson received his patients. I found that to be quite charming. I placed brochures from the local attractions on a small side table between two chairs. I also laid out printed sheets of my guest house rules, which I copied from various guest houses on the internet. Something already told me there would be some things I hadn't even considered when you bring total strangers into your home.

My cell went off showing me the name of my dear friend, Maggie.

"Good morning, girlfriend," I greeted.

"Same to you," she echoed. "I'm trying to pack for this big trip to Borna and wondered if you could give me any advice."

I chuckled. "Well, you're heading south, my dear, so the temperature is a little warmer than what you've been experiencing. I was just outside this morning, admiring my tulips. By the time you get here, my lilac bushes should be in full bloom. The weather's been great, so just bring a light jacket."

"So what about this open house. Is it going to be very fancy?" she asked, giving me another chuckle.

"Not to worry," I said more seriously. "This is an afternoon event which may go into the evening hours, but nothing fancy is required. Most folks around here are pretty casual, unless it's church or a special occasion."

"Well this sure sounds like one, if you ask me!"

"That it is!" I boasted. "Just think, you and Carla will be my first overnight guests."

"Oh honey, I wonder what that will cost?" We both laughed.

"It'll cost you some fresh blueberries from the farmer's market and some scones from the Golden Bakery," I said, surprising her.

"Consider it done!"

The thought of blueberries from home excited me.

"Carla is so excited about coming. She's not been to Missouri or any other state, I don't think. She almost didn't find someone to take Rocky, but I think her next door neighbor decided to help her out."

"Oh good, how is Rocky?" I asked feeling guilty about making her take Clay's dog when I left.

"I have no idea. Carla said she'd be happy to cook while she's there."

"Not on her life!" I insisted. "She is on vacation as a guest and I want her to enjoy it. Other than having a nice birthday dinner here, I thought I'd introduce you to the local country fare. The Red Creek Winery has great ribs and gumbo. Marv's, just down the street, has great hamburgers, chicken, and award-winning chili."

"Are you trying to fatten us up? Mark's already on my case about losing weight!"

"Never mind him," I instructed. "I know he doesn't approve of you coming, so I really appreciate you insisting. You will have a wonderful time and you're only here for the weekend. This is country living at its best. Is there any gossip from the Beach Quilters?"

"I stopped in at Cornelia's yesterday and she's still hanging in there, so I didn't ask her any questions. She's not her perky self, so I'm sure things are not good. She is sending along a fabric pack for you. It's all polka dots, because she knows you love them."

"How sweet of her," I said smiling. "I gave so much of my collection to Carla so I wouldn't have to move it all here. Polka dots make me smile and it will be a happy remembrance of her. I was thinking of polka dot curtains for my kitchen. I have to incorporate them somehow. Maybe I'll make Amy Sue something cute out of it."

"Who's Amy Sue?" Maggie asked with sarcasm in her voice.

"Oh, she's Cotton and Susie's little one-year-old," I explained.

"She is so cute. They both help me out with things around here. You'll meet the two of them at the open house. I don't think they'll be bringing her. You know, I'm not allowing guests to bring children to my guest house. Some places don't. Do you think I'm being a snob about that?"

"Not at all!" Maggie snickered. "When I travel, especially at a B&B, I don't relish sharing my time with the little monsters."

"Maggie, that's a little harsh," I said picturing monsters running about. "It adds a whole other dimension to the place, which I'm not prepared for."

"Before I forget, rumors are flying around that Sandra and James may be headed for divorce," Maggie announced.

I couldn't believe it.

"No one has seen Sandra. I heard she's been very depressed. I'm sure the divorce has to do with his drinking."

"Oh man, I'm sorry to hear it," I said. "I was never close to her. The high society image she always projected was never something I aspired toward, but I do feel her pain. I'm glad it never affected me that badly with Clay. I guess, because of his travel, I didn't see as much of his behavior as she might have with James."

When I hung up with Maggie, I felt very sad. I brushed aside the negative thoughts and wondered how different my life would be if I had stayed in South Haven.

I was startled when there was a knock at the back door. I was surprised to see it was Ruth Ann.

"What a nice surprise!" I said, greeting her at the door.

"I was curious to see if you had the quilt on the wall," she explained, as she came in smiling.

"Oh, come this way and have a look!"

We walked into the entry room. Her eyes lit up, as if she were pleased.

"It's just perfect there, Kate," she complimented.

I nodded in agreement. "You did a great job," I said, beaming. "I'm glad you signed it too. People will want to know all about it. I know it will be a great conversation piece for my guests."

"This is a great advertisement for me, too," she said grinning. "I am so honored to have it here where so many folks will see it."

"Well, let's hope so," I said cautiously. "I've never owned any kind of business before."

"That's another reason I came by, Kate." There was mystery in her voice.

"Okay, so let's go sit out back on the sunporch," I suggested. "Would you like some iced tea or fresh lemonade?"

Ruth Ann's eyes were everywhere as she looked over the rooms. "Not for me, thanks. I can't leave Mom and Dad for very long, which brings up my news." I kept silent. "I'm putting Dad in an assisted living place and Mom is going into the nursing care section. I can't physically manage them any longer. My back keeps going out. They need occasional lifting and I just can't do it. I'm so afraid they are going to start having serious falls. I feel terrible about it, but I have no choice."

"I'm so sorry, Ruth Ann," I said, feeling her pain. "You've been so good to them, and you're doing the right thing before something happens. It was such an expense for you to put in that elevator!"

She nodded. "I saw this coming, of course, and it's going to be very expensive," she confessed. "I need your advice about an idea I have."

"Shoot!"

"I'll keep the building, of course, since we've put a lot of money into the living quarters upstairs, but the downstairs is such a wasted space right now," she described. "I'm thinking of turning it into a banquet hall. We really need another choice for local people to have weddings and events besides the church halls. It already has a modest kitchen downstairs, which I'd have to update for commercial use, of course. I think I could handle the occasional activity." She looked at me with worry. "The only other person I have shared this with is my cousin, who can do a lot of the renovation for me. He's in the construction business."

"It's such a wonderful idea," I responded with excitement.

"Do you really think it is?" Her face lit up. "I have to say, when you decided to do a guest house, it really got me thinking more about it. I think we can feed business off each other."

"I do, too," I answered, excited of the very thought.

"I'd like a small room walled off in the back for smaller events. There are organizational groups that could have meetings and dinners there. I could even hang some of my quilts on the walls."

I grinned, picturing her description. "So is there anything I can do to be helpful?" I asked with excitement.

"Just your approval is all I need, right now," she acknowledged. "I think I'm going to call it Lueder's Hall, so we can keep a bit of the history going. I thought about just calling it Lueder's Mercantile, like it was called originally, but folks would think it was a retail outlet."

"You're right," I said, picturing the sign. "I like it. The ole timers around here will like it as well."

"You have brought fresh eyes to this community, Kate," Ruth Ann complimented "You have inspired me and I think your guest house is going to be very successful!"

"Thanks so much," I said, feeling proud. "I hope you keep me posted on your progress."

"After I get Mom and Dad settled next week, I'll try to concentrate on everything," she said as her mind reveled in thought.

I walked her to the car and could sense I gave her some sense of relief with my approval. There was no question we were both taking a risk in this small town. I may not have guests and Lueder's Hall may remain empty.

# CHAPTER 3

My to-do list was growing for today. There were many loose ends related to having this open house. First on my list was making a stop at Harold's Hardware. It had been my first visit when I came to Borna. I had to start cleaning my house to put it on the market, and I had no cleaning supplies. It was a revelation in learning what I needed, as I'd had a cleaning lady my entire married life. Harold was very jolly and helpful, to say the least. He saw me immediately as I walked in the door.

"Say, Miss Meyr, we got your nice invitation to your open house next week," he happily announced. "It was mighty nice for you to include us. We'll be there with bells on."

"Of course, you guys were the first on my list."

He gave out a loud, hearty laugh. "Can I help you find anything today?" he asked while finishing up a paint order.

"You know, I think I have finally found my way around the place," I bragged, and Harold gave a chuckle.

It didn't take me long to find the few things on my list, but to my surprise I had to stand in line to checkout. It was obvious he had a popular business. I had a sense that someone was watching me, so I glanced to my right and saw Ben Hecht staring at me with a big smirk on his face as he held a toothpick in his mouth. I quickly turned away. Ben had rudely interrupted me one day when I was getting a lunch order at Marv's place. He was one of Blade's nasty friends who blamed me for putting his buddy in jail. Blade had mentioned he had friends in town, and I wondered if they would be trouble for me. Only time would tell, but my friends advised me never to back down or act afraid of any of them.

"Sorry for your wait," Harold said in his friendly voice. "Say, do you think our friend Clark will make it back in time for your party?"

"I hope so," I said, picking up my package.

"I bet he will," Harold said with certainty. "He's been gone quite a while and I bet you miss him."

"Now, Harold, you have this all wrong, as I told you before," I lightly protested, "We are not an item! You were so nice to pass on his name to me for my custom woodwork. He's done a beautiful job. You'll be able to see it when you come to the open house."

He grinned at the thought. "Like I told you, Clark would have never taken your job if he didn't have a real fondness for you," he reminded me. "I heard you'd been out to his place." Harold gave me a wink. "It's something, isn't it?"

"Harold, what am I going to do with you?"

He busted out in another chuckle.

I took my two bags in hand, and Ben quickly made his way out of the door before me.

"See you, Harold," I said giving him a wave. As I headed toward my car door, there leaned Ben, right against my driver's door. "Excuse me, is there something you have to say to me?" I boldly asked, wanting to push him aside.

He smirked again. I remembered in the bar how horrid his breath smelled. He removed his toothpick. "You're a feisty one, just like I heard," he said, moving away from my car door.

I was hoping Harold was looking out the window.

I didn't respond as I quickly got in my car. He watched me pull away, and it gave me the creeps. I'm sure he was somehow reporting to his jailbird friend.

I traveled on down the road to the closest grocery store, which was very small. It was fine for most of what I usually needed. On this visit, I was pleasantly surprised to see shelves loaded with trays of flowers for the planting season displayed outside the door. I got excited, knowing there was much more I wanted to do to the outside garden area this summer. I put aside a tray of red impatiens and a few hostas for the shaded area around my patio. I also pulled aside a tray of marigolds and red geraniums. They were sure to find a spot somewhere. Loading my car was another reminder that my Mercedes would have to go. My intent was to find an SUV or a Jeep for these country roads. I could have taken Clay's SUV after his death, but the thought of him using it to see other women was revolting to me.

After I added a couple of grocery bags to my car, I was ready to head home. I passed Imy's Antique Shop thinking it would have been fun to stop, but not with groceries in the car. I did everything I could mentally to dismiss Ben Hecht's nasty encounter. Was he stalking me? Was there more to this?

As I pulled in my driveway, Ellie pulled up behind me.

"Hey, Kate," she called out as she rolled down her car window. "Kelly is doing brisket tonight. Are you up for coming out for dinner?"

"Oh, I don't know, Ellie," I complained. "I have so much to do."

"You can't be too busy to eat," she reminded. "I promise

I'll join you so we can catch up." It was hard to ever refuse Ellie as she was always so good to me.

"Okay, just for a bite to eat, maybe around 6:00 p.m.," I conceded.

"Awesome!" she yelled as she pulled out of the drive and waved.

I looked in my full-sized bedroom mirror to size up what I could wear for the evening. I decided on jeans and a denim jacket. Was this going to be my uniform for Borna? In South Haven I felt I was always being judged on my appearance, whether I was at the grocery store or country club. I pulled back my hair and sprayed on my favorite perfume. This would have to do.

I rushed down the stairs and passed the guest quilt. I smiled at the attractive addition to the house. It represented the future, as names would be added.

*It might be nice to add the year too,* I thought.

Carla and Maggie would be the first to sign it. How special to have the first guests sign it from my home town!

It was a clear, pretty spring evening as I drove along the scenic roads. Days would now become longer, which suited me just fine. When I got to the top of the hill to Ellie's winery, I had to stop and admire the view once again. She had purchased a dandy little place and fixed it up to be romantic and inviting for tourists passing by.

I walked into a fairly sparse crowd and recognized a few familiar faces. I went to the bar where I found Ellie and Trout both pouring wine.

"Hey, Kate! Good to see you again," greeted Trout. "I hear you're having dinner with us tonight."

"I am and it smells pretty good from here," I complimented.

"I have a table put aside for us over there." Ellie pointed to the best table with an incredible view. "I'll be right over!"

I nodded and walked toward the table. Each table had red checkered tablecloths and a lit candle for the evening. When I got seated, I was approached by a nice looking man carrying what looked like a computer bag.

"Excuse me," he said, holding his hand out for me to acknowledge, "my name is Carson Jones. Ellie tells me you are opening a guest house here in Borna."

"Hi, I'm Kate Meyr," I responded, shaking his hand. "It's not open just yet." He put his bag on another chair as if he wanted an invitation to sit down.

"I'm asking because I travel this area a lot and sometimes I don't get all my business done in a timely manner and need a place to stay over." He was coming across with charm, for sure.

"What business is that, Mr. Jones?" I asked, wanting to keep it short.

"I'm a wine rep," he began. "I service many of these small wineries and bars in these small communities. I've had this territory for quite a while and really enjoy all the folks around here." His voice was deep and pleasant. "I also represent wine accessories and a small amount of restaurant equipment. Ellie's been buying from me since she opened."

*I bet she doesn't mind that one bit,* I thought.

"Oh, I see you've both met," Ellie said as she brought the two of us a glasses of wine. "Carson has been a big help to us. I don't know who knows more about wine, Trout or Carson!"

"You're too kind, Ellie," he blushed. "I want to hear more about your friend's guest house." His eyes were pouring directly into mine.

"Would you like to join us for a drink?" Ellie asked flirtatiously. "Do you mind, Kate?"

Actually, I did rather mind, but I could see Ellie was delighted to make the offer.

"That's fine," I nodded.

"Thanks Ellie, but I need to be on my way," he responded, pulling out his chair. "I'll be needing a room now and then, so keep me posted when you're open. Here's my card."

*Is it always this easy to get customers?* I wondered. I took his card, reminding myself I had none to give him in return.

"Kate's place is right on Main Street in the ole Doc Paulson house," Ellie explained.

"Why yes," he quickly responded. "It's the large house that's been vacant for some time?"

I nodded with a smile.

"What a fine house and a perfect location, I might add! What have you named it?"

"Josephine's Guest House," I boldly stated. "I named it after the doctor's wife."

"I like that very much," he grinned. "I'm sure most folks will think you are Josephine, right?"

"They might," Ellie jumped in to say.

I could tell Ellie was starting to feel left out of the conversation.

"I want to treat you both to your dinner tonight, if you'll let me," he offered. "You both have a lot to celebrate. Kate, you will be a charming hostess and I wish you the best of luck with your new endeavor."

"Thank you, but your gesture isn't necessary," I said, feeling a little embarrassed.

"I insist," he said, getting ready to leave. "You girls, enjoy!"

Ellie was quick to walk him to the door, as if she had something to tell him. Carson's appearance was tasteful and impeccable, not the type you would typically see on a day-to-day basis around here. There was something a little too friendly about him, but Ellie obviously thought he was okay.

When Ellie returned, I could tell her mood had changed. She was more somber looking. "He'll make a great guest for you, Kate," she remarked with a serious tone.

"He'd make a great guest for you, Miss Ellie," I teased. "You're a little smitten with this guy, aren't you?"

She looked shocked at my remark.

"I'm afraid it shows. I don't blame you!" I tried to make light of my comment.

"Oh, Kate, he's just a great guy that has been fun to visit with when he comes around," Ellie calmly responded.

"Is he available?" I asked to get a reaction. My gut said he was married.

"Well, he's actually going through a divorce," Ellie said like she didn't want anyone to hear.

"I should have guessed," I said, quickly making a judgment. "That's usually the scenario with a traveling salesman. I can tell you all about it."

Ellie looked at me sternly. "I don't think that's fair, Kate," she defended. "Not everyone is like your Clay. It sounds like his wife has some issues, and he's tired of it all."

"I bet she does have issues!" I said sarcastically. "He's definitely charming and good looking, as was my Clay. I bet he is quite popular with the ladies." Now I knew I had spoken too bluntly, when I saw the look on Ellie's face. This was a side of Ellie I had not seen. She always indicated she had no use for any man in her life. "I'm sorry, Ellie, that was cruel and judgmental," I blurted. "You know him much better than I do."

Ellie looked down. "Let me go check on dinner," she said, leaving me at the table.

I never had a cross word with Ellie, ever. I found it very interesting the way she reacted to my impression. She never mentioned this guy to me, so there was no reason to think he was someone special. Was there more to this?

The brisket was delicious and Ellie and I continued to make small talk through dinner, as different folks stopped by our table to say hello. The topic of Carson Jones was dropped. I wanted to share with Ellie my experience at Harold's Hardware, where I ran into Ben Hecht, but we were never alone the rest of the evening. When I said good-bye to go home, Ellie was not her bubbly self. We did not exchange hugs as we so often did.

As I was driving home, I hated I was turning into a man-hater of sorts. Carson was too much of a reminder of the ladies man who cheated on me. I promised I would never bring up his name around Ellie ever again. I also hoped he would not request a reservation in my guest house.

I was sleepy from the two glasses of wine, so I went directly upstairs to shower and get ready for an early rest. I thought about calling Jack, but didn't feel up to talking to anyone. I had spoken enough tonight.

Just as I was pulling back the covers, I noticed from the street window to my bedroom there were flashing lights. I pulled the curtains back ever so slightly, and saw that there was a truck pulled to the side of the road in front of my house, across the street. I figured it was someone with car problems who had to slow down or wait for help. When I closed the curtain, I had a disturbing thought. The truck looked like the same one that Ben Hecht was leaning on at Marv's and Harold's. Was he staring up at me to see if I would respond? I sat on the side of the bed, wondering what to do. I had my alarm on, so I shouldn't be afraid of him breaking in, like Blade did. There was no one to call. I was certain Ellie was still at the winery.

I took a deep breath and reminded myself I was a grown woman who was not going to be intimated in this town, especially from such a weird guy like Ben Hecht. Would his friends ever forget about my past encounter with Blade? I had to send a message that I would be going about my usual business. All of a sudden, the truck gunned the motor and took off. Was the driver satisfied he had managed to get noticed by me? It certainly wasn't anyone with car problems.

I crawled into bed feeling very unsettled, but exhausted. I wanted to think of pleasant things. If Clark were in town, I would consider calling him for advice. He always seemed to be so sensitive to my challenges. Clark was not a cell phone person. He discouraged being interrupted with his phone going off while working. I tried to respect that request when he worked here. He told me he would show up when he could and he did. He was a simple kind of guy who was honest and caring. Why weren't there more guys like him in this world?

# CHAPTER 4

The next two days were filled with making beds with my brand new linens and double checking my list that grew each day. This would be a good test to see if I had thought of everything my guests would need. Carla and Maggie would be arriving tomorrow after a long day's drive. Company was comin', as many locals called it.

There had been no word from Ellie, so I decided I had a good excuse to call her and ask if everything was set for my catered order for my open house. She sounded like her old self when she answered, but I still felt there was some sort of wedge between us which wasn't there before. I wish she had just opened up about how she really felt about Carson and the subject would have been settled. She was a smart, grown woman. I didn't want to insinuate anything nor make her feel bad.

"Trout will deliver everything in the morning, so not to worry," Ellie nicely reported.

"Great! You know tomorrow Maggie and Carla arrive. They have heard so much about you. I was hoping you'd come by tomorrow evening to meet them, instead of waiting till the open house."

She paused. "I'm anxious to meet them," she responded. "I could probably stop by on my way to the winery tomorrow evening."

"Oh, I would love that, Ellie," I said, feeling relieved. I took a deep breath. "Ellie, are you and I okay with each other?"

I asked with some hesitation.

"Oh, Kate, we're good," she confirmed. "I was just taken aback with your impression of Carson, that's all. You made a pretty quick, false judgment about him."

"I know, and I apologize," I said sincerely, wanting to drop the subject.

"So how are the RSVPs coming along?" Ellie asked to move the topic of conversation.

"Very good, but Ruth Ann says folks around here only respond when they are not coming, so if that's true, I'd say I'll have a nice showing."

"She's right," Ellie added. "Well, if you think of anything else, give me a ring. I'll see you tomorrow evening."

"Thanks, Ellie." I hung up the phone feeling much better.

I picked up my cell to confirm with Maggie, but it went to voice mail. I then tried Carla.

"Good to hear from you, Kate," Carla immediately answered. "We're excited about the trip and Maggie said we'd be there around dinner time. This is a big step for me, I'll have you know."

I had to laugh. I loved Carla's down to earth personality. She was a godsend to me as I struggled with my marriage to Clay. I was so happy I could give her some joy after all she had done for me.

"That's why I'm checking on you guys," I said, chuckling. "I don't want you to back out!" She assured me that was not going to happen.

After hearing from Ellie and Carla, I became energized. I felt like baking, of course, but I had arranged for Anna to bring all the baked goods. She was even picking up coffee cake from Mrs. Grebing, so Carla and Maggie could have it for breakfast.

It was still daylight, so I decided to go outdoors to water my new flowers. The weather was delightful, and the forecast was holding while my visitors would be here. Cotton was doing a fine job keeping things looking nice outdoors, and Susie was satisfactory with cleaning, for now anyway. There was a lot she would have to learn. She was so worried about breaking things that she would hardly move anything that might be too fragile.

I had just put my car into the garage for the evening, when Clark pulled into the driveway with his SUV. I couldn't believe it. He got out of the car smiling, but he looked exhausted.

"Hey there, woman, how are you?" he asked in his familiar, pleasant voice.

"I'm great! Did you just get back in town?" I eagerly asked.

"I drove 650 miles today, I'll have you know," he said, taking off his hat and shaking his hair back.

"Wow, that's a long day! How about coming in for a drink? I'd like to hear about your trip."

"Oh no, I'm ready to hit the sack." He sighed. "I called into Ellie's place to have an order ready for me to take home. After I eat, I'm done for today. Say, you have a big day coming up. The sign out front looks good. Cotton did okay."

"Well, with a little guidance from me, of course," I said, blushing. "So can I expect you to come Sunday afternoon?"

He gave me his familiar pause again. "I suppose so," he finally said. "You know I'm not much for crowds and small talk." I laughed and knew it would be a stretch to see him come.

"Carla and Maggie arrive tomorrow!" I happily announced. "I can hardly wait to see them. I am very anxious for you to meet them."

"I'll see what I can do," he said, giving in to my request.

"Hey, you've done more planting since I've been here."

"Do you like it?" I looked for a response. "I couldn't resist. I wanted everything to be as inviting on the outside as the inside. We could use some rain to keep all this looking good."

"Everything looks great." He shook his head like I was being silly. "Well, I thought I'd just stop by and see how you were doing. I never know about you." We laughed, but little did he know, and that was okay by me.

"I'm glad you stopped by. Take care." I waved as he got in his SUV.

Off he went and I felt a sense of comfort knowing he was back. Whether he came to the open house would remain to be seen. At least I put in my personal request!


The next day at 4:00 in the afternoon I heard a car honking in my driveway. I looked out the dining room bay window and couldn't believe my eyes. My South Haven buddies were finally here in person! I ran out the door in excitement. They both were so busy looking about the place, they hardly noticed me. I couldn't hug each of them fast enough.

"Welcome to Borna!" I greeted with enthusiasm.

"Oh, Kate, you are in a piece of heaven, aren't you?" Maggie said when she released me from my bear hug.

"I can't believe my eyes," claimed Carla as she gave me a kiss on the cheek. "You are right smack in the middle of Main Street."

"Well, this is my new home," I blurted out. "What do you think?" They were somewhat speechless as they looked about. "Come on in. We'll get your luggage later."

"Your flowers and yard are lovely," Maggie complimented

as we walked toward the sunporch. "I just can't believe you did all this."

When we entered the sunporch, I began to explain where the original part of the house started and ended. I tried to explain the bad condition the house had been in and what had to be torn down and built. I could tell they were most impressed and yet confused. I was talking too fast in my excitement.

"I made some of my fresh lemonade which you guys always liked," I announced. "It's a little too early for a cocktail, unless you would prefer one." They both laughed and took me up on my offer of lemonade.

"Can we see the whole house first?" Maggie requested. "I can't wait to see our suite and your private quarters."

"Of course, follow me," I directed.

I explained the layout of the first floor. I told them Dr. Paulson had his office and waiting room off the first floor and that the house was built with his purpose in mind. They seemed to remember the house was named after his wife, Josephine. When we were in the entryway, Maggie spotted the guest house quilt. I explained my intentions with the guest signatures.

"You and Carla will be the first to sign the quilt, as you are my first guests," I bragged to Maggie. "The cream part of the block is where you sign your name. I'm hoping to fill many of these diamonds with folks from South Haven! I also have a guest book for you to sign that tells where you're from and the date you were here."

"What a grand idea, Kate," Maggie praised. "Whoever made this beautiful quilt did a fine job."

"It was made by my friend Ruth Ann, from the Friendship Circle," I explained. "You will meet her. She sells some of her work and lives just down the street from me." I watched how they admired the quilt. It gave me goose bumps knowing how special this quilt would be. I should have taken a photo of them standing by it.

"I love those colors, as well as your choice of area rug," Carla noted as we went up the stairs to the second floor.

They both loved the spacious hallway that led to the various bedrooms. When they saw my private section, they were amused with the large pocket doors and the beautiful woodwork throughout the house. I explained there were also pocket doors between the living and dining room, downstairs.

"Show me where you found Josephine's quilt," Carla requested.

I pointed to the upper cabinet over one of the hall doors. They asked to see it, but I put them off. I wasn't sure I would be sharing her quilt with anyone else again.

We finally arrived to the former attic, which was now converted into a suite for two people. Their compliments were immediate, and they marveled about the large open space and the view from the front window. They were surprised the new bath offered a Jacuzzi and antique reproduction fixtures. They loved the touch of fresh flowers as well as the complimentary chocolates and mints. I told them how I had purchased many of my antiques from Imy's Antique Shop. Maggie immediately told me it was on their list of things to do. They loved the cut down dining table, as I knew they would. I felt like I was showing off my children as I gloated in pride.

We wandered back down the stairs and headed to the sunporch. While I prepared their glasses of lemonade and baked goodies, they proceeded to bring in their luggage. When we all got settled, I thought about how perfect this would be if Jack were also here. We all started talking at once, as we both had many questions and news bits to share.

"You look so happy, Kate," remarked Maggie. "This country air agrees with you. I think you may have even added a couple of pounds, if you don't mind me sayin'. It's about time!"

I was shocked to hear it really was noticeable.

"I think it becomes you, don't you think so, Carla?"

She nodded.

"Well, thanks a lot," I joked. "You would be too, if you ate all this good food around here every day. If I'm not baking, someone else is."

They laughed.

"Oh my goodness, this apple crumb cake is delicious," Carla remarked as she took another bite. "I don't remember you making this before."

"Just wait till breakfast!" I teased. "By the way, I'm waiting for the blueberry scones you were supposed to bring me. You didn't forget, did you?"

They both giggled and shook their heads.

The day was flying by and I told them dinner would be simple. I popped a chicken divan casserole in the oven, as I knew it was a favorite of Carla's. I had baked a loaf of whole wheat bread the day before, so I knew they would enjoy that as well. As I was arranging their place settings, I heard Ellie arriving, as she promised.

"So happy to meet you South Haveners," Ellie greeted as I introduced her.

They smiled and hugged each other.

"We can't believe you stole our soul sister to Missouri," Maggie said. "We have been friends since grade school."

Ellie laughed and nodded. "Well, I'm not sorry, but I have

to admit there were times I thought she'd head back north after a few hurdles. Once she decided to make this her home, nothing was going to stop her," she bragged.

"What hurdles?" Carla seriously asked, but I didn't want to go there.

"Life's little adjustments, that's all," I quickly answered, hoping to change the subject. "This was all new to me."

"Kate sure weathered the storm back in South Haven, so I think she's up to any mission," Maggie noted. "I just hope we can get her back for regular visits."

"On a serious note, I was e-mailed a few new condo prospects along North Shore Drive just last week," I revealed. "There's one in the Parkshores, which seems fairly reasonable. I may have you guys check it out for me."

"We'll be happy too," Carla quickly offered. "That would be a great spot for you."

"Don't be too slow to respond," warned Maggie. "These come and go quickly."

"Well, I'd have to talk it over with Jack, first," I reminded them.

"How is Jack?" Maggie inquired.

"He's great, depending on his hot and cold relationship," I described, making them laugh. "I sure wish he could have come for my open house."

"I do, too," replied Maggie.

"I must run, but I am counting on you girls coming out to the winery before you go home," Ellie insisted. "I'm sure Kate has told you all about it by now!"

They nodded and smiled.

"You bet we will," assured Maggie. "We can't wait to check it out!"

"The Red Creek Winery is doing all the food and drink for my open house tomorrow," I announced with enthusiasm.

"Ellie, we brought you some blueberry scones as well as Kate, and also thought your cook might enjoy trying some of our blueberry barbecue sauce," Maggie offered.

"Why that is so sweet of you!" Ellie blushed. "I certainly love the blueberry wine which Kate has brought me. I'll take that straight to Kelly, my cook, right now. If you all aren't too tired, come on out tonight."

"Oh no," Maggie jumped quickly in to say. "I'm exhausted and we promised to help Kate in the morning before the whole town comes to visit."

Ellie nodded with understanding. "Okay then," she said, going toward the door. "Thanks so much for the scones and barbecue sauce! I smell something yummy coming out of the kitchen, so I'd better let you go."

Everyone hugged like we had all been longtime friends. It was so special for me to see this merging of my true friends.

We all went into the kitchen and helped ourselves to some wine while I fixed their plates. They were so excited when I told them they were the first guests to sit at my new dining room table. I had pictured this scene many times in my mind. I used my very best china, silverware, and crystal. When we were all seated, I asked permission to say grace. Their faces showed an unexpected response, as they nodded and put their heads down.

"Come Lord Jesus, be our guest and let these gifts to us be blessed. Thank you for bringing me my special friends to share my joy, amen." I prayed.

"Amen," they both added, which surprised me.

"Mealtime prayers are pretty commonplace around here,

and it has reminded me of my childhood, when we always said a prayer before we ate and a prayer of thanksgiving afterwards," I shared. "I could never leave the table without the last prayer. It really reminds us of our blessings."

"That is nice to hear, Kate," Maggie somberly said. "I would like to make a toast to our friend Kate, who has found peace and happiness."

We all took our glasses of wine and raised them in response. Right now, life was perfect.

Our meal began and so did the chatter, with everyone talking at once. I got an update on Rocky, who now had accepted Carla as his master. Maggie touched on news from the community as well as the country club crowd. She then brought up James and Sandra.

"James refuses to go to counseling, so I heard Sandra is filing for divorce," Maggie revealed. "I have to admit I feel sorry for her."

"Oh, I do too," I said, feeling sad.

"The Beach Quilters say hello and I've gotten way too many questions about whether you are dating or not!" Maggie confessed.

I was shocked at the comment, which made me almost choke with food in my mouth.

"What's the matter? Did I touch on a sensitive subject?"

I shook my head. "You could say that," I admitted. "I hope you go home to report that I am one, single, happy lady."

"You won't always want to be alone, Kate," Carla said seriously. "I would give anything to be hugged and taken care of by someone else." I did feel bad for Carla, but I wasn't her.

"I don't need to be taken care of, nor do I want to take care of anyone else, thank you," I strongly responded. "If I had a good husband like Mark, things probably would be different."

"Mark's not perfect by any means," revealed Maggie. "We will be empty nesters soon, so I hope we can rediscover each other once again."

I smiled as I pictured the two of them.

After a long day, everyone was ready to turn in. They went on upstairs as I finished cleaning up. With dinner out of the way, it made me concentrate on the coming day, which made me nervous. Would everyone come or no one? Somehow it now didn't matter as much with Carla and Maggie here.

It was midnight when I finally gave in to go upstairs. I took three steps, when I was startled by a very loud noise coming from a vehicle out in front of the house. I peeked out of the oval glass in my front door and saw Ben Hecht's truck parked across the street. I quickly stepped back, as he gunned his motor to make another frightening noise. I had just set my security alarm, but somehow I couldn't feel good about this creepy man watching me.

When I got up to my bedroom, I kept the lights off and went straight to the bathroom to get ready for bed. I wondered how long he would stay there. Could I trust he wouldn't be so stupid to assault me like Blade had done, or was he all smoke, just trying to make me feel uneasy? I couldn't help but wonder if Blade was paying him to do this to me. I crawled into bed and heard him step on the gas and speed away. I only wished I had Ellie to call when he would stalk me like this in front of my house. She could then see for herself how he behaved, but she was always at the winery. I lay awake and said my prayers, hoping we all would be safe. I wanted my South Haven friends visit to be perfect.

# CHAPTER 5

My disturbed sleep had me tossing and turning. I was drowning in Indian Creek and Clark was calling out my name. I kept trying to reach for him, but the strong current was taking me away from him. I was swallowing water and gagging. Why wasn't he coming after me? When I repeatedly called his name, it woke me up. I was shaking and sweating as I sat up. I got out of bed thinking it was morning and that I had overslept. I went to get a glass of water and noticed the clock only said 1:00 a.m. I became calm as the warm light overcame my body, telling me everything was okay. I crawled back into bed, as if I were in someone's arms and went back to sleep.

When I awoke again much later, I could hear footsteps above me. I had to concentrate for a moment and realized Maggie and Carla were right above me. I had never experienced anyone moving around upstairs since I had moved into the house. It was comforting, as I got up to dress, knowing it was Carla and Maggie. I wanted to be downstairs before they arrived for breakfast, so I went into double time, knowing this was the big day.

Since the girls were not yet downstairs, I took three vases and went outside to arrange some flowers from my beds. I was trying to arrange as I cut them. I had many wild ferns growing under the shade trees, which were great fillers to my amateur arrangements. I had just finished filling the third vase when Cotton pulled in the drive.

"Good morning, Miss Kate," Cotton yelled out as he got out of his pickup truck. "Are we ready for your big party?"

"Not quite yet, but the flowers will help," I acknowledged. "My guests from South Haven are still upstairs, so I wanted to get this done before breakfast."

"Well, I'm here to help, you know," Cotton reminded.

"That's fine," I said in relief. "I do have a few things for you to check on, but this afternoon, when you and Susie arrive, I want you to remember you are my guests. I don't want you working."

He laughed. "Yeah, Susie's quite excited," he said with a big grin. "I told her to go to town and buy herself something new to wear."

"Good for you," I said, walking into the house. "Will you bring the other two vases in for me?"

"Sure enough," he happily responded.

"Well, look who is up and about and bringing us such beauty so early in the morning," Maggie greeted. "These are beautiful! Is there any talent you don't have, my dear?"

I blushed and began introducing Cotton. Carla and Maggie acknowledged that they heard me speak of him.

"So, Carla, you're the one that has kept Miss Kate's dog, am I right?" Cotton inquired.

Carla nodded with a smile.

"I don't know why she didn't bring him here. He would have loved runnin' around this countryside."

Maggie and Carla burst into laughter.

"Cotton, my yard is not fenced in," I stated. "He's always been an inside dog. He really wasn't my dog. Besides, he's known Carla forever and has a good home."

"Maybe someday you'll decide to get your own dog or cat here," Maggie said to end the uncomfortable subject.

"Miss Kate, I'm gonna check on those things outside now," Cotton said going toward the door. "If you need anything, just holler. Ladies, it's been nice meetin' you."

"You too, Cotton," Maggie responded. "Thanks for being here for our good friend!"

Cotton blushed.

I joined Maggie and Carla at the breakfast counter as they enjoyed their coffee and assortment of coffee cakes. Maggie offered to help make the lemonade, and Carla and I began pulling out serving dishes for the occasion. The flower arrangements fit perfectly on the dining room table, living room coffee table, and the side table in the entry hall. The house was taking on a festive look that said something was about to take place.

"Let's get your signatures on this quilt before folks start to come," I instructed. "Here is the pen I want you to use. Why don't you start in this lower right-hand corner, Maggie?"

"Oh good, I'm glad you're going first," Carla teased. "I don't want to screw up."

"I want the two of you to be side by side," I insisted. "Now, I want to get this occasion in a photo. This is better than an actual ribbon cutting."

They stood side by side as I instructed different poses. As I took photos, I watched them make history for Josephine's Guest House.

"I love this quilt," Maggie said with admiration. "I want to meet this quilter. Did you say she was coming?"

"Yes, she said she would," I recalled. "She is thrilled to have her art in this house and sells some of her things now and then. She just lives right down the street and is one of the members of my Friendship Circle. I think everyone but Esther is supposed to attend today."

"Okay, let's get back to work so we have time to change our clothes!" Maggie said in her disciplined voice. "What else needs to be done?"

I fussed on small details that they could attend to.

The clock was ticking and Kelly would be here anytime to deliver the food and drinks. Carla insisted she could help serve drinks, despite me reminding her she was a guest. As soon as Kelly was finished with his delivery, we all agreed it was time to go up and change in case someone showed up early.

I changed my thoughts on my attire several times, before choosing very bright colors. I think the garden flowers had set my tone for the day. I hoped my excitement would be for the good and the afternoon would go well. I wanted both my worlds to rejoice as I celebrated Josephine's lovely home.

At 2:00 p.m. sharp, the doorbell rang at the front door. I told the girls I would stay out front to greet the guests as they arrived. It was no surprise to see my first guest to arrive was Ellie.

"I don't think I've come to your front door before," Ellie admitted with a chuckle.

"Welcome, neighbor," I said, giving her a hug. "I'm glad you're here! I'm a nervous wreck."

"No one in this town is late around here, so expect everyone to come at once," she warned. "Ruth Ann and Charlene just pulled up. By the way, Ruth Ann got her folks settled at their special care facility this past week. I bet she feels she is as free as a bird now."

"That's good to know, Ellie," I said, as I remembered my conversation with Ruth Ann. "That had to be so hard to do." I walked to my front porch. "Hello, ladies, come on in!" I greeted. "Your quilt has already been admired, Ruth Ann. Now be sure you meet my friends from South Haven as they are most anxious to meet you."

"I can't wait!" Ruth Ann cheerfully acknowledged.

"I brought you a little something," said Charlene, holding a small package.

I smiled. "Just put it on the mantle for now, if you don't mind," I instructed. "I see Esther getting out of the car."

Charlene nodded and went into the house.

"I was afraid I was not going to be able to come," Esther complained when she got to the porch. "I'm still not feeling well. It's just a sinus condition, I guess. Don't worry. I wouldn't have come if I knew this was contagious."

"I'm sorry to hear that," I responded. "Perhaps you'll feel better as the day goes along."

"I'm sure I will because I wasn't about to miss your celebration," she said as she went on into the house.

"Why hello, Anna," I yelled out as she walked from her car to the front door. "Didn't you bring that nice husband of yours?"

"Heavens no," she said shaking her head. "He's not much for these kinds of affairs, so he's watchin' the kids. I did bring you a loaf of a new recipe I just tried. It's eggnog bread. I think you'll like it! I figured your South Haven guests might enjoy it."

"How sweet, Anna," I said as I cleared the way for her to go on in the house. "I've never heard of egg nog bread. Thank you so much."

Standing in line to say hello were Harold and Milly. They both looked like they were dressed for church. They were true pillars of the community, and it meant a lot that they chose to come.

"Harold, I hardly recognized you all dressed up," I gushed. "Please come on in and look around. I know you have been most curious about what I've been up to."

He laughed. "You're darn tootin'!" he joked. "You are mighty nice to invite us. Milly's talked of nothing else since the invite came."

She blushed as they went inside.

"Hi, Mary Catherine," I said as she approached the front steps. "Don't you look nice? What did you do different?"

"Thanks, but I very seldom wear makeup," she admitted. "It's not too much, is it?"

I laughed. "You look beautiful!" I praised. "Some of the other members are here, so come on in."

"You don't mind if I do a little write up on your open house for the local paper, do you?" she timidly asked.

"Why, I wouldn't mind a bit," I answered with some curiosity. "I'm going to need some publicity for this place."

She grinned as she carried her notebook inside with her.

"Marv, I'm so glad you took time to come over," I eagerly said. He was a shy kind of guy considering the kind of business he ran.

"I can't stay but a bit. I was just curious to see the place," he explained. "I gotta get back to work. I ain't dressed very fancy. I heard so much about what a nice job you did and all. I guess I'll be getting lots more business with this bein' a guest house and all. Congratulations!"

I snickered. "Thanks. Both of us having a lot of business

would be a good thing," I responded. "Go on in. You'll know everyone but my two guests from South Haven. Just introduce yourself. I promise to bring them to the bar."

He grinned at the idea.

Betsy and Peggy arrived together, which didn't surprise me. It seemed more folks were walking to my place, than driving. Perhaps they thought parking would be a problem.

"Good to see you girls," I said, giving them each a little hug.

"My goodness, it looks like you have a nice crowd here," Peggy commented. She looked darling in a blue flowered sun dress.

"I'm thrilled," I said looking into the house. "One never knows about occasions like this."

"If you need some help, just let us know," offered Betsy.

"Thanks, but you all go in and just enjoy!" I suggested. "I know the food and drinks are great."

"Imy, please come on in," I said, giving her a hug. "You look great, all dressed up."

She was embarrassed at my unexpected compliment. She never had on anything but jeans when I'd see her. She had such a pretty face, with eyes that twinkled whenever she'd talk to you.

"My South Haven friends are anxious to get to your shop, so we'll probably stop by tomorrow if you're open."

"Oh my, yes, that would be great!" she said with excitement.

"We had dinner for the first time at the dining room table last night. I do so appreciate you finding that furniture for me. Please introduce yourself. I'm keeping busy here at the door."

"I will." She beamed. "I am so proud I was a part of furnishing Josephine's Guest House. Congratulations, Kate."

Ellen and Oscar walked up the steps with Mayor Pelker. I had sent him an invitation, but since we hadn't met, I wasn't sure he would come. I was expecting an older man, but he was very gracious when Ellen introduced us.

"I can't thank you enough for what you have done to this house and for providing a guest house, which is so sorely needed around here," the mayor acknowledged. "I'm sorry we have not met before now."

"Me, too," I responded, shaking his hand. "It's been a challenge for me, but the community has welcomed me with open arms."

"That's good to hear," he said as his eyes were inspecting the whole place.

"You all go in and enjoy the refreshments," I encouraged. "I have two friends here from Michigan who would enjoy meeting you all."

"We would be delighted," Ellen said as she took Oscar's hand.

"I am proud of you, Kate," Oscar said with a big smile. "I know this wasn't easy."

I just nodded with a smile. It meant a lot to me for Oscar to say that.

Up the sidewalk came Cotton and Susie. She was beaming in her new pink dress. They were a sweet looking couple. Cotton looked like he had on a new shirt. I had to remember this day was also a big day in their lives. I guess you could say it took a village to pull this off.

"Hi, you two," I greeted. "You both look so nice. How is Amy Sue? You really should have brought her."

"Thanks, but no thanks," Cotton said chuckling. "This is our treat today. We'll bring her by sometime next week."

"That would be great." I nodded. "Now go on in and be my guest. No working today."

They smiled as they walked up the steps.

"Oh, Sharla Lee, don't you look festive today," I said as she and Gerard arrived together. Her dress had large multi-colored flowers on it and the red scarf tied in her hair topped off her flamboyant taste. Only Sharla Lee could pull this off.

"You should talk, my dear," she came back. "You're wearing pretty bright colors yourself, today. This is a party, isn't it? I think Gerard looks pretty darn sharp in his pink shirt, don't you?"

Gerard blushed, as always.

"I did feel rather festive, and it is a happy occasion for sure." I laughed in response. "I love your style, Sharla Lee. Gerard, it's good to see you, too, looking sharp. I guess you're used to Sharla Lee stealing the show."

"No doubt about it," he agreed with a subtle laugh. "Say, Miss Meyr, this place sure turned out real nice. We'll be sure to tell everyone about it. I love the sign above the porch. You sure can't miss seein' that going by."

"Thanks so much, you two," I said giving them each a little hug. "Let's hope we'll be finding out a little more information about this mysterious lady, Josephine. I have really appreciated all your help so far."

I walked in the house with them, and their eyes immediately went to the guest quilt on the wall. I could tell this quilt was going to be a conversation piece as time evolved. I was concerned about Maggie and Carla, so I peeked into the living room for a minute and found the two of them laughing and talking like they knew everyone in the room. Behind me were the voices of Eddie Mueller and his wife.

"Hello, Miss Meyr," Eddie said with all smiles. "Thank you for your invitation. This is my wife, Clara."

"How nice to meet you, Clara," I said as I put my hand on her shoulder. "Eddie has talked about you and your good cooking."

She blushed. "I have always loved this house," Clara said with admiration. "I never knew Josephine was the name of Doc's wife, so that's lovely of you to acknowledge her."

"Thank you for mentioning that, Clara," I said with a big smile. "I thought the same thing! I don't think many know where the name came from. They may assume I am Josephine for all I know." She nodded in agreement as they walked into the house.

To my surprise, I was pleased to see Pastor Hermann arriving. His eyes were all over the building as he approached me. He was not dressed out of character. His German demeanor and smile were always the same.

"Do you have room for one more person in there?" he teased, as he shook my hand.

"I think just one more," I teased back. "I am so pleased you came. You will know most of the folks, of course."

"God bless you in this new adventure," he said before going in.

I smiled. Goodness knows, I would need all the blessings one could give.

"Mr. Brewer, welcome," I said offering my hand. "Good of you to come."

"I told you to call me Wayne," he scolded. "Kate, this is my wife, Ella Jean."

"Pleased to meet you, Ella Jean," I repeated. "Your husband has done a wonderful job with my place."

She nodded in pride. "He would tell me every detail when he'd come home at night," she reported. Wayne seemed to be embarrassed. "I really admire you tackling this place!"

All the compliments were certainly nice to hear.

"Hey, is Clark here?" he asked so innocently.

"No, he isn't, but I have hopes he'll stop by," I said trying to act casual about it.

"This probably isn't his cup of tea, bein' around a lot of people and all," Wayne noted.

I nodded and smiled, thinking he was right.

"I wanted Ella Jean to meet him. She thinks he's pretty famous."

"Emma, you made it," I said helping her up the steps.

"Oh, my darn knee," she complained. "I wouldn't miss this, honey, no matter how bad my knee talked today." I shook my head. "I don't think I've been in this place since I had my tonsils taken out as a young girl. What a treat! I'm so proud of you."

"I think this will be a more pleasant visit, so please go on in," I encouraged. "Most of the friends from the circle are here inside. Don't overdo it now."

"I'm really anxious to see Ruth Ann's quilt," she added.

"It's right in the entryway," I guided her inside. "I think she's standing in there, reaping all the compliments."

Emma snickered and went on inside, favoring her other knee.

"Have you seen my Aunt May?" Ellie said coming by my side on the porch. "I told her to stop by. She is dying to see the inside of this house."

"No, I haven't, but here comes somebody you know," I said pointing to Trout, who was getting out of his pickup truck across the street.

"Great, any sign of Clark?" Ellie asked quickly before Trout came up on the porch.

I shook my head.

"Pretty fancy digs, Miss Kate!" Trout boasted. "Hi, Ellie."

"Good to see you," I said with a hug. "The drinks are on me today, okay?"

"Fine by me," he grinned. "Show me the wine."

I was about to go in the house with them when Gabe and Helen Grebing arrived. They were walking slowly as they held onto each other. She carried a small box under her arm, and she explained it was some of her coffee cake. I was delighted.

"You didn't have to do that, but my Michigan guests will be thrilled," I said with gratitude. "Please join a houseful of folks and enjoy some refreshment."

They both slowly made their way up the steps, with Ellie giving them a hand.

"Don't you think it's time to come in and visit with your guests?" Ellie asked with concern. "Surely everyone is here but the dogcatcher!"

We laughed as I followed behind her.

When I entered the house, there was Ruth Ann, standing by the guest quilt, reaping compliments from Sharla Lee, Peggy, and Betsy. She was explaining how it was only for my guest house guests to sign, not the general public, which I appreciated. I walked into the living room to find Carla and Maggie visiting with folks. I grabbed the cell out of my pocket and took some photos. It was just great seeing everyone having a good time. Mary Catherine appeared to be interviewing Emma, as they sat together on the couch. Maybe she could find out more about this house than I could. I overheard Wayne bragging to Mayor Pelker how he was instrumental to the addition and describing what it was like before. Ellen, Oscar, and the reverend were helping themselves to the finger sandwiches and fruit when I joined them.

"Why, Kate, you truly have outdone yourself today," Ellen praised. "Your presentation is quite lovely."

"I wish I could take all the credit, but Kelly, from the Red Creek Winery, implemented exactly what I was wanting," I explained. "I'm so glad you're enjoying it."

"Oh my, yes," Oscar said as he took another bite of his sandwich. "Why, look who just walked in!" He was looking toward the living room where Clark was arriving. "How did you manage to get him here? He usually likes to avoid these things."

"I think I have an idea," Ellen said giving Oscar a wink.

I didn't want to appear anxious, so I slowly made my way toward him. My eyes didn't leave him, as he started talking to Trout and Cotton.

"Welcome," I said joining them. Clark looked extra handsome in his khakis and dress shirt.

*Does he know he's this good looking?* I wondered.

"Good turnout, Miss Meyr," he said gazing over the crowd.

I nodded and smiled. "It's so great to see this place full of people," I boasted. "You are getting a lot of compliments on your craftsmanship."

"I had a wonderful house to work with and a great boss," he admitted.

"Almost every person in this house played a part in some way," I shared. "Clark, I especially want you to meet my two friends from Michigan. You certainly heard me speak of them quite often."

I grabbed Maggie, who was standing nearby, and pulled her in my direction.

"Hey, what's up?" she responded with some confusion.

"Remember me talking about a famous woodcarver who had consented to do my custom cabinetry?" I asked as I got Carla's attention. Maggie nodded.

"Well, this is Clark McFadden and this is my best friend, Maggie," I said smiling.

"Nice to meet you, Maggie," Clark said holding out his hand to shake.

Maggie's eyes were popping in admiration. "Likewise, Mr. McFadden," she very slowly responded. "This is Carla. We came together and we both are truly amazed at what our friend has accomplished here."

"A pleasure," Carla responded with a handshake. Her eyes stared at him in disbelief.

"Kate, I think you left out a few details about your friend here, but we did hear about your incredible workmanship," Maggie remarked. "Do you have your work for sale anywhere?"

"Yes, but my main source is at the Patina Gallery in Springfield, Missouri," he revealed modestly. "I do well to keep up with their demand, so I travel there frequently."

"I was very fortunate Clark agreed to help me," I admitted. "He stopped doing residential work a long time ago, but I think he felt sorry for me."

"So do you live nearby?" Maggie asked wanting to know more than I wanted her to.

"Some ways from here, near Indian Creek, where it's very private," he described. "Kate can tell you about it."

Maggie looked at me with daggers in her eyes.

"Now, ladies, if you'll excuse me, I happen to know there's some good wine here. Nice to have met you both. Enjoy your visit." Clark walked away and the girls followed him with their eyes.

"Excuse me, girlfriend, but you have a lot of explaining to do!" Maggie joked as Carla stared at me intensely.

"He's a carpenter?" Carla asked in disbelief.

"He's an artist, and he knew I was pretty desperate to find anyone to do any custom work like I needed," I simply explained. "He's just a friend, so don't get all hot and bothered."

"He just saved your life, that's all," Cotton jumped in to say. He had obviously overheard our conversation.

"He saved your life?" Maggie asked in a raised voice. "What's that about?" Her face now looked very serious.

"Cotton's just exaggerating," I said to ignore the topic. "I need to refill some of the platters. Have you met everyone?"

Carla and Maggie were stunned as I changed the subject and walked away. Cotton disappeared as well, knowing he had spoken out of turn.

I was filling the cookie tray in the kitchen, when Ellie came up behind me.

"I have a little surprise for you, if it's okay with you," she said in almost a whisper.

"What's that?" I said looking up.

"I brought this ribbon that has Josephine's Guest House printed on it," she began. "I thought we could have everyone come out to the porch and do a ribbon cutting. The mayor loves the idea, and Trout said he'd be happy to take the picture."

"I suppose I should have thought of that myself, but if you think it's appropriate, I don't see why we can't do that." I smiled in agreement.

"We did it when the winery opened, and it's a nice gesture that makes it all official," Ellie added. "I guess I should have asked you before now, but you've been pretty busy. Before folks start drifting away, how about I ask them to gather on or around the porch."

I nodded and smiled. I placed the tray on the table, and then went in the powder room to freshen my face. Leave it to Ellie to still take care of me. I certainly didn't know anything about ribbon cuttings, other than seeing pictures in the paper once in a while. When I returned, I noticed Ellie had succeeded to gather everyone. The ribbon was too lovely to cut, so I said I would cut to the side of the wording so I would have the gold title of the guest house as a remembrance. I insisted Carla and Maggie be at my side, and next to my other side were Ellie and the mayor. I first got everyone's attention and thanked them for coming to celebrate the completion and for supporting me with the opening of Josephine's Guest House. You could have heard a pin drop when I expressed my thanks in making me feel welcome in the community.

"Now, we'll do this on the count of three," I instructed. "One, two, three!" The ribbon fell to the side and everyone cheered. I couldn't believe it was happening. When I looked into the crowd, I saw Clark near the street as he was leaving, giving me thumbs up as he waved good-bye. It was a cute and typical gesture of his support.

Everyone seemed to think this was their cue to leave, so

hugs and good wishes began happening. I walked into the house and opened the housewarming gifts that were placed on my mantle. There was more wine, food, and some darling, monogrammed guest towels with a J embroidered on them for my guests to enjoy. Maggie and Carla started making themselves useful by picking up scattered cups, plates, and glasses. There were very few guests left that had their own private conversations going. It was all a good feeling.

She slowly approached me as she was about to leave. "I visited briefly with Clark about my banquet plans," Ruth Ann divulged. "He thought the banquet hall was a grand idea and said he'd be able to advise me if needed."

"Oh, that's good," I said feeling a tad jealous. She looked exceptionally beautiful and artistic today. "He would have some good ideas of his own, I bet. Everyone certainly admired your quilt today."

"It's your quilt now," Ruth Ann reminded. "Well, maybe I better say it's Josephine's quilt, under your care." She grinned and I nodded in agreement.

The last one to leave was Mary Catherine.

"I'll let you know when this will be in the paper," she alerted. "I'm glad you cut a ribbon. That was such a nice touch. You must feel very pleased about how everything went today. I think I have a pretty good photo to use."

"Thanks so much," I said kissing her on the cheek. "Everyone has been so supportive, as I said."

"The best of luck to you, Kate." She went out the door.

I closed the front door and turned around to see Maggie and Carla staring at me. It was over. Just like that.

"What a grand afternoon, my friend," Maggie was the first to say. "Congratulations! I don't know how you managed to know so many people in such a short amount of time. I think the whole town was here."

"My words, exactly," chimed in Carla. "When you meet the mayor, the reverend, and then this hunk of a carpenter, it's pretty impressive." We all laughed. "I don't think you ever entertained that many guests the whole time I worked for you in South Haven."

"You're so right, Carla," I observed. "There doesn't seem to be a status here, which I like. The local plumber is just as important as the mayor. They are all good people who really want to help one another."

"How can we ever ask you to come back to South Haven when you have all this going for you?" Maggie said in a discouraging tone.

"Now don't you go badmouthing my hometown, girlfriend," I defended. "Borna cannot replace my memories in South Haven growing up, not to mention the beach and our little blueberry downtown. I can't and won't ever give that up."

"That's good to hear," Maggie said, feeling better. "When we return, Carla and I will check out that condo in Parkshores you mentioned."

"That would be great." I nodded with a big smile. "Unfortunately the cleaning up of this little party must begin."

"You sure have a lot of food left over, Miss Kate," Carla noted as she carried an empty platter to the kitchen.

"Oh, let's forget all that," I said, wanting to relax and relive the occasion. "If it were a little cooler, I'd make a fire like I did every day and night last winter. We could sit here and talk."

"My feet are killing me," Maggie complained as she kicked off her shoes.

"You know I haven't had a glass of wine or a bite to eat since I opened that door at 2:00 p.m.," I announced.

"Well, I'll take care of that," Carla quickly offered as she went back to the kitchen.

"Oh no, you don't," I argued. "I am now officially the proprietor of this guest house and it is my duty to wait on you."

They laughed and told me to go for it.

I merrily waltzed into the kitchen to help myself, and happened to glance out the back window. There sat Ben Hecht's truck on the side road of my house, pointed toward my sunporch. It was dusk and I couldn't see him real well. I couldn't help wonder if he sat there the whole time of my open house. It gave me a pang of nausea and my appetite vanished. I couldn't say or do anything to spoil this wonderful day. I took my glass of wine and joined my friends in silence.

"This carving is beautiful!" Maggie complimented. "It's the shape of your tree in the backyard. Am I right?"

"Yes, it is," I nodded. "I just love it and it was a gift from Clark, by the way. It's probably worth a fortune. He said he always admired that tree and had carved this some years ago."

"What am I missing here?" Maggie asked with confusion. "He's just a friendly carpenter who happens to give his clients expensive gifts? How can this happen if you're not more than friends?"

I laughed, looking down. "I hear you, Maggie, but it's an unusual friendship, I have to agree," I explained. "He felt it belonged here in this house. It's not a romantic relationship, but Clark is so sensitive and understanding. He spent many hours working here every day. He saw my frustrations, as well as my accomplishments. He particularly liked my blueberry muffins, which I provided for all the workers." Now they both were laughing in disbelief. "My talent for baking has now been fully appreciated."

"Well, I'm still confused," Maggie noted. "Why isn't it romantic?"

"Because neither one of us has wanted it or tried to pursue it," I explained once again. "He loves his lifestyle and I surely am not looking for anything more. He knows all about James and the business as well as my anger with Clay. It's been the perfect friendship for what I need."

They both stared at me as they tried to understand.

"I guess I've had a little too much wine, but I'd jump those bones in a minute, if I could," Maggie joked. "Who cares if it's nothing more?"

We all laughed.

"Maggie, Maggie, you never change," I joked back. "I don't think Clark has a clue how handsome he is. He's just so modest, in general. I'm surprised he even showed up today. He is not very social."

"He must care a lot about you then," suggested Carla.

I smiled.

"So he hinted that you somehow would know all about the place where he lives, huh?" Maggie probed.

"Yup, guilty there." I snickered. "He invited me to his place for dinner one day when I was feeling pretty low about things that had happened. He loves to cook, however, on that particular day bad storms were predicted. I almost didn't go, but then I weakened. He fixed a ton of food, so he would have been very disappointed had I not gone." They both were dead quiet to hear more. "Well, I went and the weather was so bad, there was no way to get me back home."

"So you spent the night?" Maggie asked in a raised voice. "Have some more wine, Kate."

Carla chuckled out loud.

"I did and slept in his guest room," I simply said. "It was all on the up and up."

They didn't believe me.

"No way!" Maggie teased. "Seriously?"

"Yes way!" I repeated. "I never felt threatened or uncomfortable." I wasn't about to tell her about the kiss we shared.

"Now that's the kind of friend I would like," Carla revealed.

"I agree with you, Carla," I said as I took another sip of wine. "It's so great having a male friend to bounce things off of. I may not have started thinking about this guest house had it not been for Clark asking me what my plans were for the future. He really led me to this idea."

"Well, you could have taken that as a hint about whether he wanted you to stay here in Borna or not!" Maggie surmised. "He certainly had to be happy about your decision."

I nodded.

"What did Cotton mean when he said he saved your life?" Carla asked.

"It's not a big deal, and I really don't want to go into that tonight," I confessed. "It's been such a grand day. I just want to sit here and relish the fact that so many people came to celebrate with me."

"I do want to hear more about that, girlfriend, but you should feel very pleased about everything today," Maggie concluded. "I am so proud of you!"

We talked and reminisced till close to midnight. We

were all exhausted and decided to head for bed. Carla and Maggie went upstairs, and I carried a few more dishes to the kitchen. I looked out the window and was relieved that Ben's truck was gone. I hated to reveal such craziness to Carla and Maggie.

I turned off the lights and set the alarm. As I walked toward the stairs I gave one last glance at Josephine's quilt on the wall. I did a double take as I walked closer to the quilt. I couldn't believe what I was seeing. On the opposite corner of the quilt from where the girls had signed was a set of initials beautifully scripted with the same ink pen. The initials JLP were boldly written in plain view. Who would do that? Who attended the open house with those initials? The thought of someone taking advantage was making me very angry. Did Ruth Ann know about this, since she was standing by the quilt most of the afternoon? Would this be the first of many folks who just thought they could sign the quilt?

I slowly went up the stairs in total disappointment, trying to remember the names of my guests today. The delicate initials would have taken some time to produce. Wouldn't someone have noticed?

I undressed and showered, falling helplessly into bed. As tired as I was, I could tell with my mind racing that sleep would not come easily. I tried to think of pleasant conversations throughout the afternoon, so I could distract my thoughts about the quilt. I did think about Clark and how pleased I was with his appearance. When he gave me a thumbs up before he left, I found myself smiling. I knew Carla and Maggie were not going to get off my case regarding Clark. It did make me jealous when Ruth Ann said she had shared her banquet plans with him. Would he start working with her like he did me? Ruth Ann was a striking girl who could appeal to Clark. I wanted to get off that scenario or I would never go to sleep.

It was nice to have a blessing from Pastor Hermann. I also wished I could have spent some time visiting with the mayor. I'm sure Ellen and Oscar were good friends with him since they came together. I wondered if Ellen approved of all the choices I made for the house. I'm sure she didn't miss a room or closet as I saw her roam about the place. I hoped Mary Catherine's article would be complimentary. Having publicity for the home I was actually living in sure would be challenging.

I kept rearranging my pillow as my mind raced along. Would Josephine have approved of the day's activities? Of course, Josephine! JLP were her initials, Josephine Lottes Paulson. So who decided to put her initials on there? I took a deep breath to get a hold of myself.

"Josephine, was it you?" I cautiously asked in a whisper. "Can you hear me?" I had goose bumps all over me. "If you did, I really don't mind. It's your quilt to honor you."

Somehow, I felt a sense of relief to the mystery and drifted off to sleep.

# CHAPTER 6

Carla, Maggie, and I happened to meet in the upstairs hallway at the same time the next morning. They seemed to be in a chipper mood. As we walked down the steps, I couldn't help but tell them what I had discovered on the quilt the night before.

"Stop," I said when we got to the bottom hallway. "Look at what I discovered." I pointed to the corner block that had the initials JLP and expressed my curiosity.

"Who did that?" Carla said looking closer. "That had to take time."

"What lovely, elegant work!" Maggie admired. "Whose initials are these?"

They were both now staring at me for answers.

"JLP just happens to be Josephine's initials," I revealed. "Josephine Lottes Paulson." They stared at the quilt, not really understanding what I was trying to tell them.

"Well, aren't you glad that worked out, instead of the initials belonging to your plumber or someone," Maggie joked. "Sorry, not funny, but who would take the time to do this with all the people you had around yesterday?"

"Let's get some coffee, shall we?" I said, leading the way to the kitchen. I knew they would never understand. I poured them coffee and arranged some pastries on a platter, while they remained silent. We went out to the sunporch to get comfortable.

"What a beautiful day," Maggie finally said. "It'll be a great night at the winery."

"It will," I agreed. "We can stop by Imy's Antique Shop and then I'll drive you around and show you Saxon Village. Sharla Lee wants me to bring you by the museum as well."

"So, Kate, back to the quilt," Carla reminded.

I took a deep breath. "There's reason for me to believe that Josephine herself put the initials on the quilt," I said watching their faces erupt.

"Did I hear you correctly?" Maggie said as she put down her coffee cup.

I nodded. I began explaining how mysterious things had begun happening when I found her quilt. I told them about the quilt showing up in different places. I confessed it was a message to me that she didn't appreciate me airing her private pain to others in the community. They were listening intently. I think Carla was getting more and more spooked.

"I know she approves of me in this house, don't get me wrong," I explained. "There's another experience I haven't shared with you."

"Now you're freaking me out!" Carla expressed.

"I thought you said the place wasn't haunted," Maggie said in a raised voice.

I told them it wasn't haunted in a bad way like folks like to think, so I explained the warm daylight that sometimes happens on the middle of the night.

"Oh my lands," Carla responded, "I've never been anywhere around ghosts!"

"It's not like that, Carla," I corrected. "The locals have used the haunting story as an excuse for the house not selling for such a long time, but I am telling you it is full of love.

There is nothing creepy about this place. I feel very safe and happy here!"

The looks on their faces showed they were not convinced.

"You are never afraid?" Maggie asked like she had doubts.

"No, I'm not." I made myself clear. "I have found by talking to her directly, it gives me comfort and I think she feels I am not ignoring her. She's been ignored most of her life!"

"Mercy! Kate, I don't know how you've gotten yourself into this," Maggie said, shaking her head. "You are so calm and brave about everything."

"I have gone through a lot to get this place up to par and have made many friends here," I bragged. "I am not going to let a few unexplained happenings scare me."

"Obviously not, and you've never seemed happier," Maggie admitted as she got up to refill her coffee.

"Josephine must be pretty special to you to name this house after her," Carla said, taking another slice of coffee cake. "You don't think she'll do something goofy to us up in the attic, do you?" I laughed.

"Oh mercy, I sure hope not," Maggie chimed in.

"Relax, you two," I said, shaking my head. "Ellie and I think that's where she spent most of her time when she remained out of sight. I guess the two of you had better behave up there." I snickered even louder, which made them stir.

After everyone dressed for the day we hopped in my car and headed to Imy's. We told her we were coming, so when she saw our car, she came out to greet us. We each went our own way as if we were on a scavenger hunt. There were a few others in the shop, but it didn't stop our aggressive shopping. Imy was answering one question after another. It seemed the shop was even fuller with merchandise than the last time I had visited. Imy even had a few things sitting outside the building.

The girls started commenting about her reasonable prices as they gathered things in their arms.

"It's a good thing we have a car to take us home instead of an airplane," Maggie noted. "This vase is Royal Doulton. Did you see this marking, Imy?"

Imy smiled and nodded. "I know the price is cheap, but I only mark up from what I paid," she explained. "It makes my bookkeeping easier. If I get a bargain, I pass it on."

"Okay, sold!" Maggie said, putting the vase on Imy's counter. "I also love this Lone Star quilt, but it's purple and I hate purple."

"Imy gets pretty nice quilts now and then," I shared.

"Yes, Emma told me yesterday that she is planning to bring some quilts in to sell," Imy said as she refolded the star quilt. "I can't wait to see what she has. Her family members were all good quiltmakers."

"This is a genuine Tiffany lamp, isn't it?" I asked Imy.

"It is, and it isn't cheap," she admitted. "I had to pay a lot for that, but I have a dealer that comes through who will buy that in a second. He takes things out east and gets a pretty penny for good stuff when I find it."

"Well, I have been eyeing that ever since I've started coming in here," I claimed. "I just love it, but didn't have a clue where it could go, plus I didn't know why it was so expensive. I'm thinking it would be perfect on my side table in the entry hall. All I have is that overhead light. What do you think, girlfriends?"

"Go for it," encouraged Maggie, not paying much attention.

"Is it about 1910 or so?" I asked now picking it up.

"More likely, 1920," Imy corrected. "It'll be perfect for your house."

"Well, happy birthday to me," I said putting it on her counter. "I'd like to leave it here and pick it up later, if you don't mind."

"Wow, happy birthday, Kate," Imy said as her face sparkled. "I didn't know it was your birthday. I'll give you a generous discount."

"Not necessary, Imy. Please don't," I insisted. "You have been such a help to me, and I don't want you losing income by selling it to me instead of your other good customer."

Maggie came to the counter and looked at the price. "Boy, I'm glad I didn't offer to buy that for you as my birthday present," she joked. "That's a pretty penny! Does it mean the beach house is off the table now?"

We laughed.

"Well, I'm not in their league," Carla said complaining to Imy. "This will be all for me. This Mickey and Minnie pair of shakers is so cute and perfect for my collection."

"You collect salt and pepper shakers?" I asked in shock. "How did I never know that?"

"There's a lot you don't know about me, boss lady," Carla teased.

Imy took special care to wrap Maggie's vase and a few other small items in heavy paper for travel. Carla took her small package and tucked it into her purse. We all were thrilled with our purchases and we made Imy's day.

# CHAPTER 7

We knocked on Anna's door when we arrived at Saxon Village. Anna and her family lived in the farmhouse located on the Saxon Village grounds. I knew she would give us a great tour, highlighting the outdoor oven I had talked about so much. Maggie and Carla were quite busy taking photographs as we visited all the cabins. We took a break at one of the picnic tables, when Anna brought out some cold lemonade and pound cake for us to enjoy.

"I could stay here all day," Maggie said, fanning herself. "It's so peaceful and I can't believe how much history there is around here. It's so secluded."

"Anna can tell you about this whole county," I bragged. "I don't know how she runs this place and raises those three little ones she's got." Anna blushed. "Her husband takes care of the grounds here and farms some of the land. How about we head to Marv's for a late lunch?" I asked the girls. "Don't eat too much of that cake."

"If we're going to the winery in a few hours, I'm not sure that's necessary," complained Maggie. "I'm not hungry at all. I think I could have a nap. This fresh air really gets to you."

"I agree with Maggie," Carla chimed in. "We certainly don't need more food."

"Okay then, we'll go earlier to the winery," I announced.

We thanked Anna and went on our way towards Dresden. We drove past the historic log cabin where the first

Lutheran college was located, as well as the nearby Heritage Museum. I told them Sharla Lee wanted us to stop by, but the girls wanted to keep moving. They loved meeting her and said I should be sure to apologize about not stopping. I continued driving because I wanted them to see some of the surrounding villages and finally circled around on the road leading us back toward Borna. The redbud trees were almost past their peak, but the scenery with all the new greens was heavenly. Carla had an interest in the old barns we passed. I told her I was fascinated by them as well. I pointed out Harold's Hardware store, my church, and Ruth Ann's enormous building where she wanted to put a banquet center. They were impressed she was willing to take on such a major project.

When we arrived home, the girls tended to linger in the backyard among the red and yellow tulips, which were looking spectacular. Carla was snapping photos with her camera.

"So where is that tombstone you were telling me about?" Maggie asked.

Carla looked shocked at the request.

"Oh, it's over here," I said, walking toward the small barn.

They carefully followed me as if we were now walking on sacred ground. It took me a while, but then my toe hit the edge of the uneven stone. I brushed back the fresh weeds so they could see the slight carving.

"My goodness, it is worn," commented Carla. "I bet this was made for a pet that died here. People used to bury their pets behind their houses, you know."

"No one ever said the Paulsons had a pet," I added. "There is so much I don't know about them."

"With folks keeping their pets outside back then, nobody may have known," offered Maggie. "This looks so old, it may go way back before the Paulsons even lived here, Kate."

Maggie stooped down and tried to brush the stone clean. "It looks like there are five letters at the top here," she said softly. "That says to me it's a pet. It would have the full name if it was a person. I can't make out anything, can you? You may want to do a rubbing on it and see what you'd come up with."

"I think one of the ole timers around here told me that before this house was built, it was just farmland. But that may not be correct," I added. "We'd better get cleaned up if we still intend to go early!"

"Let's get a few more pictures, first," Carla said as she positioned her camera. "How about you and Maggie stand in front of the amazing tree?"

We all took turns, including getting some shots of the spring tulips. Some photos were silly, just like when Maggie and I were in high school.

*It was such a fun day,* I kept thinking. I didn't want their visit to end. I couldn't wait to give Maggie my birthday present. It wasn't the birthday get together we typically had, but being together to celebrate here in my new home was very special.

As we went up to change, they joked back and forth about what they were supposed to wear. I teased them that they needed to look hot and sexy for the evening. Carla thought I was serious and started to rebel. Maggie and I giggled like we had done many times through the years. I finished dressing before the girls, wearing simple jeans with a denim jacket. I knew we may end up sitting outdoors, so come evening I wanted to be prepared. When I came downstairs, I placed Maggie's present and card on the coffee table in the living room, where she would be sure to see it. Finally, my cheery friends joined me and Maggie immediately noticed the big gift. They both carried medium-size gift bags, a reminder that I, too, had a birthday to celebrate.

"I'm treating you all to dinner tonight," Maggie announced. I shook my head and Carla and I both said her offer wasn't necessary. "It's part of my birthday treat."

"I didn't get you much, Kate," Carla said apologetically. "I had no idea what you wanted or needed!" She handed me her gift bag.

"I'm sure this is very special," I responded. "Can I open it now?"

Carla nodded with a big smile.

From wrapped tissue, I pulled out a framed photo of Rocky and Carla posed on her front porch. I smiled at how personal it was.

"We didn't want you to forget us," Carla explained. Part of me felt badly that I left poor Carla with Clay's dog.

"You crazy girl," I said, giving her a little hug. "This will be openly displayed somewhere. It makes me happy to see the two of you together. I'm going to put it right here on the mantle, like I would any family member."

Carla smiled with approval. "I already gave Maggie her gift before we came," she noted. "Now will someone open this big, lovely package?"

"It's for you, Maggie," I happily announced.

She looked surprised and began tearing at the paper.

"Don't you know you're supposed to open the card first?" Carla teased.

Maggie tore into the package and her eyes lit up when she saw the crazy quilt.

"Oh, Kate, this is beautiful," Maggie said as she unfolded the quilt. "This is too much. This is way too much!"

"I'm glad you like it!" I said, helping her unfold it. "I loved the embellished border, which I thought was unique. I found it at Imy's."

"I love it!" she said aloud. "I can't top this, for heaven's sake. I didn't spend the big bucks like you did, but here's my gift anyway." Maggie handed me her gift bag.

"You saw how reasonable Imy's prices were," I defended. "It didn't break my bank, plus I figured one more crazy quilt in your collection wouldn't hurt. Doesn't this make about six of them?"

We all laughed and she felt embarrassed.

I opened Maggie's gift bag and the first item I pulled out was a framed photo of Maggie and me on the beach when we were teenagers. What great times we'd had and it certainly made me smile. We were prettier and thinner then, for sure.

"Man, can you believe we ever looked like this?" I asked laughing. "This is great! Look how skinny I am. This will also go on my mantle. No one will ever guess this is me."

"Those were the days, my friend, and I don't want you to ever forget them!" Maggie joked.

I felt something else in the bag and pulled out a book of some kind. I unwrapped more tissue to discover it was a guest book that had *Josephine's Guest House* printed on the cover in gold letters.

"Wow Maggie, this is awesome," I responded, looking at it closer. "How did someone do this?"

"I saw one given at a bridal shower and thought of you,"

she explained. "Of course, I didn't know at the time you already had a book and were using a quilt for your guests to sign."

"Both are excellent," I said, hugging her. "My book is a cheap one I picked up at a drugstore, The only names in it are you and Carla, so be sure to sign this one. The quilt is supposed to be a conversation piece more than a record of guests. This also has room for comments, which will be so helpful. I love when people share their experience. Thank you both so much!" I felt incredibly blessed. "Having the two of you here with me is the best gift of all. Happy birthday one and all!"

"Well then, let the party begin," Maggie cheered. "Carla said she'd be the designated driver, so we'll take our car."

As we drove up the hill to winery, the girls marveled at the scenery and how secluded it was from the main road. After we got out of the car, they couldn't seem to get enough of the view.

"It's nice enough to sit outdoors, if you want!" I offered.

"We all brought jackets, so why don't we?" Maggie suggested. Carla nodded with approval.

"Welcome, ladies!" Ellie greeted as she came out to meet us. "I hear we are celebrating some birthdays this evening."

"That's right, Ellie, but we have said what happens in Borna, stays in Borna!" Maggie teased.

We all laughed in agreement.

"If you want to eat out here, that's fine," Ellie conceded. "We have some balloons and decorations we'll bring out. Trout will be out shortly to take your order."

"Oh great, now everyone here knows about us, Maggie," I teased. "I forget what a small town this is. I don't think there are many secrets here, like how old everyone is."

Maggie and Carla laughed it off.

We picked out a table for six, and Trout came to tell us about their wine choices and the history of Red Creek Winery. I wondered how many times a day he had to recite his charming information. After we gave him our wine order, he encouraged us to go inside and look around. The girls showered Ellie with many compliments as we followed her inside. The place was still rather empty at the early hour. I went to the bar and told Trout I wanted to pay for two bottles of wine with the Red Creek label on it for Maggie and Carla to take home.

Our mood was quite jolly as we got seated back on the patio. Trout reminded us of the wonderful sunset we'd be seeing. He told us he had barbecued ribs and pork steaks that afternoon and that everything was as tender as a baby's cheeks. The girls laughed and I added that his gumbo was as hot as a firecracker on the fourth of July. We watched as others started arriving at the winery and the conversation and laughter stated flowing as we consumed delicious wine.

"Does Clark ever come here?" Carla asked out of the blue.

"Now and then, but usually just to pick up food orders to go," I answered. "Why do you ask?"

"Well, I just thought it would have been fun for him to join us," Carla said politely. "You should have asked him."

"Nice of you to suggest, but he's not a social butterfly," I explained. "I hope Ellie can come out and join us soon."

Just as I wished, Ellie came out to take our food order and told us that dinner was on the house.

"Oh no, Miss Ellie," Maggie jumped in to say. "I'm treating my dear friend here for having us this weekend."

"Well, I want to treat Kate's friends and welcome you all

to Borna, so I'm sorry but there will be no tab," Ellie insisted. "You all enjoy!"

Maggie threw up her hands and blew her a kiss.

"I'd like to raise my glass to toast all my dear friends," I began. "This has been a memorable visit I will never forget. Here's to friendship. Forget the birthdays!"

They all raised their glasses, including Ellie, and shouted "friendship!"

"Why can't men seem to understand what friendship means?" asked Maggie more seriously. "Men don't seem to have a need for a really good friend."

"Here, here," I responded. "Women are survivors, but we value our friends."

"My husband doesn't have a best friend, can you believe it?" Maggie sadly questioned.

"I sometimes feel sorry for myself since I've been alone for so long," Carla said in a serious tone. "I have somehow survived with good friends."

"So, Ellie, you must meet a lot of eligible men in this business," Maggie remarked.

Ellie shook her head, as she sat down to join us. "That rarely happens, Maggie," she said, taking a sip of wine. "We have a lot of locals who mostly come here, and they have a good time teasing me about being single. I have to remember this is my business."

I couldn't help but wonder what Ellie was referring to.

"Good for you," Carla said as she enjoyed her diet soda.

"Kate had me believe no single folks existed here, but when I met Clark McFadden, I thought she must be blind," Maggie said.

Everyone snickered.

"Don't start, Maggie," I warned.

"I'm not always sure where Kate's coming from," Ellie claimed. "I've watched her take on some incredible challenges and take some hard knocks, but she stays focused and look at her now. A new business owner to the community, not every woman can do that."

"Here's to our buddy Kate and to all women who need support out there!" toasted Maggie with a slight of a slur in her voice.

"To women!" we cheered, as others were now starting to look at us.

"Did I hear a cheer for women in this direction?" a man said, joining us. It was Carson Jones. I couldn't believe his bad timing.

"Yes you did, mister," Maggie bragged. "There's been quite a bit of men bashing here, so be careful how you proceed."

We all laughed.

"These gals are celebrating a couple of birthdays," Trout explained as he filled our glasses with more wine.

"We sure are!" Ellie confirmed. "Kate is celebrating with her friends, Maggie and Carla, who are here from South Haven, Michigan. This is Carson, ladies. He is a friend of mine who happens to also be my wine distributor."

"It's my pleasure, ladies. However, I've already met Miss Meyr, here," he bragged with a big grin. "I understand you had your official ribbon cutting, so I'm pleased you are now open for business." He flirtatiously looked at me and I barely nodded. "Congratulations and whatever you're drinking, the next round is on me!"

The girls shouted a thank you.

Trout brought our food, but instead of Carson excusing

himself, he pulled up a chair as if he had been invited to join us. No one seemed to care but me. He told Trout to bring him an order of ribs. Ellie seemed thrilled to be in the social environment with him.

*Is she really falling for this guy?* I wondered.

The food was certainly delicious and the girls raved to Ellie about her chef, Kelly. I continued to ignore Carson, but saw him continually looking at me.

"Well, I'm sure sorry I missed the ribbon cutting," Carson voiced as if he'd been invited. "I plan to stay there as soon as I know my schedule next week."

I pretended I wasn't listening to him as I engaged Carla in conversation.

"We were Kate's first guests," bragged Maggie. "We were treated like royalty, as I'm sure you will be as well."

Why on earth did Maggie say that? She was showing her alcohol. I knew her too well.

"I sure hope so," Carson responded. "It's a beautiful place and the owner isn't too shabby either."

I was very embarrassed and I couldn't get myself to look at Ellie, who had to be very uncomfortable.

"I have a special dessert for you ladies," announced Ellie as Trout came our way with a birthday cake. "I bet you didn't know that you could bake a blueberry, chocolate cake, did you? Carson, these ladies are from blueberry country."

"Oh, Ellie, how sweet," I praised from across the table. "This should be quite yummy."

"More wine with this anyone?" Trout asked as he refilled Maggie's glass.

With more wine, Maggie started to sing Happy Birthday to us. They all joined in and I wanted to crawl under the table.

"Cut her off," I instructed Trout. "When Maggie sings, I know she's had way too much alcohol. This is the first year she's ever allowed singing to happen at our birthday dinners. We always insisted no hats, no balloons, and no singing! Well, guess there's a first for everything."

They all laughed.

"This is most delicious!" bragged Carla as she ate her cake. "Carson, would you like a slice?"

"I would indeed," he answered, looking at me for some approval.

"Carson, why don't we leave these gals to their little party and go inside," Ellie strongly suggested.

*Good for her,* I thought.

"If that's what these ladies want!" he teased, as if we were going to beg him to stay. The girls remained silent, thank goodness.

When Ellie and Carson went inside, I explained how uncomfortable I was with Carson's attention and that Ellie seemed to have a thing for him.

"Well, even I could tell he only had eyes for you, my dear," Maggie teased.

I shook my head. "I really don't want him staying at the guest house," I confessed. "I know it will make Ellie worry. Even though I have shown no interest, I can tell it bothers her. I wouldn't do anything to ever hurt her."

"I thought he was pretty presumptuous to just invite himself to our group, but then I don't know the players here," Carla expressed.

"Exactly my point," I agreed.

"Oh dear, I hope I didn't encourage anything," Maggie said in a more somber tone.

"You were both just being gracious, as always," I said to comfort them.

"He is rather full of himself," Maggie observed. "Even with my wine influence, I picked up on that. I know a lot of his kind of men from the country club."

"Good eye on that, girlfriend," I said, laughing. "I think we should go. I'll go in to settle up with Trout on my wine and say good-bye to Ellie."

When I walked inside, I headed for the bar, but out of the corner of my eye, I saw Ellie and Carson in a private conversation that looked pretty intimate. I hated to see her get hooked on him, but I knew it was too late. Goodness knows how long she had a thing for him.

"Trout, I need to settle up on wine for the girls," I said, still watching Ellie. "Did they tell you what kind they liked?"

"Yes, ma'am, it's all ready to go," Trout stated with a smile. "Leaving so soon?"

"We're not as young anymore since we just had a birthday, remember?" I teased. "We ole gals have to get our sleep and besides, they're leaving early in the morning."

I hated to interrupt, but from a distance I shouted to Ellie we were leaving. She immediately came over to give me a hug good-bye. I thanked her for treating us all to a wonderful meal. She followed me out the door, as we left Carson inside.

"Sure nice to meet you, ladies, since I've heard so much about you both," Ellie happily confessed. "Please come back anytime."

Each of them took time to give Ellie a hug and thank her for being such a good friend to me. It was comforting to see. Friendship was truly the basis of this past weekend. What would I do without it?

After we got home, we all agreed that we had a perfect little birthday celebration. Maggie started getting more sober and decided it would be helpful for them to load the car with a few things tonight, rather than wait till morning. When Maggie came back in the house from taking a handful to the car, she told me there was a truck parked across the street and asked what I thought about it. I didn't want to go into any explanation, but knew it had to be Ben Hecht with his usual stalking routine. I satisfied her concern when I told her I looked out the window and recognized the truck from seeing it around town. I told her he might be waiting for someone, or perhaps he'd had a bit much to drink. That seemed to satisfy her curiosity.

"I'm really beat," announced Carla as she kicked off her shoes. "I'm ready to turn in."

"Me, too," added Maggie with a yawn. "I'm not used to all this social activity! I'm glad Mark wasn't with us."

We laughed.

"I sure hate to see you guys go," I sadly admitted. "I hope you'll give me an honest critique of the guest house since you were my very first guests. It has meant so much for you all to be here and see the direction of my new life. It all seems more real now that you have been here."

They grinned.

"Well, since you gave me permission, I'll have your agent show me that condo she has in mind for you," Maggie shared. "We have to get you back for a visit real soon."

I smiled and nodded.

After a couple of good night hugs, the girls retired for the evening. I turned off the lights and set the alarm as always. I went to the front window to see if Ben was still parked across the street. I felt much better when I saw he was gone. What a strange life this man must have to be so obsessed with what I was doing. I figured Blade must be paying him to do such nonsense.

I went upstairs reliving my events of the evening. I sure hated the thought of Ellie getting involved with this Carson guy. He just didn't seem her type, despite sharing their interest in the wine business. I found it odd and unflattering that he seemed to flirt with me, if he had a relationship with Ellie. The more I thought about him, the more I hoped he would not call to book a room.

As I prepared for bed, I realized how long it had been since I heard from Jack. I hated being this far away from him. I decided I would call him tomorrow and tell him I was getting close to securing a condo in South Haven.

Where had Clark been tonight? I sure was hoping he would have stopped by the winery, as he frequently did. What was he up to and how did he spend his nights? I now was pleased that I hadn't shared with the girls the story of the horrible night when Clark saved my life. Would Clark want to know about Ben stalking me? He probably would have some good advice. I was also glad I had kept Ben's stalking habits from Ellie, so far. I didn't want her worrying about me, nor did I want the word to get out around town. There were times I felt so naïve in this town. Wasn't I supposed to be this city girl who was wise and street smart? I wondered if Josephine approved of my life so far.

# CHAPTER 8

The morning was very difficult for me as I prepared breakfast for Carla and Maggie. As I watched them finish loading the car, tears were already flowing down my cheeks. They were like family to me, since my parents were no longer living and I had divorced myself from the Meyrs. I could tell they were anxious to get on the road, so we took one last photo in the backyard before we gave our last hugs. We were all in tears as I watched them drive away.

I went inside to pour myself another cup of coffee and sat down in my favorite wicker chair on the sunporch. I always seemed to gravitate to the sunporch. The only things on my schedule today were cleaning the attic suite and meeting with the website guy Ellie had recommended. I knew exactly what I wanted him to do, so I felt the meeting could be accomplished quickly. I was about to get up when Ellie suddenly appeared at my back door.

"Hey, good morning," I greeted.

"I saw your friends leave and thought I'd walk over to cheer you up a bit," Ellie said with her great smile. "I'm sure you're feeling a bit sorry for yourself about now."

I nodded and wanted to tear up all over again. "I hate good-byes," I said sadly.

She gave me a kind look of understanding. "Well, you better get used to it, my dear, since you are now in the guest house business," she teased. "Folks are going to be leaving all the time!"

I had to laugh at the truth of it all.

"Your friends are just as special as you described them, Kate," Ellie praised.

"I know, and it's made me realize I need to get busy securing the condo so I can visit them more frequently," I admitted.

"I think it's a grand idea, because I'd love to vacation on Lake Michigan, myself," Ellie revealed as if she really meant it.

"Oh, that would be wonderful," I responded. I was definitely cheering up. I also felt somewhat brave to ask Ellie some personal things. "Ellie, you and I have known each other quite awhile now," I began. "I need you to share with me what might be going on between you and Carson. It may be none of my business, and you can just tell me to back off if you don't want to talk about it."

She looked surprised at the question and paused before she spoke. "I guess you do know me pretty well," she admitted. She looked away as she continued. "I didn't realize that my feelings showed." She paused again. "I think I always was that strong and independent businesswoman, and then I fall for a guy who doesn't want any part of a commitment. It's been years since I let any of my emotions get out of control like this. At first I was attracted to his independent nature, but then I realized I want more for some reason. I hate myself for that!"

"There's nothing wrong with wanting a commitment, especially if this has been going on for some time," I declared. "I just guess you wonder about any traveling salesman. Do you trust him?"

She nodded shamelessly. "I know he comes across like this ladies man, but it's just part of his salesmanship," she defended.

I wanted to tell her right away she was wrong, but kept my mouth closed.

"He said he loves me because I don't crowd him or make any demands. He also loves talking business strategy with me. That's how we got started in all this, you know."

None of this sounded very good to me.

"He loves you?" I softly asked. She nodded. "So you also love him?"

She was silent for a bit. "In the worst way, and it makes me crazy," she said, looking restless. "I think Trout is the only one that knows about this. It's been pretty hard to keep it from him at the winery. Trout is rather protective of me and he doesn't care much for Carson."

*Good for Trout,* I thought.

"So what do you think of me now, Kate?"

I sure was hoping she wouldn't ask such a question.

"I don't know him very well, Ellie," I began to explain. "We all need different things in our life at different times. If you are willing to hang in there, it's your business. You're a big girl and can handle whatever happens, I'm sure."

"Oh, Kate, I'm so glad to hear you say this," Ellie said in relief. "I thought you might give me a lecture. He may change his mind in the future. He is very jealous when he thinks others are flirting with me."

"I've never seen his car at your place next door," I noted.

"I know," she said, nodding. "You know what a small town this is, and I don't want anyone talking. We usually meet up at my winery or go for a drive and have dinner somewhere else."

*How awful,* I thought.

"Hey, how about some coffee?" I said to move on from the conversation. I could hardly stand to hear more.

"No thanks, Kate, I need to get going," she explained. "Let me know how you like Frank, the computer guy. He's pretty sharp! What time is he coming?"

"Around 1:00 p.m., I think," I said, looking at my watch. The morning was slipping away. "I have to get the attic cleaned. The more I think about it, I better put Susie on call when I have guests. I don't think I'll make a very good housemaid."

Ellie laughed and agreed.

We said good-bye and I couldn't decide if I was happy I had asked Ellie about Carson. It made me sick inside. How could any relationship be so unhealthy? How stressful for her to have to keep this such a secret. How could someone so smart be so dumb? No, that wasn't Ellie. She just got caught off guard, which could happen to anyone.

Throughout the week, I tried to put Ellie's relationship aside. I convinced myself it was none of my business. If I sensed he was hurting her, I would certainly advise her differently. To distract myself from her situation, I concentrated on business concerns like printed material, my website, and putting finishing touches on the house. There was part of me that was happy no one was reserving a room. Perhaps I just liked the thought of owning a guest house, instead of the ritual of entertaining guests. It was soon to be my turn to entertain the Friendship Circle. I felt more confident now that the house was ready, and I was anxious to see them again. I decided to bake up a storm with all my favorite blueberry recipes. They should get a kick out of that.

I decided it was time to make a decision about my home in South Haven, so I called my real estate agent and settled for a second story condo, on a street that lined the shore of

Lake Michigan. I remembered visiting there years ago with a friend, and it had a nice view of the lake. Maggie's account of the place was appealing and the price was right. This gave me a sense of relief, and I would start contacting painters to give the place a new, clean look. The thought of another decorating assignment was somewhat exciting. Carla, Maggie, and Jack were excited, of course, when I gave them the good news. I also was pleased to catch up with Jack. He as much confessed he wouldn't be visiting Borna anytime soon, but he would make it a point to get right home once I started working on the condo. South Haven would always be home to Jack. I now realized that.

I took my first reservation over the phone. It was a referral from Anna at Saxon Village. It was from a couple were who were spending a few days touring all the county sites and needed one night in Borna. I responded so professionally, it caught me by surprise. Who was this businesswoman? They booked the Wildflower Room, across from my bedroom. Next to that room was the Forestroom. With a bigger group, these two bedrooms could be open to each other. I called the small single room downstairs The Study. It was small and wanted to be more masculine because it used to be Doc's office. I had to name the attic after Josephine by calling it Josephine's Attic Suite. As far as I was concerned, that would always be her room. I was starting to feel relaxed about my new role as a hostess till I got the call from Carson, who booked two weekend nights. I kept my professional voice and avoided any conversation. I wished he could have been here when I also booked the Stevens. I booked him in The Study, on the first floor.

I finally ran into Clark when I went into Harold's

Hardware to get a few supplies. He seemed to be glad to see me. He was in a hurry, but did ask how the guest house was doing and said that he missed having my blueberry muffins. It was an opening to invite him to stop by anytime. Of course, Harold was listening to our conversation. I knew he thought there should be something romantic going on between us, but he was badly mistaken. I had to admit that when Clark came around I had schoolgirl butterflies in my stomach.

Summer was now in full swing after a short spring. My flowers were gorgeous, thanks to my insistence of daily watering. There were now endless events and happenings around the county. The East Perry Fair was the biggest event of the year, and that's all folks were talking about. I couldn't wait to experience it.

# CHAPTER 9

On the eve of my first guests' arrival, I saw Ben Hecht's pickup truck parked across the street. Surely others had to see his truck around my place and found it odd. I peeked out the front window as always, only this time when I looked for his face usually staring at me, he seemed to be slumped over as if he had fallen asleep. It was barely dark, so I was surprised to see him parked there so early. I went about my business of checking e-mails. I got up to pour myself a glass of wine, and decided awhile later to see if Ben's truck was still there. Nothing had changed. Something wasn't right. It didn't look normal. I decided, wise or not, to go out and confront him. I crossed the street and his body didn't move as I came nearer to him. I hesitatingly knocked on the window. It was a hot night with his window up and the truck not running.

"Mr. Hecht, Mr. Hecht," I shouted as I continued to knock on the window. All of a sudden he leaned to the right on the seat. "Are you okay?" I yelled, knowing there was something terribly wrong.

I bravely opened the unlocked door and saw his face staring at me in horror. He groaned lightly as if he wanted to say something. He was definitely stricken with a heart attack or a stroke.

"Don't worry Mr. Hecht, I'll get some help!" I frantically shouted.

At that time a car was going by. I quickly got in the street to flag down whoever it might be. As luck would have it, it was Oscar Meers. He saw my panic and pulled to the side of the road.

"Mr. Hecht is seriously ill! Can you call for help? It's a stroke or heart attack!"

Oscar nodded and immediately called the first responders in Borna that were available for emergency calls. Oscar helped me lay him across the seat. The inside of the truck was hot and smelled like cigarette smoke. I told Oscar how I spotted his truck and saw him slumped over. There was no way I was sharing more information about him being parked here.

When two responder guys showed up, they said an ambulance was on its way. I felt relief and wanted to run back into the house. I tried to comfort Mr. Hecht, but the horror in his eyes made it difficult. I took his hand, telling him everything would be all right. By the time the ambulance left, a small crowd of locals gathered who wanted to know the scoop.

"It's a good thing Miss Meyr spotted him slumped over. He may be dead right now," Oscar told the onlookers.

"Thank goodness you came along, Oscar," I said with gratitude. "I truly didn't know what to do first."

"I'll have one of my guys take his truck home," Oscar said as he prepared to get back in his car.

We said good-bye and I asked him to inform me if he heard anything about his condition.

As I walked across the street, Marv walked up the hill in my direction and asked me what happened. I explained the chain of events. He admitted he had seen Ben's truck there before. I just nodded, not wanting to explain that Ben was stalking me. Before Marv left, he reminded me that Ben was a mean, tough, ole bird who would probably survive.

I closed the front door, feeling all kinds of emotions.

I couldn't help but feel sorry for Ben. I knew the look in his eyes was fear of losing his life. Was he also afraid that I would reveal about him stalking me? Ben had obviously gotten carried away defending his friend Blade by scaring me. Ben had to be in his late seventies, even looking older. I said a private prayer that he would be all right.

I had to concentrate on the arrival of Mr. and Mrs. Stevens' arrival. I was mixing up ingredients for a quiche, when my cell phone rang. It was Ellie.

"We just got word here that Ben Hecht had a stroke in front of your house!" she stated before I could say hello. "I hear you found him. Is that right?"

"Boy, word sure spreads fast," I said.

"Yeah, the bread truck guy drove by the ambulance and told us when he dropped off his delivery," Ellie explained. "Is he still alive?"

"He was when he left here," I reported. "Thank goodness Oscar was driving by. I flagged him down to help me."

"Well, you may have saved his life, Miss Meyr," Ellie said sarcastically. "Aren't you expecting guests soon?"

"Yes, I was just preparing some quiche when you called." I shared.

"Hey, I got a visit from Ruth Ann this afternoon," Ellie announced. "She wanted to go over some of her plans and ask me about some things."

"Good, I hope you encouraged her to follow through," I said in a positive tone.

"It really does sound great, and she's going to pile a lot of bucks into the place," Ellie recalled. "She bragged about how Clark is helping her with some things and commented that he didn't come cheap."

"Sounds like she can afford it, so I'm happy for her," I stated, without meaning a word of it.

"I think she's got a thing for him, frankly," Ellie said. "She is looking a lot better since she's living alone. Have you noticed that? She looks like she has a new lease on life starting this project and all."

I didn't respond and just told Ellie I had to get back to work. Ellie had to know I would be uncomfortable with her telling me about Ruth Ann having a thing for Clark. She used to want to tease me about him. Was she expecting a rise out of me? Clark had to make a living and he obviously saw an opportunity. It would take quite the female to get Clark off the dime in a relationship. Somehow, I doubted if Ruth Ann was up to the mission.

I came out the back door when I saw the Stevens arrive in the driveway. They were a well-dressed looking couple that looked to be in their sixties. They immediately admired the house and flowers before coming inside. I gradually led them to my office, where I took care of payment and gave them proper materials. It felt very strange taking payment for staying in a house I lived in.

Mrs. Stevens started admiring the quilt on the wall, and I explained it was for my guests to sign. They were delighted and offered to sign it immediately after they signed the guest book. I took them upstairs to the assigned Wildflower Room, which was waiting for them. Their compliments were overwhelming.

"Are we the first to stay in this room?" Mrs. Stevens asked. "I know you just opened."

I nodded with pride. "I hope you will enjoy it and let me know if there's anything you need," I assured them. "You are welcome to come down and have a cocktail before you leave for dinner, if you like."

They explained they were on a tight schedule and had dinner reservations with some distant relatives. I wished them a good evening and told them I would see them at breakfast. They left for dinner within the half hour. I reminded myself that I couldn't set my alarm at night till all my guests were in for the evening. I wondered if I should stay up like parents do when their children are out. This was going to take some getting used to.

Before I went upstairs to bed, I called Maggie. I missed her and wanted to talk to someone.

"Glad you called, girlfriend," Maggie responded. "I just told the Beach Quilters all about my visit to Borna. They all said to tell you hello when I talked to you again. They were especially happy when I told them you finally made a condo choice and would be visiting soon."

"Oh, it would so fun to see them again!" I happily said. "Was Cornelia there?"

"Yes, she was," Maggie confirmed.

"Any more talk about her selling?" I curiously asked.

"Not right now, anyway," Maggie noted. "She still always has such new things. I don't think she wants us to think she's going anywhere. Actually, the gossip of the day was Sandra's divorce becoming final. That was pretty quick, don't you think?"

"Oh my," I said in surprise. "I'm sorry to hear that. James has not only screwed up the business, but his family."

"They say she looks horrible and has lost a lot of weight, which she didn't have to lose in the first place. I just want to remind you that your painters are going to be in the condo this week. After they finish, the rest is up to you."

"That's kind of exciting," I said, moving my thoughts away from Sandra. "I've been looking online at some of the modern furniture they have at Country House Furniture. I want light, simple lines for easy upkeep, since I won't be there much. I want it to look like a lake house, I think."

"Sounds good, and I love Country House Furniture," added Maggie. "You know you can always lease the place when you're not here."

"No way, don't go there," I stated firmly. "This is my home away from home."

Maggie laughed. "So how is Borna and my new friend Ellie?" she inquired.

I told her Borna had some excitement today with Ben's attack in front of the house. She wanted to press me for more information about what he was doing there in the first place, but I didn't go there. I told her he may not recover, based on how serious it looked. She finally dropped the subject, but it reminded me that tomorrow I needed to check on him. We hung up with our usual messages of love. I always felt better after talking to Maggie.

I sat there thinking about how I had a friend for life. Did Sandra have a friend to cry with I wondered? I never had much in common with her, but we did marry into the same family. I'm sure she felt betrayed with James' drinking and who knows what else. The way he harassed me over the Borna settlement, I couldn't imagine how brutal he might have been with her. When she approached me about trying to be reasonable with James, I bet she didn't have a clue as to what was really going on. I decided to give her a call when I went back to South Haven. We certainly had a few things in common right now.

# CHAPTER 10

The Stevens couple was up bright and early, which somewhat surprised me. I served my first official breakfast at the dining room table with some of my best china. They were quite impressed with my veggie quiche and fruit salad, but most of all my blueberry muffins and Mrs. Grebing's apple crumb coffee cake. I couldn't take all the credit, of course.

"You should come up with your own cookbook to sell which has all of your special recipes," advised Ms. Stevens.

"When I have some spare time, I might consider that," I graciously responded. "I hope you both have a wonderful day and please come back again."

They got up from the table and Mr. Stevens paused.

"We certainly will," he said nodding. "I had the best sleep last night. I am generally not a good sleeper."

"I did, too, and it was kind of strange, because we both woke up from a bright sunlight coming in the room. But the clock only said it was midnight," Mrs. Stevens described with a chuckle. "I couldn't believe it."

"Yeah, I went into the bathroom and saw it was still dark outside," he said in disbelief. "We had a laugh about it and easily went right back to sleep. It was the craziest thing."

I knew exactly what they were talking about.

"I've never felt so refreshed, and that was a wonderful breakfast," bragged Mr. Stevens as he stretched his arms.

"Thank you so much," I said, seeing them toward the door. "I'm kind of new at this, so I'm pleased you were happy with your stay."

"We'd love to come back for the fair everyone's talking about, but we have another commitment," Mrs. Stevens shared, going to the car.

Off they went, as I waved from the back steps. I was pleased with how my first experience went. However, I was a bit surprised that Josephine was going to be active across the hall. Thank goodness they were happy with the end result. Would all my guests get this special treatment from her?

Now the unpleasant part began with the cleanup, plus I dreaded Carson's visit in the evening. I got on the phone and called Susie to see if she could come in Monday morning to clean after Carson's visit. She was delighted. I knew she would be because she sometimes came with Cotton when he did the yardwork and hinted for odd jobs.

My phone rang as I began to strip the sheets in the Wildflower Room.

"Hey, how did your first guest visit go?" Ellie happily asked.

"Great, really great," I reported. "I think it will actually be more fun when I have a mix of folks here at the same time. They could visit among each other without me trying to entertain them."

"It might!" she agreed. "Remember, not everyone that comes to stay will want to be entertained. By the way, Ruth Ann said some of her quilting friends were on the internet and signed up for a little quilting retreat with her. She has a sister that's part of the group. They will probably stay at your place, which should be fun. Anyway, the reason I'm calling is to invite you to have dinner with Carson and me tonight. We're having Italian night, so I know it'll be great."

"Oh, no thanks, Ellie," I immediately answered. "I am quite behind here. So you suppose Carson will check in before dinner or after?"

"Probably before, but I wish you'd change your mind," she insisted.

I finally convinced her, plus I knew exactly what she was trying to do. I would be the cover for their little romantic dinner, and I didn't want to have any part of it. I had to make sure this visit from Carson was going to be all business. There was something about him I didn't like or trust.

I had just gotten back to arranging my laundry, when my phone went off again.

"Miss Meyr?" the faint, elderly female voice asked.

"Yes, who is this?" I asked.

"It's Mrs. Hecht, Ben's wife," she struggled to say.

"Oh, Mrs. Hecht, how is Mr. Hecht doing?" I asked with concern.

"He's still with us, but can barely speak," she described. "He had a terrible stroke and he's paralyzed on one side. His heart has always been weak, so I'm very worried about him."

"I'm sorry to hear that," I said truly feeling bad for her.

"He wanted me to call you," she finally revealed. "He'd like to thank you in person for saving his life."

"That just isn't necessary, Mrs. Hecht," I sadly stated.

"He said not to take no for an answer," she insisted. "He's in Perry County Memorial Hospital in Room 212. Can I tell him you'll come?"

I paused. "I'm expecting guests tonight, but perhaps I can come by tomorrow," I said to ease her mind.

"That will be fine. So I'll tell him right away," she said before hanging up.

What a strange request from a man who tried to scare me. There was no way I could turn her down, but I sure wasn't looking forward to going face to face with her husband. I felt myself getting all tangled up in this community of characters. Would I be able to be myself and satisfy everyone's demands? I now had a public facility that would require even more of my attention. At least I didn't have to be afraid of Ben anymore. I was glad I kept his behavior a secret from everyone. At least I think I did, anyway.

I went about my day, pondering Ellie's information about Carson arriving early before dinner. Would he open up about this relationship with Ellie? Was I supposed to play dumb to another secret going on?

After baking another batch of muffins for Carson's breakfast, I realized it was 5:00 p.m. It was a day of many domestic duties and I was tired. Fifteen minutes later, a knock on the front door startled me. Through the oval glass in the door I saw Carson. He saw me, too, so there was no time to check myself in the mirror.

"Did I come to the right door?" he asked as I opened the door for him.

"Why sure, come on in," I greeted. "Most folks park in the rear and use the back door."

"Wow, Kate, this is beautiful!" Carson said, eyeing the place from the entry hall.

"Thanks, I'll show you around," I said in a professional manner. "If you'll step in here, we can get you registered. "This is where Doc's patients waited, by the way."

"I see," he said, looking everywhere. "The place looks like

it was beautifully built for that period of time. I understand you have three floors here for guests." I nodded as I took his charge card.

"You asked for a single room, so I put you in what I call The Study, right here next to this room on the first floor," I explained. "That's the room where Doc Paulson saw his patients. It's perfect for one person. I think you'll like it. Here are all the particulars for breakfast and checkout time."

"I'm sure all will be fine," he said, checking out the living room. "This is even better than I thought it would be. So how do you like being a guest house hostess, so far?"

"It's a little too early to report," I said with a slight smile.

"Ellie said you were not able to join us for dinner tonight," he complained. "I'm sorry to hear that, as we both would enjoy your company."

"Thanks, but perhaps another time," I said briefly. "Here's your room and there are two entrances to the kitchen. Just let me know if you need anything or have any questions." I turned away, as if I were busy.

"Thanks, I'll just quickly change and be off," he reported. "I hope you'll still be up when I return."

I ignored his comment and assured myself I would not be. As soon as he went into his room, I went upstairs to mine and locked the door. I turned on the evening news and would stay there till I heard his car leave. It felt strange feeling somewhat captive in my own house. This arrangement would take some getting used to. I told myself I would not be one of those hostesses that stayed with her guests.

I heard the shower running and waited till I thought Carson had left the building. I quietly began my way back downstairs, then I suddenly stopped as I heard his voice.

*Do I go back upstairs?*

His door must have been slightly open, since I could hear him. I assumed he thought I was still upstairs. I could barely hear him, as I quietly stayed in the hallway.

"No, hon, that's not the deal," he said in a defensive voice. "I know I said I thought I'd be home tonight, but we're not finished here."

It was then silent, as I strained my ears. Who was he talking to?

"I understand," he began again. "Don't worry, I'll be there. How are the kids?" More pause. "Damn it, I told you, so let up, will you!" There was another pause. "Okay, I'll forget it," he continued. "I love you, too." He hung up and I turned quickly to get back up the stairs.

I couldn't believe what I just heard. I would stake my life if that wasn't a husband talking to a wife. He asked about the kids and was trying to explain why he was not coming home. The message of I love you was the kicker. Mr. Carson was indeed a married man, and now I wondered if Ellie knew this or she just didn't want to tell me.

I finally heard the front door close. So now he was off to have a cozy dinner with his girlfriend, my friend. I guess that was the part of the day he couldn't get quite finished. What a creep! Thoughts of Clay's deceitfulness with me crept quickly into my mind. Surely Ellie did not know about this. She had such good values. I wanted to call him more names, but I knew that wouldn't accomplish anything. I headed to the kitchen to pour myself a glass of wine. My appetite had just vanished for dinner. I took my wine to the porch to sit and think. This scenario reminded me of when I was in high school. I found out my friend's boyfriend was cheating on her, so I told her. We were so close and I felt I was doing her a big favor. As it turned out, it ruined our friendship forever because I caused her so much pain. I was the messenger and I paid the price. I regretted it ever since. Ellie was a big girl and very smart. I had to trust this would all be revealed in some way.

I took my frustration, glass of wine, and a jar of peanut butter and crackers upstairs to my room. Not knowing when Carson would return, I wanted to be out of sight. I grabbed one of three books I had started and got comfortable. If I got lucky, I would fall asleep and leave the disappointments of the world behind.

# CHAPTER 11

I awoke, as always, around 7:00 a.m. thinking it would be plenty of time to start breakfast. My brochure said it would be served at 8:00 a.m. I had everything ready. When I finally came downstairs, I saw Carson's door was closed, which was a relief. I did a few things in the kitchen and then set the table for one in the dining room. I suddenly felt eyes on me and quickly turned around. It was Carson, standing right behind me. I dropped a spoon on the floor, I was so surprised.

"Oh, good morning," I quickly said, picking up the spoon.

"You're not joining me for breakfast?" he asked in a teasing manner.

"No, I'm not much of a breakfast eater. Plus, I am the hostess, remember?" I said with a bit of humor.

"And a pretty and efficient one at that!" he complimented.

I poured his coffee and ignored his comment. "So how was your dinner last night?" I asked with a straight face.

"It was great!" he claimed. "Kelly put out a nice spread and Ellie hired a small band that was terrific! It got to be a late night, so I'm glad you didn't stay up for me." I wanted to gag at that remark. "You don't have any recommendations for a hangover, do you?"

"I guess I should be prepared for that, shouldn't I?" I said, shaking my head with a snicker in my voice.

"Oh, these must be the famous muffins I keep hearing

about," he teased. "Do you mind if I pass on breakfast? My stomach isn't quite ready for food as of yet."

"I'll be happy to wrap some for you to have for later, if you like," I offered.

"Sure, thanks," he said with a wink. "I'll just have my coffee here and visit with you!" I heard a knock at the door, so I did not respond.

"Oh, good morning, Cotton," I said, going out to greet him.

"Good morning, Kate," Cotton responded, cheerfully as always. "I wanted to make sure your guests were up before I started mowing the lawn."

"Go ahead and thanks for checking," I answered with relief that he was close by. "I have extra muffins this morning, so when you're finished here, be sure to take some home."

He lit up with delight.

Right behind me was Carson, listening to every word. He certainly made me nervous, and I think he knew it.

"You seem to have a lot of help around here," he commented as he sipped his coffee.

"I'm very fortunate," I said as I got back into the kitchen.

"So do you have any suitors hanging around also?" he asked in a provocative tone.

"No, Carson," I answered angrily. "I am a recent widow, and that's the last thing I need. This new business and house are plenty to keep me busy."

"But you're still a young and attractive woman," he said, hoping to get a response.

I pretended I didn't hear him as I busied myself. "So do you have a lot of appointments today?" I asked just to hear his excuse.

"No, not many," he claimed. "I told Ellie I would stop by

this morning and help her with a computer problem." That was a new excuse since she had a computer guy.

"Well, if you'll excuse me, I have an appointment to get ready for this morning," I explained as I started to walk away. "Feel free to relax on the porch. There are a couple of newspapers from this morning."

"Thanks, I will," he said sitting down in my favorite chair and putting his feet up. I was hoping for a different answer.

I went upstairs to shower and change for my visit to see Ben Hecht. I had decided not to leave till Carson left the house. He was certainly not the type of guest I wanted to leave alone in the house. I got on my phone to check e-mails. I was pleasantly surprised to get a text from Jack.

> Congrats on the condo, Mom. When will you be there? I will try to join you.

That was a good question, and I knew I had to decide in the next week.

When I finally decided to go downstairs, I opened my bedroom door to find Carson standing there in the hallway.

"I'm just checkin' the place out," he quickly explained, as if he were a little boy caught in the cookie jar. "Do you mind showing me the attic?" It appeared he was going there with or without me. "I may want to stay up there next time."

"Sure," I reluctantly said.

He followed me up the stairs and I felt as if he were staring right through me.

"Nice, nice," he said as he went in and walked around.

I stayed by the door. "It's very quiet up here and bigger than I imagined. So this is where your friends from South Haven stayed?" he asked with curiosity. I nodded and started heading down the stairs.

"You look mighty nice today, Kate," he complimented as we went down the stairs. "Where are you off to?"

I really wanted to give him a nasty answer, but didn't. "Several places," I simply answered when we got down the stairs in the entry hall.

"Oh, I just remembered to sign the guest book and this lovely quilt, as the brochure told me to," he noted as he picked up the pen.

I then remembered I had not personally asked him to sign either one. I saw Cotton about to leave so I went to the back door to give him his muffins.

"Say, too bad about ole Ben Hecht," Cotton commented. "I understand you found him. Mighty good timin', if I do say so," he said, taking my muffins. Cotton then saw Carson behind me.

"I'm out of here, Kate," Carson said passing by us on the steps. "I'll see you this evening."

I waved and felt a sense of relief he was gone. It was then I realized that my guests would have a key to my home.

"Thanks again, Miss Kate," Cotton said, ignoring my guest. He drove away happy, with his muffins.

When I arrived at the second floor of the hospital, I stopped at the nurses' station to ask where to find Mr. Hecht's room.

"Are you family?" she asked as she removed her reading glasses.

"No, I'm not," I said, feeling guilty about coming. "I was asked to be here by the patient and Mrs. Hecht."

"I'll have to check," she said as if she didn't believe me. She walked down the hall and disappeared into one of the rooms. The whole place was unusually quiet. Perhaps everyone was napping. She returned very quickly. "Okay, Miss Meyr, you may go in to Room 212 down the hall," she instructed. "Please keep your visit short."

"I will, thank you." I made my dreaded steps down the hall. When I entered the room, I saw an old man that looked like he had already passed away. His eyes were closed. Mrs. Hecht was huddled at his bedside and another younger man was standing by her. I was really interrupting something personal, and I had no business here.

"Oh, Miss Meyr, so good of you to come," she said getting up to greet me. "This is our son, Edward."

"Nice to meet you, Miss Meyr," he said graciously. He was a well-dressed man that certainly didn't look like a son of Ben Hecht's. "I understand you found Dad slumped over in his truck. He must have started feeling badly and pulled over to the roadside."

I nodded, not wanting to say more.

"Ben, Ben," Mrs. Hecht said as she nudged Mr. Hecht in the arm, "Miss Meyr is here to see you now."

He turned his head my direction and opened his eyes. I then remembered how penetrating those scary eyes were when he first approached me in Marv's bar. Mrs. Hecht raised the bed slightly so he could see me better. His eyes were red and watery and his mouth was twisted on one side from the stroke. He attempted to speak, but only a grunt came out.

"I hope you are feeling better!" I leaned down and said in a loud voice, so he could hear me.

"I, I, want to say, I'm sorry." He forced the sentence out of his mouth in a loud whisper. He then raised his unaffected hand for me to take.

I took his brittle hand in mine, which was shaking. I wanted to tell him his apology wasn't necessary, but didn't want to interrupt his chain of thought.

"You're a nice lady."

I smiled and squeezed his weather-worn hand. "Thank you, Mr. Hecht," I responded with a smile. "Apology not needed. I'm glad I was helpful and now you just need to get better." I wanted to cry, but took a deep breath instead.

"If I can help in any way, Mrs. Hecht, just let me know."

She smiled with tears flowing out of her wrinkled, dried eyes.

"Thank you for coming, Miss Meyr," Edward said as he offered to shake my hand. "Dad can be pretty stubborn sometimes, but I hope he'll do what he's told."

"Where do you live, Edward?" I asked with some interest.

"Outside of Chicago," he explained. "I don't get here to visit as often as I should. Could I please speak with you for a moment out in the hall?"

"Sure," I said looking back at Mr. Hecht, still watching me. "You take care now." I followed Edward into the hallway.

"If you don't mind, Miss Meyr, I'd like to know why my dad felt so compelled to tell you he was sorry for something," Edward asked in a quiet voice. I wasn't prepared for this.

"It should all be forgotten, Edward," I answered. "Your dad was very angry about his friend Blade having gone to prison." Edward looked confused. "Blade broke into my house and attacked me. Some of his friends didn't take it well when I put their friend in jail. Please know your father did nothing to harm me. He was just bitter about the experience."

"I'm sorry to hear that," Edward said, looking bewildered. "Mom said something about a guy named Blade awhile back, but I don't remember the story."

"For everyone's sake, all should be forgotten, so I better get going," I said, wanting to leave. "Take care of your dad. I wish I still had my dad around."

He gave me a sad smile. "It meant a lot to him, so thanks for coming," he said as I walked away.

I left to go home, feeling sad and yet comforted that Ben was in good hands. I really wanted to put Blade and Ben out of my life and out of my mind. I decided to stop for gas in Unionville before I turned on the road leading to Borna. Across the street was a house I admired immediately on my first drive here. It sat close to the curved road and it looked to have been built in the Civil War era. The framed white house had tiny paned windows with green shutters. It was a storybook house which only needed red geraniums to make it perfect. It appeared to be empty.

I went inside to pay cash for my gas, and asked the cashier if he knew the owner of the house and if it was for sale.

"Nope, not for sale that I know of," he said, shaking his head. "It's been in the Hopfer family for as long as I've known, but nobody lives there."

"What a shame," I said staring at the house out the window.

"Once in a while somebody will come around," he added. "The guy over there keeps the grass mowed for them. He may be part of the family."

I nodded and thanked him for the information. I wanted to walk around the property and look in the windows, but decided that wouldn't be wise. Word would spread quickly that the guest house lady from Borna was snooping around in Unionville. I continued my trip back home, admiring its summer beauty along the roadside. My mind now began to wander back to the reality of my day-to-day life. I needed to make plans soon to get back to South Haven. The summer would pass before I knew it. Perhaps by then, Ellie would have wised up to her married friend. I sure dreaded him spending another night at 6229 Main Street.

It was now dusk, and I really didn't want to go home just yet. I hadn't eaten all day, so I decided Marv's was the perfect place to stop and pick up dinner before I went home. As always, the parking lot was packed with cars and trucks. I finally squeezed in at the edge of their parking lot. This place used to intimidate me, but not any longer. I walked in and immediately saw Marv behind the counter, which always made me smile. I took a seat at the crowded bar counter. A lot of these faces I had never seen before.

"Hey, neighbor, glad to see you back here again!" Marv greeted.

"I'm starved, and I remembered this is the night for your pork chop special," I recalled.

"That's right and Clara's strawberry rhubarb pie," he bragged. "It's her best. You have to try it."

"I better pass on that and just settle for a glass of Cabernet," I ordered. "Give me the usual sides that go with it."

He nodded with a big smile.

"Make that for two!"

I turned around to see Clark standing behind me.

"Hey you!" I said with a big smile. "Are you trying to crash my dinner?"

He grinned. "Bring it over to the corner table that's empty over there," he instructed Marv.

Marv grinned and nodded.

"Does this mean you're buying?" I teasingly asked.

"I might," he said giving me a wink.

I followed him to the corner table, where it was rather dark, but less smoky. "I thought you just ordered food to go," I joked as I followed him.

"Not when I see a pretty lady to have dinner with," Clark joked back. "So you're not cooking tonight?"

I shook my head. "I just came back from visiting Ben Hecht in the hospital," I said.

He looked shocked. "Well, I did hear you were the Good Samaritan that found him," he shared. "Say, I've seen his truck around your place more than once. Am I wrong?"

I shook my head once more, reminding myself again what a small town this was. It was interesting to know that Clark had observed Ben, but never said anything to me. I reluctantly confessed the continued stalking of Ben and how I really didn't want anyone to know. He was all ears, and I could tell he didn't know it was that frequent. He seemed to be pleased when I told him Ben was sorry for his actions. We were then interrupted.

"Here's the best food you'll find in East Perry," Marv announced when he presented our food.

"No question!" I smiled.

"This goes on my house tab, Marv," Clark instructed.

"Got it," Marv said with a wink.

We then went to lighter topics while we ate our delicious dinner. I caught myself just staring at him at times. When he smiled, I smiled.

"So what brought you by here, besides food," I asked in hopes of knowing more about his schedule.

"Business," he briefly said. "Speaking of business, how is it going at Josephine's?" He sure had a way of avoiding telling me about his life.

"I don't really have an honest assessment of the picture right now," I admitted. "It takes getting used to. I know I won't always be able to pick my guests, that's for sure." He laughed. "I thought you told me I would be in complete control with a business like this!"

"Well, you do and you don't," he confessed. "You have to eat, so sometimes it means going out of your way to make a buck or two." He was right about that, and no one knew better than he.

"Right now I have Carson Jones staying one more night at the house," I divulged. "I don't like that man!"

Clark chuckled.

"I guess I should keep opinions like this private, right?"

"You're not the only one with that opinion!" Clark added. "Trout has plenty to say about that guy. I don't know him. I've just seen him around the winery now and then."

The wine was making my tongue wag more than I liked, as I shared with him what I had overheard Carson saying on the phone. I told him it was very hard not to pick up the phone and call Ellie.

"So what happens at Josephine's Guest House doesn't stay at Josephine's Guest House?" Clark asked in a teasing manner.

"It's going to be very difficult!" I said, watching the waitress take our food away. "Seriously, Clark, Ellie's a friend of mine and she needs to know."

"You're right, but you cannot be the one to tell her or your friendship will suffer," he concurred. "She may already know."

"So should I just decide to drop it?" I asked with a straight face.

"I say leave it to me and Trout to fix this guy," Clark offered. He had a grin on his face.

"Oh boy, you'd better not tell me about it." I snickered.

"I would be thankful, because none of us wants to see Ellie hurt, even if it's a little too late for that."

The hours were passing as I shared the news of purchasing a condo. He also revealed he was helping Ruth Ann design and build a fancy bar for her banquet center which he found challenging. The place was now becoming empty with only a few people left.

"I can't believe it's almost midnight," I said looking at my watch. "Maybe my unwanted guest will be fast asleep when I get home."

"Last call," Marv yelled across the room.

"We'll pass," Clark yelled back.

We both got up and headed toward the door as Marv yelled for us to come back real soon.

"I'll walk you to your car," Clark offered, taking my arm. "Why are you parked way over there?"

"Because it was the only place I could find," I explained, being totally aware of his arm in my arm.

"You would have been closer if you'd parked your car at home and walked over," he teased.

"But if I did that, my unwanted guest would know I was home," I responded. He shook his head and laughed. Just then, Marv turned off the outside lights and we were in pitch darkness.

"Thanks for dinner," I said in a soft voice.

"My pleasure, Miss Meyr," he said as he leaned into me against my car. "There is only one more thing that would make this evening even better." He turned up my chin and gave me a wonderful kiss. We took a moment to look into each other's eyes before anyone spoke.

"Not bad." I blushed when he stepped back a bit. "It's the best dessert I've had in a long time." He liked that comment.

"Are you sure you can get home okay?" he asked looking deep into my eyes. Did he want me to say no? Was he hinting to come in?

"I hope I won't be pulled over on my long drive home," I teased. He smiled and I thought he was going to kiss me again but he didn't.

"Let me know when you decide to leave for South Haven, and I'll keep an eye out for you," he sweetly offered.

"That would mean a lot," I said taking a deep breath.

He kissed me on the forehead and softly said good night. I wanted to just stay there to replay everything, but I finally gathered my emotions and got into the car. It was only two houses to my place, and I watched Clark observe me till I arrived in my driveway.

Carson's car was parked at my house, so when I walked into the house, I did so very quietly. The same lights were on as when I left, and Carson's bedroom door was still partly open as it was before.

*How odd,* I thought. I walked past as if I intended to go to the kitchen and saw that his room was empty. Surely he wouldn't be so brazen as to choose another room to sleep in.

"Carson, are you here?" I finally yelled out. Why was his car here? The only other reason was that he may have left it here and then went with someone else. That someone else was likely Ellie. Could he be at her place next door and left his car here to avoid any talk or scandal? It made me feel uncomfortable.

I didn't set the alarm since I had no idea when Carson would return. I went upstairs to my room and locked the door. I had to admit, now that I was home safe, it brought back a smile on my face, like the one I had at the parking lot at Marv's place. I wanted to giggle like a schoolgirl getting her first kiss. I reminded myself it was not the first kiss from Clark. I instigated the first kiss when we were at his cabin in the dead of winter. It was too precious when Clark and I watched the deer being fed outside his door. His acts of kindness were always touching. I think this kiss was just as terrific as the first one.

The most wonderful thing that Clark and I shared more than anything else was the ability to communicate with each other about most anything. I think that's what most women want. Did I always feel like this? I think if Clay would have been more of a friend to me, I would have been totally satisfied. I never had this kind of trust and ease with any other man. To me, this was better than any wild and passionate relationship. I don't think he had a clue how attractive and somewhat sexy he was. Did he know how I could have melted in his arms if he reached for me? He was very smart in not pushing for more. I guess he knew me pretty well. I could still detect his smell, which I remembered from being around him here at the house when he was working. It was manly, yet sweet. He would die if he knew I had described him this way.

As I dressed for bed, I was reminded of how protective he was with me. Offering to keep an eye out for me while I was in South Haven was huge, in my opinion. Perhaps it came from his effort in saving my life from Blade. We both would never forget that.

I took my pleasant thoughts to bed with me. I couldn't help but wonder if Clark ever envisioned having a lover. He was so secretive, for all I know he could have one in another location as he traveled around on business. I wasn't going to let myself think about that. I was pleased how he described his business relationship with Ruth Ann. Now when I thought of the two of them together, it would not be a good match. I guess I was just a little jealous when I heard he had agreed to help her.

I dozed off in Pleasantville till I heard a sudden noise like a door closing. Since the beginning of having outsiders in my house, I was more susceptible to noises. It was an old house, I had to remind myself. There were always sounds of the house settling, as they often say. I sat up quickly and decided it must be Carson getting home. I got up and quietly walked across the hall into the Wildflower Room, where I could peek out the window facing Ellie's house. There now was an outside porch light on that wasn't on when I returned home from Marv's. I now felt like a nosey neighbor, so I turned around and went back to my room.

As I tried to go to sleep, I picked up a smoky bar smell. It was from my clothes on the chair, which I had worn to Marv's. Despite my disgust for the smell, it brought back memories of a very pleasant evening with my friend.

# CHAPTER 12

The next morning came quickly. I dressed and thought about my breakfast plan. If I was lucky, Carson would sleep late this morning. A steady rain was now falling and the clouds were dark. Perhaps we were due for a storm. I went ahead and prepared some egg cups for breakfast, even though Carson's door was still closed. It sounded good to me, and for some reason I had an appetite this morning. I was hulling some fresh strawberries when Carson made a groggy appearance in the kitchen.

"Don't go to any trouble for me, Kate," Carson said in a crabby tone. "Coffee is all I need."

"Well, you're not allowing me to do my job," I teased as I kept working.

"I'll be on my way shortly," he noted as he picked up the newspaper. "I'll call you next week to book another overnight."

"I'm afraid I won't be here, Carson," I informed him. "I purchased a condo in South Haven and I need to get moved in."

"Guess you can't totally take the beach out of a country girl, after all," he joked. "Well, it goes something like that."

We both had to laugh.

"You're probably right, Carson. I love the beach, and I don't cherish the winters here."

"I'll give you a call anyway to see if you're back," he said, not giving up. Carson took coffee to his room and returned within ten minutes to be on his way. "Thanks for everything, Kate, and try to stay out of trouble," he said as he opened the back door.

"Take care of that hangover," I said, shaking my head. He wanted ME to stay out of trouble?

When I closed the door, I was very relieved his visit was over. I sat down to enjoy my yummy breakfast and plan my weekend trip to South Haven. I began by texting Jack to see if he could get a flight home at the same time. As planned, Susie arrived at my back door to do some cleaning for me and I eagerly let her in.

"I have plenty of breakfast left this morning, Susie," I revealed. "I hope you'll take a minute and have something to eat with me."

"Oh my," she said grinning. "That does look mighty good. What a treat!" She put down her purse and gladly joined me.

"How's Amy Sue this morning?" I asked her while I poured her coffee.

"She's growing so fast, I just can't believe it," she claimed. "She's trying to talk and it's hilarious! Time is moving too quickly."

"I know what you mean," I said in agreement. "It just seems like yesterday my Jack was just a little tyke." She smiled and nodded. "I want you to know I'm going to South Haven on the weekend. Since I don't know my return date, I'll have to call you."

"Does Cotton know you'll be away?" she curiously asked.

"No, I'll call him when I know something for sure," I said as I started to clear the dishes. "The downstairs bedroom just had a guest leave, so I want you to start in that room," I instructed.

"Sure will," she said, nodding. "How are you likin' folks stayin' here, Miss Kate?"

"The jury is still out," I responded.

She laughed and nodded, like she understood.

I was pleased to see how fast I received a text back from Jack. There was no doubt he seemed excited about going back home. I responded back telling him I would have beds there for us, but nothing else. I was now getting really excited.

I decided to go upstairs to make my call to Maggie. I wanted to give her an update on my plans. I was about to go up the stairs, when I did a double glance of the quilt on the wall. Something was different. I walked up closer and then discovered that Carson's name was no longer on the quilt. That was bizarre, because I had watched him sign it. I then checked the guest book to see if his name was still there, which it was. This was another unexplained occurrence that was so confusing. I couldn't be telling others about this kind of activity. I had to admit, removing Carson's name from Josephine's quilt was just fine with me. Was she going to screen which guests could remain on the quilt?

Maggie answered my call from her cell phone. She was on her way to get her hair cut. She was delighted I was arriving the next weekend and told her I was having two beds delivered for Jack and me ahead of time.

"I don't know why you both don't just stay with us while you're furnishing the place," Maggie pleaded.

"Thanks, but this is a good time for Jack and me to be together," I explained. "I am counting on his help, for a change. He only has a couple of days, but I plan to stay there till most of it's furnished."

"That's wonderful," she said with excitement. "I'll call the quilters and we'll make our meeting a luncheon at my house, so we'll have plenty of time to visit."

"If you want," I agreed with excitement.

I hung up thinking how organized this visit was going to be. This time, I would be taking things from Borna to South Haven, instead of the opposite. The thought of decorating a whole new place was renewing my spirit.

I couldn't wait to follow up my plans with Ellie, so I gave her a call at the winery.

"Come on out and have dinner with me tonight," Ellie suggested as she did so often.

"I think I'll pass on the idea, but if you could stop by in the morning for breakfast before you go in to work, I could make you one of my guest specialties!" I enticed.

"Okay, breakfast it is," she confirmed. "I can't wait to taste what you've been serving everyone."

I continued to stay up in my room to take care of business, like arranging for South Haven utilities and dealing with the condo's office. It was hard to remember what the condo was really like when I was there as a guest, but I wasn't worried. I did know they were well respected owners. So far they were very helpful. I also answered a couple of phone calls regarding reservations. I felt guilty turning them down because of my schedule, but those were my special rules I had made with myself. Ruth Ann called, however, to book all the rooms for her quilting friends coming in a few weeks. It would be the first time for a full house and a real experience, I predicted. I had a feeling it would all be a lot of fun. I may even pop in on the classes at Ruth Ann's. I really missed working on quilt projects on a regular basis.

When I went back downstairs, I double checked the guest quilt to see if I had mistaken my earlier observation. Carson's name was nowhere on the quilt, just as I had observed. I had to keep this incident a secret or no one would want to sign the quilt. A true test would be when all the girls would be staying here.

"Miss Kate, do you want me to do anything upstairs?" Susie came to ask. She watched me as I stared at the quilt.

"No, we're good up there," I responded. "If you're done down here, you can leave. I'll be leaving as well. I need to pick up some things from Harold for my new condo."

I gave Susie the dates to plan for, and she had many questions regarding my condo. In the back of my mind, I thought about how cool it would be if Susie and Cotton could vacation there some day. I followed Susie out the door and welcomed the sunshine that followed the rain.

I had a list with me when I entered the hardware store. When I couldn't find one of the bathroom accessories, I asked Harold for some help. He didn't seem his bouncy, friendly self.

"Here you are," Harold said when he found what I was looking for.

"Oh thanks," I said with a grin. "I should have asked you right away."

"I guess you heard about ole man Hecht dying last night," Harold said, taking me by surprise.

"No, I hadn't heard that," I somberly responded.

"Their neighbor, Fred Mueller, was in here early this morning and told me."

"I feel so sorry for Mrs. Hecht," I said sadly. "I'm so glad she has her son."

"Me, too," Harold nodded. "Maybe they'll start spending some of the ole man's money for a change." I looked at him with curiosity. "He was a very wealthy man, but you'd never know it by the way they live. He owns acres and acres around this county, but he'd come in here and harass me about wanting some things half price. He's had that ole pickup truck since I've known him. He could afford to have any fancy vehicle he wanted."

"Very interesting," I noted. "To each his own." I neglected to add that he was not only poor looking, but smelled and looked dirty. "I'm glad I went to see him at the hospital when I did."

The look on Harold's face was like he had seen a ghost. I realized then that I shouldn't have mentioned that. Before he could question me, a customer interrupted us and took him in another direction. I walked out of Harold's without my usual, happy bounce. How sad the whole Hecht family must be right now. I'd have to send them a card and find out if there would be a wake.

Ellie's breakfast visit the next morning was just what I needed to remind me how much I cared for her and this wonderful community. I told her how impressed I was that Harold seemed to be really sad about Ben's passing when he really didn't like the guy. She reminded me that this community stuck together when there was grief or problems. I avoided talking about Carson. She was bringing me up to date on the latest Friendship Circle meeting at Peggy's house. She said Emma made a request for us to help out quilting at church. They were overwhelmed with orders and Emma was the only one from our circle who quilted at church.

"I do want to visit them some time," I revealed to Ellie.

"I don't think I want to be a regular quilter, but I certainly wouldn't mind helping them once in a while."

"I'm sure they would love to have you," Ellie said. "You'll never catch me there, but I know some of you girls know how to quilt. You'd certainly be filled in on the latest gossip and the town's history."

"That's a good enticement for me. I still want to find out more about Josephine and this community. The church seemed to be the only place she'd be seen now and then."

"So what did you decide to do with her quilt?" she asked, catching me by surprise.

"It's put away where I found it, which is what I think she wants," I described. "Please keep any activity we experienced with the quilt to yourself, Ellie. I don't want anyone to think she is haunting this place."

"Mum's the word," she promised.

"I sure hope you'll come to visit my place in Michigan, someday," I said, wanting to change the subject. "I know you have slow times at the winery. I think you need to get away once in a while."

"You have more snow in the winter than Borna, so I don't think I'd want to go in the dead of winter," she explained as she shook her head.

"It's the idea of just seeing something different," I noted. "You are welcome there any time of the year."

"Well, just look who pulled into your drive," Ellie called out. I looked out the bay window and saw it was Clark. "What could he possibly want?" she winked at me.

"Oh stop it, Ellie," I said, going to the door to meet him.

"Good morning!" I said as I cracked the back door. "Come on in. I'm just having a cup of coffee with Ellie."

"No, I better not," he quickly responded. "I hope that's going well." He snickered. "I was heading over to Ruth Ann's place and wondered if you were still trying to leave on the weekend."

"I am, and I was going to let you know," I revealed. "You sure you don't want to come in?"

"I'm on a mission, but thanks," he said with his gorgeous smile. "Tell Ellie hi for me. You have a safe trip, and I hope all goes well with the condo."

"I'll give you a full report when I return," I said, hinting to get together.

"Sounds like a plan," he said, getting into his SUV. I went back into the house.

"So what was that all about?" Ellie asked when I joined her at the table.

"He's offered to keep an eye on things while I'm gone," I said matter of factly. "He wanted to know the exact date I was leaving."

"He only has eyes for you, my dear," Ellie teased. "You should act on that before it's too late."

"Stop," I said, shaking my head. "I don't know what you mean by that, but we have the perfect friendship right now."

"What are you so afraid of?" Ellie asked. "You both are so darn stubborn and independent!" I laughed. "One of you just needs to make the move, that's all. You both are probably worried one or the other is gonna mess things up, I guess."

"Now you have a good point there, girlfriend," I said, snickering. "I like the way things are right now."

"You know what they say, *if you're not growin', you're dyin',*" she quoted.

# CHAPTER 13

The next few days passed quickly as I planned to be gone indefinitely. I knew Ellie, Cotton, and Clark would look out for my place. I texted Jack the night before I left, to make sure he was able to get a flight. He was going to rent a car from the airport, despite me having one. The forecast was going to be in the mid 90s for Borna, but a delightful 70s to 80s for South Haven. It would be nice to get away from the Missouri humidity.

As I left town Saturday morning, I called Ellie when I stopped to pull over for gas.

"Be sure you stay in contact, Kate," Ellie scolded. "I'll think of you having fun decorating your place. I know you'll love having that time with Jack."

"Thanks, Ellie," I responded. "I am really looking forward to it. I'll miss you for sure! Just remember if anything looks out of the ordinary at my place, call me."

"I will, but don't worry," she comforted. "I think the whole town knows you're leaving, so everyone will be watching." I didn't know if that was good or bad.

"I'll remember to bring you all the blueberry goodies you ordered," I said as a cheerful reminder. "I love you, girlfriend." Little did I know I would have another friend as wonderful as Maggie.

The hours flew by as I drove the familiar route to South Haven. Having my new friends in Borna made me want to return to my home as soon as possible. Borna was now my real home, for sure.

Finally, I arrived in South Haven, approaching the beautiful flower-lined drawbridge. It had traffic stopped because the bridge was drawn for high sailboats passing by. It was neat to see again. As a former resident, I hated when I had to wait for the bridge to go down, but now it was revisiting a fond memory. It was a welcome home for me. After it went down, I drove a little farther before turning left on North Shore Drive. Tourist season was truly in full swing, as folks lined the sidewalks going to the beach. I had to check in at the office before going to my condo to pick up the keys. They were happy to see me and told me to let them know if there were any problems. My new address was 1113 B. I had to snicker as I always considered the number 3 my lucky number. I forgot to ask them if the downstairs condo had sold.

When I arrived at my condo walking from the parking lot, I had forgotten that the pool was very close by. A few children and what looked like grandparents were enjoying the pool. I wondered what the noise would be like.

The downstairs condo appeared to still be empty, which pleased me. I got up the stairs and punched in a security code before I could use my key. It did make me feel more secure since I was now living close to other people. I entered a room of stale air when I opened the door. The first large room was a substantial kitchen that opened up into the grand living area. It was clean and most everything looked new and freshly painted. All the colors were cream or white. The living room opened up to the double doors leading to the deck, which showed a nice view of the beach. The breeze was delightful, so I kept everything open to air the place out.

I went to check out the two bedrooms which were separated by the kitchen. One was larger than the other. I was pleased to see the beds had arrived and were placed, waiting for linens. The third room was the upstairs loft, which had spiral stairs going up from the living room. When I got to the top of the stairs, I could see a nice little office or studio. The skylight would be perfect lighting for sewing or reading. It could also hold a day bed if I needed one. I loved it! So far, there were no surprises to my new home away from home. Now I just had to unload and find myself some dinner.

Everything from my car was now placed in the middle of the living room, except my personal suitcase and my hanging clothes. I sent a text to Jack telling him I had arrived, and he replied he was on his way from the airport. It would be nice to wait till he arrived so we could get a bite to eat together.

I walked about the place to envision what I might like it to look like. I wanted to keep as much white color as I could and decided touches of the aqua sea would be lovely. There was so much open area that now had to be tied together. This would surely be a contrast to my antique home in Borna.

Twenty minutes later, Jack knocked at the door. Seeing his dark twinkling eyes was like heaven on earth. He had his father's big wide smile and was sporting a beard, which I wasn't prepared for. He looked so much older and a lot like his father.

*Clay should see him now,* I thought. I couldn't stop hugging him.

"Wow," Jack finally responded as he looked about the place.

I stayed silent to hear his initial reaction. From what I was hearing, he certainly approved.

"So do you want me down here or up in the loft or the smaller nursery?" he asked as a joke.

"You pick!" I happily said. "You can have the master bedroom if you like!" I offered.

"I think the smaller bedroom would be best, Mom," he said, walking in that direction. "So are you happy with it?"

"I haven't fallen in love just yet," I admitted. "When I can start putting my personal touches on the place, I'm sure it will happen. I do wish the views were larger, but I have to remember we are sharing it with others! If there's anything you'd like to have or see in your room, speak up while you are here. I'll be doing some power shopping."

"You always do a fine job," he conceded. "I'll be more interested in just my bed, most likely."

"So let's go eat. I'm starving," I complained. He agreed wholeheartedly. We both agreed Clementia's was the place to go for a quick meal.

As we were going to the car, I sent Maggie a text telling her I had arrived and would see her at the Golden Bakery in the morning. When we walked in the door at Clementia's, I asked Jack about Jennifer, the girl he had mentioned. He was silent and didn't respond till we were seated.

"I needed this break from her, Mom," he revealed. "I won't go into it now, but I really don't know how to answer your question."

As I looked over the menu, I knew the food would never be as good as what we had in Borna.

"Are you happy with your guest house?" Jack asked as he drank some water.

"Everyone has been asking and, as I told others, the jury is still out," I shared. "I guess what's hardest to get used to is having strangers in your private home."

"Yeah, I can imagine!" Jack said nodding. "I hope you're not too upset that I haven't come to visit yet."

"I understand your time commitment, Jack," I lovingly said, putting my menu aside. "South Haven will always be OUR home. Someday when I get you to Borna, I think you'll appreciate it. You may not appreciate it like I do, but you'll begin to understand why I love it so much. I really had to remold my life after your father passed." I didn't want to tell him much more. He listened intently.

"I know Dad wasn't perfect, but I do wonder why you had to move so far away to get on with your life," Jack expressed so calmly.

"I found myself to be very angry with him," I explained without telling him too much. "The reasons are not your concern. I hadn't planned it to be this way, as you recall, but when I got there, I couldn't leave. I felt needed, and I fell in love with the house and the whole community. Does that help?"

"I suppose so," he replied with a puzzled look on his face. I knew he had plenty more questions about his father.

"New York has certainly been a distraction for you, hasn't it?" I bluntly asked.

"No question," he responded. "Jennifer has helped, of course, but I guess I'm now beyond that part of my life." I found that comment to be interesting.

"Does she have any idea how you feel?"

"I think she is figuring it out," he described, as he looked about the room. We were sitting near their crowded bar, so it was difficult at times to hear him.

"I know what I want to order, do you?" he asked, handing the waitress his menu. I nodded.

"Well, I can't believe my eyes!" said a girl's voice from the bar. "Hi, Jack and Kate!" It was Jill, Maggie and Mark's daughter. Jill and Jack had grown up together, but barely kept in touch.

"Hey, Jill," Jack said jumping out of his chair. "How's it going?" His face was beaming.

"Really good!" she said smiling ear to ear. "Meet my friend Alice."

"It's nice to meet you," Jack politely said. "I think I remember you. Did you date Harry Mueller at one time?"

"I did," Alice blushed. "You and Harry used to hang out with Ted Maxwell, right?"

"Oh, right," Jack said laughing. "Boy, this is going back. Hey, good to see you both, but I'm here having dinner with my mom."

"How about we all hook up tomorrow night?" Jill asked in her cute voice.

"Yeah, maybe," he said with some hesitation. "I'm not here for very long, and I promised Mom I would help her get settled in her new condo."

"My mom is so excited you'll be here now and then," Jill added, grinning at me. "So I guess that means you'll come around too! My mom really misses you, Kate. Here's my card, Jack. Let me know what your plans are, okay?" He gladly took her card.

"I will," he said as he sat back in his seat. "Good seeing you both."

Our food was served, and Jack didn't hesitate to bite into his favorite choice of the Captain's Hamburger served with onion rings. It was fun to watch him devour it.

"I can't believe that was Jill," Jack said with his mouth still full. "When did she start looking hot?"

I had to laugh and shrug my shoulders, as I hadn't seen much of her myself. "She has always been pretty darn cute, if you ask me," I casually responded.

"I may meet up with them for a drink tomorrow night, if you don't mind."

I could tell his mind was spinning. "Not at all, sounds like fun!" I said, giving my permission.

As I described to Jack my mission for the next couple of days, he barely heard me. Every now and then I caught him glancing at the girls at the bar, every time they laughed or made a noise. It all told me that Jennifer was on her way out, and a new adventure may be beginning with Jack.

# CHAPTER 14

The next morning I anxiously met Maggie at the Golden Bakery. Before I looked for her, I stopped at the counter to order six blueberry scones to take home with me. They were so large and plump with the biggest blueberries I had ever seen.

"Couldn't wait for me, huh," Maggie said creeping up behind me. She grabbed me for a hug.

"It's so good to see you," I cheered. "I think I'm in heaven."

"No, you're in South Haven, not heaven," she laughed.

"Good one, Maggie," I responded.

We found our usual table and sat down. The place was certainly emptier than during the Blueberry Festival.

"You look great," Maggie said looking me over. "Borna is certainly agreeing with you. How is everyone?"

"Great! They all said to tell you hello." It was neat for her to acknowledge them.

"So how do you like the condo?" Maggie asked, drinking her coffee.

"It's pretty bare right now, but I think it will work out nicely!"

"Hey, did you know that the Blueberry Bay Shop is having a sale?" Maggie informed. "I know how you love that place. You may want to check it out."

"I didn't know about the sale, but that's where I'm headed," I said, taking a big bite of my scone. "Do you have time to go with me?"

"If I keep it brief," she answered. "Jill is here for the weekend, and I want to spend some time with her."

"You'll have to compete with Jack, I'm afraid," I said catching her by surprise. "When Jack and I were eating at Clementia's last night, they ran into each other. Jill was with her friend Alice at the bar. They're all meeting up tonight somewhere. Jack couldn't believe how she has changed."

"Yeah, ever since she started this new job, she has completely changed her style," Maggie added. "She is looking much more sophisticated. Well, that's great they may be getting together."

"I hope so. She is very beautiful, Maggie. What is she doing now? Where does she live?"

"About six months ago, she moved to Benton Harbor to work for a company that designs props for department stores," she explained. "It's really a good fit for her fashion background. She loves it. She even has an assistant now, which is really a big deal."

"How wonderful, and she's still pretty close to home," I observed as I had another sip of coffee.

"She's here in South Haven almost every weekend," she divulged. "All her friends are here, which pleases me, of course. You know Jack never paid attention to her growing up, remember?"

I nodded with a slight embarrassment. "Well, I don't think he'll propose to her tomorrow night, but it's a start," I teased. We both doubled over in laughter. "You never know these days."

We stayed in the bakery talking way too long. Maggie had to be on her way and my list was not getting any shorter.

Blueberry Bay was located in the middle of downtown. Their taste was impeccable, especially when it came to area rugs and accessories. It was all overwhelming when I walked in, but one area rug did get my attention. I took a photo on my phone for future reference. I made some mental notes and decided I needed to keep looking. My next stop was the outdoor furniture store around the corner. I fell in love with a grouping of furniture perfect for the deck. The good news was it could be delivered tomorrow. We now had a table and chairs, at least. This was beginning to be fun!

When I got home in the late afternoon, Jack said he would be having a bite out with his friends for dinner. He took time to hear all about my visit with Maggie and what Jill was now doing in her life. He listened with an extra amount of interest.

"So what do you have planned for the evening?" Jack asked with concern.

"I'm really beat," I complained. "Nothing is more exhausting than shopping. I think you'll like the deck furniture, which arrives tomorrow, but I'm afraid that's all I got accomplished today. As far as I'm concerned it's the most important room in the house right now." Jack laughed. "I have a hunger for some of Tello's pizza, so I might go pick some up."

"Oh hey, that sounds pretty good," Jack said enviously.

"I'll order plenty so there will be some leftovers!" I said, feeling hungrier.

Jack wasn't gone ten minutes when I freshened up and headed out the door to Tello's. Before I got in the car, I called Sandra Meyr to see if she was up for a visit the next day. I was glad it went to her voice mail. It gave me more time to think about meeting her. She would either be glad to hear from me, or ignore me completely. I had a feeling she didn't have too many friends left in this town since the divorce.

When I walked into Tello's, it was like I had never left

South Haven. Many tables were filled with folks, but there wasn't anyone at the bar. Since I had no place to eat at home, I decided to eat here and enjoy my pizza. I ordered a glass of red wine with a name I couldn't pronounce. The bartender assured me I would like it. I regretted not bringing a book to read, but pulled out my phone to check e-mails instead. I was hoping there would be one from Ellie.

The last time I was here, I ran into Will Cummings, who had worked with Clay. He was newly divorced and I didn't want him to think I had any interest in him personally, but wanted information about Meyr Lumber. The bartender was nice enough to make small talk as I ate my pizza. I wanted to ask him where the single women went in this town to meet people, but didn't want to leave the impression I was one of them. I knew it wasn't the Country Club, unless they were playing golf. The older widows would occasionally come to dinner and play cards at the club to pass the time. Neither of those activities was something I cared for. As much as I enjoyed my pizza and this morning's scones, it didn't compare to the German food I was enjoying in Borna. I left a nice sized tip, took my leftover pizza, and headed for home. Jack would love finding the pizza in the refrigerator.

I walked into my dark condo and turned on the ceiling light in the kitchen, which lit up most of the first floor. It didn't take me long to find my bed and make up the sheets, so I could crawl inside them. The bed was surprisingly comfortable, but then the wine had relaxed me for a good night's sleep. I had almost dozed off, when my cell phone, lying on the floor, started ringing.

"Kate?" the female voice asked.

"Yes, this is Kate," I answered. I then saw it was a local number calling.

"It's Sandra," she stated, like I should have known her voice.

"Oh, it's good to hear from you!" I said in my half asleep voice. "I wasn't sure you'd be speaking to me, but since I'm here for a visit in South Haven, I thought I'd give you a call." There was silence. "How are you?"

"I don't know how much you know," she said in a somber voice.

I wanted to ask about what, but didn't.

"Well, my friend Maggie said you got divorced," I stated calmly.

"I guess that doesn't surprise you, does it?" she said sarcastically.I could envision her angry face.

"I'm sorry, Sandra," I consoled. "We both have been through a lot of heartache and disappointments. If I can help you in any way, let me know. I may understand your situation more than anyone,"

"I doubt that," she said so negatively. "Where are you staying?"

"I bought a condo on North Shore Drive. Jack and I wanted a place to stay here in South Haven when we come to visit. As you probably know, I moved to Borna, Missouri, and really love it there."

"Well, good for you!" she said in an insincere tone.

"Are you up for meeting for lunch tomorrow?" I finally asked. There was a long pause.

"Sure, but I prefer to meet here at the house," she suggested. "I will have Noreen fix us something. I'm sure the tongues will wag if we meet in public."

"Okay, I'll be there about noon then," I said wanting to end the conversation.

After I hung up, I was sorry I had opened this old wound. Sandra was obviously bitter and hurt. I could certainly feel her pain, but I wasn't sure if she considered me part of her problem. She was still in their big house, which surprised me. It was a status symbol she was probably not ready to give up. I remembered she had a housekeeper named Noreen, so she was able to keep her as well.

How could I now relax to go to sleep? Why did she call me so late? Was it an afterthought and why wasn't she nicer to me on the phone? I sure hoped I wouldn't regret making contact with her.

# CHAPTER 15

I slept so soundly, I didn't hear Jack come home. At an early hour, I staggered into the kitchen to make some coffee. I remembered when I arrived in Borna how important a coffee pot could be, so I made sure I brought one. The scones would still be good, and Jack would be thrilled that I had them.

Jack's door was closed. So much for all the help he'd be on this visit. With some luck, I'd be able to have dinner with him tonight. It was 10:30 a.m. when a knock came at the door. It was my furniture delivery, which made me very pleased since I didn't want to leave for shopping till it arrived. Jack finally came out of his room and assisted with the arrangement. After the delivery guys left, Jack and I had a cup of coffee as we set on my new deck furniture.

"So how was last night?" I finally asked.

"Good, Mom, good," he said between yawns. "We went a few places, but ended up at Alice's apartment downtown."

"Oh, where?" I was curious.

"It's actually above one of the clothing stores on Phoenix Street," he described. "She's got it fixed pretty cool."

"So are you free tonight for dinner, since you're leaving tomorrow?" I bravely asked.

He paused. "Can we make it pretty early?" he shyly asked.

I should have anticipated this.

"Sure, whatever works for you. Your plane leaves at noon, right?"

He nodded. "I've asked Jill out, so could we make it around 5:00?" Jack suggested. "I really want to see her again before I leave. We really hit it off after all these years."

"Well that's great," I said with amazement. "I guess you're not too concerned about Jennifer?" He just grinned. "I'm having lunch with your Aunt Sandra today," I said suddenly.

"Really? How is she doing since the divorce?"

"I guess I'll find out," I sighed. "I just don't want to continue to have bad feelings about her. I know it's rough for her. She is still in their big house, which surprised me."

"Tell her I said hello," Jack added. "As soon as I shower, I need to pick up some dress pants for tonight. All I brought with me are casual clothes."

"Oh, good idea," I encouraged. This was an important date, for sure. "I'm headed to the big box stores after lunch. Are you sure you don't have any special requests for your bedroom?"

"Nah," he said shaking his head. "That's your territory. I'm sure whatever you pick out will be just fine. I guess I wouldn't mind if you had one or two of your quilts for my room."

"How sweet of you to suggest that, Jack," I noted. "I just might have to make you one, once I know what the colors will be."

"Well, you better get busy then," Jack said as he went into his room.

I loved the thought of Jack liking my quilts. His father could have cared less and preferred I not use them on our bed or decorate with them. I jumped when my cell phone went off. It was Ellie.

"Hey, neighbor, nice to hear from you," I greeted. "Is everything okay?"

"Sure, what about there?" she repeated. "I sure miss you!"

*How odd,* I thought, *for her to say that.*

"Well, it's been a hectic couple of days and I'm not making much progress," I reported. "So what's up in Borna?"

"Not much," she said in a sad voice.

"What's wrong, Ellie?" I finally said. "You don't sound like yourself."

"It's Carson," she said in a shaky voice like she might start crying.

"What about him? Is he all right?" I asked impatiently. She was silent again. "Have you seen him lately?"

"No, and it appears I have lost my wine distributor," she stated very slowly.

"Why, what happened?" I asked, knowing it couldn't be good news.

"I've been such a fool, Kate," Ellie admitted sadly. "I won't go into it now on the phone, but I thought he and I had a pretty special relationship over this past year. I guess there's no fool like an old fool."

"How so?" I interjected.

"He is very married and has young children!" she finally spilled in her shaky voice.

"Oh dear," I said calmly. "I'm sorry to hear that." I really was at a loss for words.

"Trout and you were the only ones I shared my feelings with," she confessed. "I've always known that Trout didn't care for him."

"How did you find out?" I curiously asked.

"Trout has been dropping hints for some time," she started to explain. "The other night, when Carson was here, I had a few drinks and decided to confront him about his situation."

"So did he deny everything?" I asked hoping he didn't.

"No, he didn't," she said bluntly. "I couldn't believe it. What really hurt was he thought we had an open relationship of convenience where it didn't matter. Can you believe that one?"

"Oh my goodness," I replied in shock. "Listen here, Miss Ellie, you better stand up for yourself. You are an intelligent, strong woman. You deserve better than that!"

"I know, I know," she muttered. "I just didn't expect that response."

We didn't talk much longer, but in that amount of time I understood she told him that the relationship was over. Oh, I wished I could be there in person to comfort her. She didn't deserve this kind of treatment. I suppose we are all vulnerable at times throughout our lifetime.

My heart was aching for Ellie. I couldn't believe the strong woman I knew let Carson control their relationship. Knowing her, she'll never trust another man again. It made me wonder if strong women were turned on by strong men who liked control. If a woman made decisions on her own all day long, I supposed it would be a relief to have someone else make decisions now and then. Clay had been a controller. I knew it from the day I met him. Through the years, I learned to pick my poison on issues we did not agree upon. I knew where my strengths were, and I knew I couldn't change some things about him. At that time, I didn't think it was such a big deal.

I went on ahead to Sandra's, thinking of Ellie. Noreen, the housekeeper, answered the door.

"Hi, Noreen, good to see you again," I greeted. She smiled and nodded. No conversation there! Noreen was an African American who had worked for the Meyr's as long as I can remember. She looked much older and much more stressed than I remembered.

"Miss Sandra is on the sunporch, ma'am," she said so businesslike. I followed her. The house was just as beautiful as I remembered. Sandra was on a lounge chair and barely turned to acknowledge me.

"How are you?" I began the conversation. She looked pale and withdrawn, ignoring my question.

"You look great as always," she said sarcastically, instead of answering my question.

"Here you are, Miss Sandra," Noreen said as she handed Sandra a mixed drink. "What can I get for you, Miss Kathryn?"

"Iced tea will be fine," I answered as I watched Sandra take big swallows of her drink.

"Noreen has set us a table out here, if that will suit you," Sandra noted, pointing with her mixed drink.

"Oh, sure. It has such a pretty view of your flowers," I complimented. "You always had such lovely gardens."

"You don't know how lucky you are, Kathryn," Sandra said as she moved up from her lounge. "Your husband died and you had the perfect excuse to start a new life."

"Sandra, how could you say such a thing?" I said in shock. "What on earth do you mean by that?"

"I wish James was dead!" she bluntly stated. I couldn't believe what I just heard. "He's made my life miserable and he's figured out a way to continue badgering me, even though we are divorced."

"I'm sure this change is difficult, but you certainly have an opportunity now to do your own thing," I countered. "You don't have to live here. Haven't you thought about what you'd like to do after all these years? Now is the time!" She snickered, like I was joking. "I gave you a lot of credit standing up to my James," she said smiling for the first time. "No one ever does that and gets by with it. You made him so angry. He is not used to not getting his way."

We were then interrupted by Noreen placing our food on the glass table, which was elegantly set.

"Thanks Noreen," I said before she walked away. "Let's have a bite to eat, shall we?"

Sandra slowly got up and didn't say a word. When we sat down, Sandra stared at her food, like she was waiting to be fed.

"This looks delicious," I said taking my first bite of chicken salad. "Noreen has always been a good cook, hasn't she?" Sandra continued to stare at her plate.

I finally spoke. "How long have you been depressed like this, Sandra?" I bravely asked. She shook her head like she didn't know. "How are my nieces and nephews?" I asked to change the subject off of her.

"I haven't seen them lately," she simply explained.

"If I recall, James was training James Jr. to work in the business," I said taking another bite. It was delicious, and I wasn't going to let her get the best of me.

"He had to get away from the monster, too," she said in a gruff voice. "He now lives in Canada."

"My goodness, a lot has happened since I left," I said as I wiped my mouth with the white linen napkin. She still wasn't eating. "So is the company managing to hang in there?"

"I could tell you plenty, but yes, the company is still there, if that's what you're asking," she said now in a raised tone. This visit was not going well. "Yeah, nothing a little bankruptcy couldn't fix."

"Bankruptcy!" I repeated. "When did that happen?"

"Right after you left town, I think," she stated as if she were uncertain. "You got your money out of the company at the right time." Now I had lost my appetite and wanted to leave.

"I am so sorry, Sandra," I said shaking my head. "I had no idea. Look, I probably shouldn't have come," I apologized. "This all is tragic, but you shouldn't let it get you down like this!" Now she gave a laugh out loud. I wondered how many drinks she'd had.

"I really am a bit tired, Kathryn," she said pulling back her chair. "You were brave and thoughtful to contact me. Thanks for not gloating about your wonderful, perfect life you have now."

"That was not my intent in seeing you, Sandra," I explained.

Noreen was now in the room to see what was happening.

"Noreen, would you see Kathryn to the door?" Sandra said in a low voice. "Thank you for coming by."

I was speechless for a moment when she turned away from me. I followed Noreen to the door without a proper good-bye.

"Please take care of her, Noreen," I said as she opened the door for me to leave. She simply nodded without a smile.

I drove away in disbelief. I had no idea the afternoon would turn out like it had. I wanted to cry. How could things be so bad that she'd wish her husband dead? I was hoping my visit would make amends, but it only made her feel worse, I'm afraid. Instead of hitting the stores to shop, I went by Maggie's house. There was no way I could concentrate on shopping. I had to talk to someone. I found her in the kitchen fixing meatloaf for their evening meal.

"Well, I'm surprised to see you," Maggie said wiping her hands clean. "What's up?"

I took a deep breath, not knowing where to start. "I just came from Sandra's house, which was supposed to be lunch," I started to explain. "I think I had one or two bites."

Maggie gave me a strange look. "What happened?" Maggie asked as she nodded for me to sit down. "How about some iced tea?"

"Sure," I said as I sat in the kitchen chair near her counter.

I didn't know where to start explaining the chain of events. Maggie listened in shock as she too was in disbelief. She paused before she replied.

"Sounds like she really needs some professional help, Kate," she finally advised. "I can't believe I didn't hear about the bankruptcy, but maybe Mark did. There has to be more to this!"

"I'm puzzled on why she agreed to see me if things were so bad," I said, taking a swallow of the cold tea. "I really didn't think she'd return my call."

"I think she wants help," Maggie sadly stated. "Did she say if she was on any medication?"

"Honestly, Maggie, she said very little to me," I explained. "I do know she has taken up drinking since I saw her last. What is it about that family and alcohol? I was doing most of the talking, and then before I knew it she asked Noreen to show me to the door. Poor Noreen said nothing, and I'm sure she knows plenty. I can't imagine what she has to put up with."

"Sounds like your plans for the day have been shot," Maggie sympathized. "Would you like to stay for dinner?"

I finally smiled, feeling bad that I had just dumped everything on her. "Oh no, I have an early dinner date with Jack," I quickly said grinning. "He has a date with your lovely daughter tonight, so I've been bumped to the senior dinner hour!"

She laughed. "Really?"

I nodded. "Evidently last night went pretty well."

"She's been gone all day, so I had no idea," Maggie said with a big smile on her face.

"He leaves tomorrow, so it'll be interesting to see where this goes," I added. "Well, now that I've cried on your shoulder, I really need to get on home. I really do love my new deck furniture, by the way. It's a start! You'll have to come see everything."

"Good idea!" Maggie agreed with excitement. "How about I pick you up in the late morning, have some lunch, and get some serious shopping done?"

"That would be a big help, Maggie," I said with a sigh. "I feel my visit is getting away from me."

Leave it to Maggie to cheer me up after such a pitiful visit with Sandra. Growing up together, she was always the one to make light of things and remind me not to worry.

I was climbing up my steps to the condo, when I noticed a man carrying in boxes to the condo below. So I assumed it must have recently been sold or rented.

I felt I had to get busy and accomplish something for the day, so I pulled out the shelving paper I had bought at Harold's before my trip. I needed some busy work to get my mind off of Ellie and Sandra. It was a good reminder of how lucky I was to have left South Haven.

Before my shower, I took a break on the deck to breathe in the perfect air.

"Hello up there," a man's voice said below. "I'm your neighbor John Baker. Just thought you'd want to know what all the noise was about."

I leaned over the deck to give him a welcoming smile. "Hi, I'm Kate Meyr," I happily said. "I just moved in here as well."

"How do you like it so far?" he said with his neck bent as far back as he could.

"I love it!" I shouted. "I only have a bed and some deck furniture right now, but it works!" I laughed.

"I wish I had your situation," he replied laughing. "I brought way too much stuff. I left a good-size place and didn't get rid of as much as I wanted. I wanted a place near the lake, so this seems perfect. Is it just you up there?"

"No, I have a son from New York that's visiting right now, but yes, it'll be just me when I'm here. I live in Borna, Missouri. How about you?"

"Just me," he said, putting his hands in the air. He sure seemed to talk with his hands!

"Well, thanks for the intro," I said with a wave." Good luck with the move."

"Nice to meet you," he said as he went inside.

*Well, it appears I have a nice, friendly neighbor,* I told myself. He sure was nice looking with his blonde hair and blue eyes. What a shame he was a lot younger. I'm sure I'd be seeing lots of pretty women going back and forth from his place.

I heard Jack come home while I was in the shower. I was feeling kind of guilty that he was resigned to having dinner with his mother. We both came out of our bedrooms looking pretty spiffy. Jack looked great in his new pants and suit coat. I could feel his excitement, and it was a treat to see him all dressed up.

Jack wanted to go to Tello's because of his fondness for Italian food. Since it was early when we arrived, the place was nearly empty. I didn't want to bring a downer to our dinner, so I just said that Sandra was quite depressed since their divorce. Jack didn't want to reveal any details of his evening plans, so I did most of the talking. I told him Maggie and I hoped to find lots of goodies for the condo on our shopping trip tomorrow. He just laughed and said to have fun. He did repeat once again how happy he was that we had a place in South Haven. He said he'd probably use it more than I would. I knew it would be some time before I would get him to visit Borna.

After Jack dropped me off, I couldn't help but notice lots of boxes crowding the windows of my neighbor downstairs.

The night was young, and here I was, practically alone in South Haven. I missed my Borna home, but did look forward to seeing the Beach Quilters the day after tomorrow. Perhaps some of them could shed some light on Sandra's depression. I poured a glass of wine and went to the deck to see that wonderful sunset once again. I missed Ellie, so decided to call her at the winery.

"Hey, Kate," greeted Trout. "How's everything up north?"

"Pretty nice, actually," I responded. "I am out on my deck watching a gorgeous sunset."

"Nice, very nice," he said. I could just see his cute smile.

"How's our friend Ellie doing?" I bravely asked. "Can you talk?"

"She's fine," he said in a serious tone. "She didn't take the news well about Carson and didn't want to take my advice some time ago, so it is what it is."

"I'm glad I wasn't the one to tell her," I said in relief. "I feel so bad for her!"

"Hey, Clark asked about you last night and wondered if I heard when you were coming back," Trout said in a teasing tone.

"Oh, he did now?" I responded with a smile. That was nice to hear. "I'm afraid I can't say just yet," I reported. "If I can get this place half furnished, it'll be next week. I'm anxious to return and get back to Josephine's."

He laughed. "Well, I'll tell him that when I see him again," Trout assured me. "Hey, I bet you called to talk to Ellie."

"Yes, as a matter of fact, I did," I said with a chuckle.

"She was here over the dinner hour, but now she's at Ruth Ann's place," he recalled.

"That's good," I said. "Please tell her I called, okay?"

"I will, and please hurry back now, you hear?" he ended the conversation.

I smiled to myself. When I hung up, I couldn't help but wonder why Ellie went to Ruth Ann's house. Was she wanting a friend to talk to and I wasn't there for her?

I leaned my head back to look at the stars. I said a prayer for Ellie and Sandra, knowing how difficult their lives must be right now. I realized I was hearing very pleasant jazz music in the background. It was definitely coming from the condo below. It was just loud enough to create lovely background music. This close living lifestyle would take getting used to. At least he wasn't blaring hard rock music. I would never be able to hear music from Ellie's house next door in Borna.

# CHAPTER 16

The next morning I heard Jack stirring in the kitchen, so I put on my robe to join him.

"I'm eating the last scone, so I hope you don't mind," Jack said as I joined him.

"I think I know a place where I can get more!" I teased, as I also helped myself.

"So how did last night go?" I asked pouring my coffee.

"Good, real good," he reported. "Jill is gonna try to get to New York soon. She has some contacts through her work she can go see!"

"Seriously? How nice!" I said surprised. "So Jennifer is not a concern?" I bravely asked.

He just shook his head as he opened up the double doors to the deck. As we sat down on our new furniture, I reported to Jack about meeting our neighbor, John Baker. When I teased that he was good looking, but too young, he looked at me almost in disgust. I got a kick out of seeing his reaction.

When Jack brought his luggage out to the door, I started to feel alone for the first time in quite a while. I really liked having him around. Jack was so much like his father. He was never still for a minute and had his future focused. I was glad he made contact with Jill. Perhaps it would bring him home more frequently.

We hugged and kissed good-bye. He said he liked saying good-bye to me from South Haven. When he walked out the door, I went to the deck to follow him go toward the parking lot. It seemed like yesterday that I watched him go to meet the school bus.

I went back into the house and tried to seriously get a grip on what to buy for these empty rooms.

Maggie arrived on time and was thrilled to finally see my new digs. She marveled at all the space to fill and had some suggestions, which I agreed with. We both thought live greenery would be awesome with all the light, but would die between my visits. When we came down the stairs to leave for shopping, my neighbor was reading on the patio.

"Good morning, Kate," he said putting his book down.

"Good morning, John," I responded cheerfully. "We're off to buy some furniture today."

"Well, good luck with that!" he yelled as we walked away.

"Well, well, well, Kate, is that your new neighbor?" she asked with a suggestive tone. "What a nice-looking, young man!"

I laughed. "Yeah, and single," I added. "Let's see, he should not be far from my son's age."

"I don't think so," assessed Maggie. "He certainly will make a nice decoration around here for you."

We continued with much laughter as we visited a few places Maggie suggested. By the time we decided to stop for lunch, we had purchased barstools for the counter bar and two matching chairs for the same room. I was pleased, but it took too much time. Our late lunch was at a downtown eatery called Taste. It offered delicious tapas, which we enjoyed choosing. We were about to select our dessert, when my cell phone went off.

"Miss Kathryn," the shaky voice asked. It sounded like Noreen.

"Noreen, is that you?" I asked concerned.

"Yes, ma'am," she said. "I'm so glad I found you. I got your number out of Miss Sandra's address book."

"What's wrong?" I asked impatiently.

"Miss Sandra's done a terrible thing," she said with a broken voice. "I found her this morning in the bathroom with blood everywhere. I think she done fainted from the cuts on her arms and wrists."

"Oh my goodness, Noreen," I said in a panic. "Is she all right?"

"I called 911, and when they took her away she was still alive," Noreen said with tears in her voice. "I called Mr. James, and he was gonna go directly to the hospital. He told me to stay away and didn't want me to tell anyone. Now that's not right, Miss Kathryn. I thought you had to know since you cared enough to come see her."

"Thank you for that," I said feeling lightheaded. "I'm sure she'll be okay. I'll find out what I can."

"Please don't do that Miss Kathryn," Noreen begged. "Mr. James will be very upset with me."

"Don't let them keep you away from her," I warned. "You are the only one who cares for her. She would want you there."

"Oh, Miss Kathryn, I just don't think that poor soul will make it!" Noreen cried into the phone.

Maggie looked at me as she tried to figure out what had just happened. I wanted to throw up, but broke into tears instead. I shared what had just happened between my sobs. I just couldn't believe it, nor could she! We put money on the table with our check and left the restaurant, so we could go outside and talk.

"What should I do, Maggie?" I asked trying to get ahold of my emotions. "I'm no longer family, so I just can't show up like I belong."

"Oh, Kate, I just can't believe she was so desperate that she would take her own life," Maggie said in a loud whisper. "Did she threaten anything like that when you were with her?"

"No, not at all. She did wish her husband dead, however." I said shaking my head.

"I'll call the hospital and see if they will give me an update on her," I suggested in a panic mode.

It took a while for me to get through to someone in the emergency room. When I did succeed, they told me they were not authorized to give out such information. I clicked off my phone.

"Can you believe James told Noreen to stay away?" I said in disgust. "She is probably the only poor soul, besides her children, who cares about her. It's going to be hard with them living out of town."

"Do you want me to take you home instead of doing more shopping?" Maggie asked in despair.

"Let's go by the emergency room, Maggie," I said with determination. "If I ask to see her, I'll know soon enough how she is doing."

"They won't let you see her, Kate," Maggie warned.

"That's okay," I nodded. "I will just have them send word that I am praying for her."

The hospital was nearby, and I planned to use my last name like other family members to find out any information. Maggie dropped me off and decided to wait in the car. I didn't recognize anyone when I got there. I looked for a kind face that might be helpful.

"Excuse me, my name is Kathryn Meyr and I'm here to see my sister-in-law, Sandra Meyr, who was just brought in recently," I asked politely.

She looked at me strangely. "Step over here, ma'am," she said taking my arm. "You must not have heard that Miss Meyr passed in the ambulance before they got her here. The immediate family has already left. I'm so sorry."

I looked at her in shock. "I can't believe that," I said wanting to sit down before I fainted. "What family was here, do you know?" She took a second to answer.

"Mr. Meyr was here and I believe a sister of hers," she recollected. I then remember Sandra having a sister in South Haven. No children, nor Noreen present. How sad!

"Thanks so much," I said wanting to get to the car as fast as I could. I felt sick with grief and disbelief.

Maggie could tell from my face what the story was. As soon as my car door slammed, I burst into more tears. Maggie started crying as well, even though she barely knew her.

"I should have done something, Maggie," I stated in anger. "I had no idea she was in such a terrible state! I must call Noreen!"

I looked to see the number in my phone for when Noreen had called me. When I rang for her, there was no answer. If she knew, she was likely grief stricken. I left a message for her to call me right away.

"You cannot feel guilty about anything, Kate," Maggie said in comfort. "You went to see her, which had to mean a lot to her."

I nodded as I wiped and blew my nose. "It obviously didn't help, but she did thank me for coming," I mumbled. "I hope God has mercy on her soul. She had to be in a terrible place to do such a thing."

"The mind does crazy things sometimes," Maggie added. "You don't know what the final straw was that made her do such a thing. Bystanders just cannot be held responsible."

I wasn't sure I agreed with that, but Maggie was trying to make me feel better.

"I should have asked her more questions," I said. "I may have gotten her to talk about what was on her mind. Instead, I was selfish and feeling uncomfortable, so I just wanted to get out of there when she started being rude. You know I keep thinking about that mixed drink at lunch, which pretty much indicated she had a drinking problem. I wonder if that contributed to her suicide."

"Life is so short," Maggie consoled. "Humans let disappointments and challenges get us down. Some can handle it better than others. Sometimes it's hard to think about a way out! That's when faith and the power of prayer come in handy." It made me wonder whether Sandra had such a faith.

"You know, I was in a pretty dark space myself after Clay died," I shared. "What saved me was prayer and knowing that others had been in my place before. Besides being so sad, I was angry on top of it, which she probably was as well."

"That is all natural behavior, Kate," she said putting her arm around me. "You took the time to grieve, but then you went on living! I just can't believe a divorce and a jackass ex-husband would be a reason to end your life."

The next day I tried several times to contact Noreen without success. It felt so strange to be disconnected from the family I used to be so fond of. I reminded myself to keep checking the paper for any memorial tributes.

As I wasted away my day with sporadic cleaning, I thought

of Will Cummings, who still worked at Meyr Lumber. I still had his number in my wallet. I found my cell and called his number before I could change my mind.

"Will, Kate Meyr," I announced.

"Kate, what a nice surprise!" he responded with that flirtatious tone. "What did I do to deserve this honor?"

"Now, Will, I'm calling on a serious topic," I stated. I took a deep breath. "I'm calling in regard to Sandra Meyr's death." He was silent. "You know she just died, right?" More silence.

"Yeah, sorry to hear that," he finally said in a somber tone.

I explained how I had gone to see her the day before she killed herself, and that I had no idea how depressed she was. Then I asked him if he knew any further details or if there would be any kind of service.

"What little I know is secondhand, Kate," he reluctantly admitted. "I was told she died and was cremated."

"That's it?" I asked in a louder tone. "What is James saying? What about their children?"

"I know, I know, but we were told, because of the nature of her death, we were not to say anything," he defended. "I know James seems pretty upset."

"He certainly should be!" I said spontaneously. "Is he still drinking?"

"Boy, you are on a scavenger hunt, aren't you?" he teased. "Look, I've been pretty disappointed with the company as of late, but I still have a job and a pretty darn good one, too, so it's just none of my business. That's all I can say."

"Okay, I get it," I said in frustration. "Will you call me if you hear about a service?"

"I'd be happy to call you anytime, my dear," he flirted, once again. I hung up in disgust.

I decided that was a wasted call, other than to learn how hush-hush this really was. Who had made such a quick decision to have her cremated so quickly? Was it in her will? My next move was to call Jack and tell him. I hated to bother him at work, but he needed to know. The news made him feel very bad for his cousins, and he told me not to worry about what I could have done differently. It helped to hear, but didn't make me feel any better.

Tomorrow I would be seeing the Beach Quilters. Perhaps they would have heard something. My appetite was gone for the day. It was a beautiful Michigan evening, so I poured myself a glass of wine and sat out on the deck. I once again picked up the sound of light jazz playing from below my condo. John's patio doors must be open. How cool it was that he appreciated such fine music. I wondered why music had left my life. I used to have piped in music at our home, but then Clay started his drinking and it was no longer soothing. Tonight though I laid my head back to enjoy John's music and turn off the ugliness of the world.

# CHAPTER 17

I was the last to arrive at Maggie's the next day for the quilter's lunch. It would be good to see everyone, but Sandra's death was certainly having a somber effect on me. The chatter was loud, and already their show and tell had begun. They all gave me a cheery hello, and some had to give me a hug. I had to admit, once I started munching on some veggies and catching up with each of the girls, I was falling into the practice of where I was before I moved from South Haven. It was nice to know that I still belonged.

When I sat down next to Cornelia to ask her about the shop, she brought up Sandra's death.

"What do you make of it, Kate?" she asked in a whisper. "I didn't know her like some of you may have. We were talking about her before you came. It's such a shame."

"We didn't keep in touch since James was being difficult about the Borna property," I explained. "I did go see her a few days ago, and she did seem pretty depressed. Something went very wrong in that marriage and the aftermath. I suppose a lot of it had to do with James drinking, just like Clay had done, but surely there has to be more to this."

"It's just such a shame she didn't get some help," Cornelia added. "Many families have some kind of addiction, but to take your life makes me also think there had to be more to the story. By the way, on a more pleasant note, Maggie said your place by the lake is so nice!"

"It will be when it's all furnished," I noted. "After this happened with Sandra, I just couldn't shop."

She nodded in sympathy.

Maggie got everyone's attention so they could discuss the Blueberry Festival raffle quilt. They were thrilled when I told them I would try to send a quilt block. Emily then showed a quilt she had just finished. She always wowed the group at each meeting with her talents. It was a hand appliquéd sampler quilt of different lighthouses. How perfect for South Haven. I wondered if Jack would like something with lighthouses on it. I should think more seriously about his request for a quilt.

There were many questions about my new house in Borna. I told them about Ruth Ann and how I commissioned a guest signature quilt from her to put in my entryway. They all thought it was quite clever. I told them that next week I was expecting a group of quilters that would be staying at the guest house. I said they should all consider such a trip in the future. It did spark some conversation about the idea.

"So what do you do for fun in such a little town?" Emily asked as she folded her quilt.

"Well, my first social experience was to go to a winery which my next door neighbor owns," I described. "I also joined a small group we call the Friendship Circle. There are a few quilters in the group, but they are all different ages with different backgrounds. It's pretty cool."

"Okay, we asked Maggie if there was a man in your life, and she said to ask you," Emily teased. They all laughed.

"I do have a male friend, but not a romantic one," I said, thinking of Clark. I think I was blushing. "He did a lot of carpentry for me at the house, and we really enjoy just talking to each other."

"I'd like that kind of man in my life," voiced Marilee. "Once they become a husband, the talking and listening stop."

They all agreed in laughter.

"Will you be back for the festival?" Maggie asked as she poured more tea for everyone.

"I don't know," I confessed. "I now have a business to consider when I get home."

"Did you hear her say home, you all?" asked Emily with her hands in the air. "We've lost her!" They all smiled.

It was a good moment to pass out the brochures of my guest house I had brought for each of them. They had many responses, including one about ghosts, which I ignored.

"Want to stay for dinner, Kate?" Maggie asked when the meeting was concluding.

"No thanks, Maggie," I answered. "I think I'll go by Country House Furniture and purchase that glass dining room table and chairs we looked at. I think it'll be perfect for that space. The realtor can let them in for a delivery."

"Oh, I loved it!" remembered Maggie.

"I better get going," I said grabbing my purse. "Be sure and give me an update on my son and your daughter, if you should learn anything."

"Oh, I will," she said as she gave me a big hug. "We better not wish for too much, or it won't happen." I nodded with laughter. We told each other "I love you," before I went out the door. Maggie was the best.

# CHAPTER 18

I was able to leave South Haven around 8:30 a.m., after I had picked up my order of blueberry scones to take home. My trip certainly hadn't gone quite as planned, but I could certainly shop for accessories most anywhere, even at Imy's. She was quite clever in making something into what you were looking for. Now I had to concentrate on my quilter guests who were about to arrive. This would truly be a test to my capability as a guest house manager.

When I stopped for gas, I called Ruth Ann to confirm the girls' arrival. She was thrilled I was on my way home. She confirmed that they would be arriving after 5:00, when their class was finished. She also told me how pleased she was on the progress of the banquet center. I wanted to ask about Clark, but didn't want to her to take the inquiry the wrong way. After I hung up, I called Susie to make sure she could come tomorrow to clean. She was planning to do so, and said that Cotton had been there to do yardwork. It was good hearing the voices from Borna. My next call was to Ellie. I was hoping she'd be in a good mood.

"I was just telling Trout last night that I'd bet you'd be here soon," she quickly replied.

"I miss you all," I admitted with a smile. "Why don't you come by for coffee tomorrow morning? I brought some of those famous scones home."

"You don't have to ask me twice!" she answered with

excitement. "You be safe now, and I'll see you on the early side."

"Great!" I had to chuckle at how folks there referred to early or late side when it came to the time of the day. This meant I could look for her around 8:30 a.m.

The day's travel was good for me to think. The trip went quickly, and when I got to Unionville to make my turn, I glanced again in admiration of the white house with the green shutters. I just had the feeling it was waiting for someone like me.

Since I didn't have food at the house, I stopped at Marv's to pick up a sandwich to take home. The place was nearly empty. I placed my order with a waitress new to the place. I ordered a beef brisket sandwich with some of his great potato salad. She gave me a glass of water while I waited.

"Are you that lady that lives in Doc's old house?" she asked shyly.

I smiled.

"I am," I said nodding. "I'm Kate Meyr. What's your name?"

"Mary Sue Hecht," she said, pouring me more water. Of course she'd have two names. "I just started working here," she noted. "I work the evenings so my husband can take care of my two little ones."

"That works!" I responded. "Were you related to Ben Hecht that just passed away?" Her face turned to stone. "My uncle," she simply stated.

"Oh, I'm sorry," I regretted bringing him up.

"Well, if you're sorry, you're the only one. That's all I can say." She walked to the kitchen to bring my food. She returned with it shortly.

"Nice to meet you, Mary Sue," I said taking my bag. I left a nice tip and left.

When I got in my car, my mind jerked back to the corner of the parking lot where Clark and I had shared a kiss. It gave me a silly schoolgirl feeling as I thought about it.

The air in my house was stuffy, to say the least. I left my car out on the drive so I could unpack and, of course, let the whole town know that I had returned. Before unpacking, I sat down in my sunporch to enjoy my dinner. Next to my chair was my mail neatly stacked that Cotton had brought in each day. I scanned through quickly before going out to get the rest of my things. In the stack was a letter from my Aunt Mandy, who lived in Jacksonville, Florida. It had the new change of address stamped on top of my South Haven address. I tore it opened immediately, wondering why I would be hearing from her. Since my father died, I only received Christmas cards from her.

Her handwriting was a little shaky, but as I read the letter I could hear her sweet voice. She told me that her son Charles had died from a long battle with cancer. She felt bad that perhaps no one had told me. Charles was her only son and must have been about my age or so. She said she was quite lonely and thought perhaps a visit to see me would be a good idea while she was still able to travel. I figured she had to be about 78 years old right now. She apologized for not coming to Clay's funeral, but she was not about to leave her son in his condition. My heart sank as I remembered getting a sympathy card from her. My state of mind did not pick up on Charles' illness as the reason for her not coming.

I had always liked Aunt Mandy, and she was very close to my dad. They had two other siblings who died at young ages.

My dad would travel to see her more than she traveled to South Haven. Her letter brought back many memories, and now I was feeling bad that I hadn't notified her of my move to Borna. I would write her immediately and tell her where I now lived. A visit from her would be delightful. We could catch up with family news, what was left of it, and I had the perfect house to entertain her.

On my way upstairs to do my task, I turned on the entry hall light to say hello to my guest quilt. Thankfully, there were no surprises while I was gone. All the signatures were in place. I brushed my hands over Josephine's initials and said aloud, "I'm back!"

It was great to see Ellie the next morning. She loved that I remembered how much she loved the blueberry wine I brought her, as well as the yummy scones from the Golden Bakery. She didn't bring up Carson's name, which was a good sign to me. She was pleased the quilters were coming to the winery for dinner on one of the nights. She wanted me to join them, but I wasn't sure I would be able to go. Before she left, I told her about Sandra's suicide. She had never known anyone to kill themselves and thought that it was very unfair for those who were left behind to blame themselves.

"I know you said her husband was a jerk, but even he didn't deserve this," Ellie noted. "Can you imagine how difficult this will be on her children? They will carry this burden the rest of their lives!"

"You have a very good point, Ellie," I considered. "I may just give a call to James. I'm sure many folks are pointing fingers at him." She nodded in agreement.

When Susie arrived to clean, Ellie went on her way. After I insisted she sit and enjoy one of the scones, we both went to work putting fresh linens on all the beds. I told Susie I wanted fresh bouquets, bottled water, mints, and a bottle of Red Creek wine in each room. I was now getting excited about their arrival.

Susie didn't leave till about 5:00 and we were both very tired. I settled for a frozen pizza and a glass of wine which I took to the sunporch to relax. With the evening news playing in the background, I heard a light knock at the back door. I jumped and saw Clark's face through the glass. He had a paper bag in his hand.

"Hey Mr. Wood Man," I teased. "Come on in."

"I didn't see any cars, but saw your light on," Clark said with a gleam in his eyes.

"Have a seat. What's in your hand?" I curiously asked as he came in.

"You know how much my recipe makes for Brunswick stew, so I thought I'd bring you some, since you enjoyed it so much," he said, giving me a wink.

"Awesome!" I replied, taking it from him. "What can I get you to drink?"

"Got beer?" he asked with that gentle grin of his.

"Sure!" I nodded. "Cotton likes a beer now and then when he's here working, so I try to keep it on hand."

I went to get his beer and wondered what on earth I must look like this time of day, with no makeup on. Clark, of course, looked neat and tidy as always, which I never could understand. We talked on the sunporch for about two hours, just catching up. He teased me about a younger man living under my condo when I described what the place was like. I had to admit, it made me blush. When I told him about Sandra he felt it was very unfortunate, but we didn't dwell on the topic.

ANN HAZELWOOD

He described how he had just finished carving a piece for
a corporation and hated giving it up. It was of some kind of
horse, which he always admired. He felt he had brought it to
life. I guess that's what he did when he decided to carve the
tree in my back yard. I was very fortunate to have it.

"You know, quilters feel they bring layers of fabric to life
when they start quilting," I added.

"I can see that!" he nodded.

When I told him about the five quilters that were coming
to stay, he said he had already heard about it from Ruth Ann.

"So how much longer will you be working at Ruth Ann's?"
I couldn't resist asking.

He chuckled and shook his head. "Well, she's a little like
you, Kate," he remarked. "When I'm in the building, she can
think of all kinds of things she needs advice on. The bar is
finished, and we're at the staining stage on other woodwork.
I hope to be done soon. You should come to see it all."

"I plan to," I said with excitement. "It's an ambitious
project, and I'm certain it'll be successful."

"Hey, you have got to be exhausted, so I better let you go,"
Clark said getting up from his chair.

"Thanks so much for the stew," I said with a big smile.
"That was very sweet of you! How about a nice South Haven
blueberry scone for tomorrow morning?" He grinned as he
gave approval.

When I handed him the wrapped scone, he pecked me on
the cheek with a sweet thank you. I watched from the porch
as he drove off. I guess I was wishing the peck on the cheek
could have been more. Was he truly just a friend, or was I
wanting it to be more? This was starting to get confusing.

# CHAPTER 19

The next day Ruth Ann called to say the girls had arrived and that they would finish their day by 5:00. They would be driving to my place to check in and freshen up before their dinner at the winery. I had to admit I was a bit nervous about the whole visit. I figured they were nice girls like I had in my quilting group, so I shouldn't be worried about anything.

Like clockwork, they arrived in two cars, traveling with an abundance of luggage and lots of laughter. I went out the back door to introduce myself and welcome them to Josephine's Guest House. When the compliments starting coming about how beautiful the house was, my anxiety was relieved. They gathered in the living room, where one of the girls said she would introduce me to everyone.

"Kate, I'm Carole, Ruth Ann's sister," she began. "I've heard so much about you. These are my friends: Kathy, Linda, Joan, and Tina. We all live not too far from here, and of course, we are all quilters like you, I understand." I nodded and smiled. "We have wanted Ruth Ann to teach some classes for some time, but she's been so tied down with her parents and this renovation. We are thrilled to be staying here. This is a real bonus to our trip. It's just as beautiful as Ruth Ann described!"

"Well, I am thrilled to have you," I responded. "We need to do a little housekeeping first before I show you to your rooms. Here is a sheet explaining our house rules, and in here is my little office where you can take care of your payment. I also have a guest book I would like you to sign as well as my guest house quilt." Their voices swooned as I pointed to the quilt. "I have a special pen to use and you may want to sign your names in a cluster of the blocks, so I will remember you as a group. You may already know that Ruth Ann made this quilt for me." From their reaction, they did not know.

"Oh, this is a grand idea!" voiced Carole. "We should sign ourselves as the Misfits, because that's what we usually call ourselves."

"Really?" I had to ask. "Why so?" They laughed.

"We call ourselves that because we don't fit in with any of the other quilters and guilds," she explained as the others started signing the book. "There are a lot of mean girls in those groups who think they are high and mighty. None of us competes. We just like to have fun making what we feel like."

"Yeah, most are overachievers who only want to impress the other quilters in their cliquish group," jumped in Tina. "They have their way of making fun of other people's work too, which is just mean!"

"Oh my!" I said in surprise. "I didn't think quilters could be mean."

"Think again," Kathy said with a laugh. "We all do what they wouldn't think of doing. Well, almost anything!" More giggles erupted like there was an inside story.

Tina especially asked for the downstairs single room, so on the second floor I put Kathy in one room and Linda in the other. Joan and Carole were thrilled to share the attic suite. They all had to see each other's rooms and marveled at the fresh flowers and décor. It made me feel so proud.

They didn't take long to change their clothes and shower themselves with various smelling colognes. It was strange how I would pick up on the smells. I told them to follow me to the winery, or they would get lost. I reminded them that I would be leaving after I had a bite to eat.

When we arrived at the top of the hill, they marveled at the view before heading to the bar. Trout was ready to please them with some wine tasting and flirty comments. The place was filling up with other customers, and a young man was setting up to play music with his guitar later in the evening. I tried to be helpful to Ellie, who was trying to arrange their table. It was fun to see all the excitement.

Ruth Ann had instructed Ellie not to let the girls have more than two glasses of wine each. I was pleased to hear that, as I didn't relish having to clean my rugs the next morning.

As we were enjoying Kelly's good barbecue, I asked about each of the girls. Tina claimed she was out of work, but wasn't in any hurry to find anything. Carole said she worked in the local bakery. I knew that famous bakery and hoped she would enjoy my muffins. Perhaps we could share some baking tips. Joan lived further out in the country. She said she loved all the little towns in East Perry. She was pleased to have a weekend away from cooking, she noted. Linda was a secretary for a local attorney, who was located on the town's square. She appeared to be the most conservative one in the group. Kathy said she and her husband owned an independent care nursing home where Ruth Ann's parents were now living. She too was thrilled to have a few days away from her stressful job. Their conversations jumped all over the place. Evidently, they had a lot of fun designing and sewing their table runners that day in class. They decided Joan had made the prettiest one of all.

After I ate, I sneaked out to head home. I knew I would have to wait up for them before I could turn on the alarm. This waiting up till my guests came home reminded me of when Jack would go out for the evening.

When they finally arrived home, their laughter and joking continued as they separated into their rooms. It did make me happy that they were having a great time. Finally, I arrived at my bed and set my alarm early to prepare fresh fruit, omelets, and my blueberry muffins.

Tina was the first to arrive in the kitchen that morning. She seemed full of energy and had lots of questions which were a bit distracting to my kitchen duties. I knew now I would have to think of a way to keep my guests out of the kitchen while I was preparing breakfast.

"Ruth Ann's place will really be awesome, don't you think?" she said as she helped herself to some orange juice.

"I haven't seen it since the major work started, but I'm sure it will be," I responded as I placed food on the table. "She has good taste."

"Yeah, she's got good taste in her workers," Tina teased. "Have you seen this guy Clark that works there? He is quite the dude, if you ask me." I nodded and wasn't sure I should respond. "I love his work. Ruth Ann said he's a famous woodcarver and sells his work all over the world. We all told Ruth Ann we'd love to see or buy some his work, but she told us flat out we couldn't afford him."

"So what was he working on yesterday?" I asked very innocently.

"Not really sure," she answered as she picked her chair at the table. "We just met him when she gave us a tour of the whole place. He's not very talkative. Ruth Ann said he's kind of shy. We told her she should make a play for him. He's not married, you know." I sure hoped Ruth Ann would not take the advice, or maybe she already had.

"What did she think about that?" I couldn't wait to hear.

"She just laughed," Tina said as she greeted Joan and Carole.

"I have everything ready if you want to start," I announced.

"Oh Kate, this is lovely," Carole noted. "I can't wait to taste those muffins."

"This is really fancy," complimented Joan. "Holidays are the only time I set a table like this."

"I'm starved," shared Kathy. "I don't know how that could be with all that I had to eat last night."

They all sat down with hearty appetites and chirping voices. It was hard to concentrate.

"I couldn't help notice that tree carving on your mantle, Kate," noted Kathy. "Is that by chance some of this woodcarver's work we heard about?"

"As a matter of fact, it is!" I bragged. "He carved the tree in my backyard long before I moved here. He said he had always admired it. He gave it to me as a gift, since he did most of the carpentry work here at my house. He thought it should live at this house, which was sweet of him."

"Man, wonder what that would sell for?" Tina asked with a serious tone.

"Plenty," jumped in Linda.

"It's beautiful!" Joan praised. "You are very lucky. I wonder if he'll give Ruth Ann something." They all giggled. I wanted to say that he'd better not, but didn't want to go there.

The girls were running late for their class and reminded me they would not be returning here till after dinner. Ruth Ann was doing an Italian meal at her place, so they could work longer. When they left, I was emotionally drained from all the chatter and trying to be a gracious hostess. I hadn't had to clean up so many pieces of china, crystal, and silverware in quite some time. It was kind of nice touching it all again, however. I hadn't entertained in years. In South Haven it was just easier to go to the country club.

That afternoon, after driving back home from getting groceries, I stopped at Imy's Antique Shop. As always, she was happy to see me. She was unloading some things from her truck that she had just purchased at a farm sale. I kept telling her I wanted to go with her some time. I helped her carry in some old crocks while she struggled with two wooden boating oars that looked terribly old.

"My goodness those oars are worn," I noticed. "They have to be quite old."

"For sure, but folks like them like that," she noted. "They hang them on the wall or think of some other way to decorate with them."

"Really?" I asked in wonder.

"They can be kind of cool with some fish netting or starfish to create a nautical theme."

"I see," I said, trying to picture it. "Where does one even buy fish netting, anyway?"

"Oh, Harold has some," she quickly answered. "Some guys around here use it for fishing, even though it's illegal."

My imagination started working, and I wondered if such an arrangement would be clever in my beach condo's loft or in Jack's room. Just feeling the patina, they had to hold a story. I wondered how many years they were used and with what kind of boat.

"As soon as you put a price on them, I think I'd like to buy them for my condo," I announced, surprising myself. She looked at me strangely. "I think I have a couple places they may work."

"Sold," Imy said giving me a wink.

"Who said I couldn't furnish my condo in South Haven from Borna?" I teased. She laughed, shaking her head.

When I got back to 6229 Main Street, I put the oars in the hall closet and started stripping the beds. I tried not to look at their personal things in their rooms, which would take some getting used to. When I went up to the attic, I couldn't believe how the two had made themselves at home. I guess the two glasses of wine at the winery weren't enough. They had opened the guest bottle of wine, and their personal things were strewn about everywhere.

At 10:00 I heard the cars pull into the drive. Their faces of excitement had turned to faces of exhaustion.

"We really had a full day!" Joan described. "Where is my pillow?"

"Yeah, serving the wine slowed us down, I'm afraid," noted Carole. "I was not very productive after that!"

"Linda and Kathy were troopers and kept sewing," said Tina as she went toward her room.

They all agreed to hit the sack, as Carole put it. That was just fine with me. The early hour would be here soon enough. Tomorrow I had to be up early enough to make baked French toast.

I climbed into bed, visualizing my oars in South Haven. It would be a nice reminder of Borna in my second home. I really wanted to call Maggie and tell her all about them, but I was just too tired. The next thing I knew I was dreaming of trying to use my old oars in Lake Michigan.

# CHAPTER 20

This was the girls' last day with Ruth Ann. They were all much quieter at the breakfast table this morning.

"So what will you be learning today?" I asked with curiosity.

"It will all be about finishing techniques!" Carole quickly answered.

"My head hurts," complained Tina. "I hate to tell you, Kate, but you have some horrific ghost in this house." Everyone stopped eating to hear more. "The first night, I just thought I had too much to drink. But last night this huge white cloud hovered over my bed that gave me the creeps." All eyes and ears were waiting to hear more. "I put my pillow over my head and somehow went to sleep. Who is that ghost?"

"I've never had anyone tell me this before," I claimed. That didn't sound like my Josephine.

"You were probably dreaming!" accused Carole, as she took another muffin.

"Well, I'm just glad I am not having to spend another night with whoever it was," she added. Some of the girls were snickering at her as they dropped the subject.

"So what time do you think you'll be back to pick up your things?" I asked as I started to clear the table.

"About 4:00 p.m. I think," Carole answered as if she was their spokesperson. "We don't have far to go, thank goodness."

When they all went out the door, I congratulated myself for getting through two nights and two breakfasts without incident.

I couldn't help but wonder what Tina's experience was all about. Could there be more than Josephine's spirit in this house?

As I was cleaning off the table, Susie and Cotton arrived to see what would need to be done after the guests left. We sat on the porch to catch up, as I offered them some of the leftover breakfast goodies. They gladly accepted. It was hard for me to waste prepared food. It may as well be eaten by folks who appreciated it.

I thought Cotton would get a kick out of seeing the new, old oars I had just purchased, so when I went through the living room to get to the hall closet, I noticed something was different. I stopped in my tracks. It was the blank space on my mantle. Clark's tree carving wasn't there! Did one of the girls pick it up to admire it and set it down somewhere else? I called Cotton into the living room and explained what was missing. He was speechless. We both looked around the room carefully as well as in my little reception room.

"It was there a couple of days ago, because one of the girls had admired it and asked if it was done by Clark," I reported. "I really don't want to panic. There has to be an explanation."

"Were any of those girls left alone in this room that you can recall?" Cotton asked, walking around.

"No," I said firmly. "I was the last to go to bed each night, so I could turn on the alarm. Oh, Cotton, I can't let Clark find out this is missing."

"Of course you can't," Cotton consoled. "Let's not panic. I'm sure there's an explanation." Susie now entered the room, as she heard our conversation.

"Let's go look in their rooms if they're not locked," I suggested.

"Like it's going to be sitting on their dressers?" Susie said sarcastically.

"I know it's silly, and we can't go through their things," I warned. "Oh, Cotton, I can't tell Ruth Ann that one of her quilting friends is a thief, but it had to be one of them. I don't know what to do."

"Well, you can ask the girls about it when they come back for their luggage," Susie suggested.

"I just don't think I can do that," I added. "I have no proof."

How could a quilter steal, I asked myself. Maybe one of them was a mean girl after all.

After Cotton and Susie left, I went to the attic which was unlocked. Their two suitcases were near the door, but nothing else looked unusual.

When I came back down the stairs to check Tina's room, I went by the guest quilt. Once again, my eye noticed something different. A name was missing from the group of signatures. It was Tina's name. I thought I saw her sign it. It reminded me of when I discovered Carson's name had removed. That actually pleased me. I gave credit to Josephine. Did Josephine remove Tina's name, too, and why?

When I went to Tina's room, the door was locked. I had a second house key, but there was no way I was going to snoop and possibly get caught. So did the ghost in Tina's room know what she was up to? It had to be her! She was the one that mentioned she wanted to buy something from Clark.

I wanted to turn to Ellie for advice, but knew she would have left for the winery by now. I couldn't do anything, so I decided I would pay Ruth Ann and the quilters a visit.

I waited till after lunch to go to Ruth Ann's place. It was a beautiful day so I decided to walk there, since it was less than a mile away down the road. My mind now had to decide what to say and what not to say. I opened the unlocked door to the first floor where men were working. Some were nailing down flooring, and one was painting some baseboards. I looked for Clark, but didn't see him. As the men acknowledged me with a nod, I spotted the magnificent bar that Clark had designed and built. The massive ornate structure was magnificent. Ruth Ann must have had to pay a fortune for it. It would be the conversation piece for her business. I couldn't help but run my hand across the smooth patina on the wood.

"May I help you, ma'am?" Clark's voice surprised me from behind. I think I may have jumped.

"Where did you come from?" I asked in surprise.

"I've been in the basement, cutting columns," he explained. "So do you like it?" His eyes were gazing at the bar in pride.

"This is truly amazing!" I praised. "You did a wonderful job." It was the first time I saw Clark a little messed up from sawdust, and his hair wasn't perfect.

"Does Ruth Ann know you're here?" Clark asked, wiping his brow.

"No, not yet," I clumsily answered. "I really hate to disturb them in class, but decided to take a walk and check things out here."

"Did you notice she put in an elevator?" Clark pointed out.

"Yes, how nice," I admired. "Those steps are a killer."

"She had the elevator started before her folks moved out," he explained as he dusted himself off. I couldn't help but smile, seeing him like this.

"I best get going and see what the girls are up to," I said, not wanting to hold him up any longer. "You better get back to work!" He nodded.

"Good to see you," he said as if he didn't want me to go. "The scone was delicious, by the way."

"I'm glad you liked it," I agreed. "I plan to have your stew for dinner tonight."

I felt his eyes on me as I walked away toward the front entrance where the steps to the upstairs were. As I climbed the wide and long staircase, I understood her need for an elevator. I knocked at the beautiful new door and waited for Ruth Ann to answer. She seemed quite surprised to see me.

"Why Kate, come on in," she greeted.

"Well, I don't want to interrupt anything," I said shyly. "I guess I was just curious about what you all were up to, and I wanted to see how the renovation was coming along. Clark gave me a little tour. The bar is simply gorgeous, Ruth Ann." She gave a prideful smile.

"I love it, and it's all getting to be pretty exciting," she admitted with a big smile. "We were just taking a little break. Why don't you have a cup of coffee with us?"

"No, thanks, but I will say hello and peek at what you're doing," I conceded.

I walked into the spacious area she now used for her studio, and it was perfect for this class size. The girls were mingling about, but I was looking for Tina.

"Hey, Kate," Carole yelled from across the room. "Come take a look! Can you believe this place? Did you ever see her fabric stash?"

"No, I never have," I answered with some interest.

"I told the girls I'm one of those midnight internet shoppers that likes shopping in her pajamas," Ruth Ann joked. "When I need a piece of fabric, I can't travel miles and miles to get to a fabric store."

"I told her she needed to open a quilt shop after the banquet hall is up and running," teased Joan. Ruth Ann just laughed the comment away.

*What a great idea,* I thought.

"This is unbelievable," I said, trying to take in all the neatly arranged fabric that was in color order. "Now I know where I'm going to go if I need anything."

"You'd be very welcome to do so," Ruth Ann responded. "Over in this room I am making an office. I figure I am going to need one with this new business."

"I'm overwhelmed," I said, taking a deep breath. "Ruth Ann, I am going to have to talk to you about something after the girls leave. Could you give me a call?" Her face turned serious.

"Why sure," she nodded.

"See you girls later," I yelled to them. I noticed the whole time I was there, Tina did not look at me. As I walked back home, I couldn't help but feel proud that I had urged Ruth Ann to make this big investment. I knew it would be successful and even help my business. I just couldn't spoil their little get-together by asking them about my missing tree.

I worked nervously around the house till the girls returned around 4:30 to get their belongings. I made some light snacks in case they wanted to socialize a bit more. I especially wanted to keep my eye on Tina.

"Oh, Kate, this is such a nice place to stay," praised Linda. "I really want to come back here real soon and see more of the sights around here.

"Me too," voiced Kathy. "I want to bring my husband to see this cute little town."

Tina remained silent and walked toward her room.

179

"Tina, I noticed you didn't sign the guest quilt," I reminded her.

"Oh, you're wrong, I did sign it," she argued.

"Go see for yourself," I said, leading the way to the quilt. "I couldn't find it." She looked at me strangely. "I'll show you." She followed me.

"I saw her sign it," noted Kathy.

Tina stared at the quilt like it was lying to her. She placed her hands on her hips. "Well for heaven's sake, give me the pen," she said in a huffy tone.

"Thanks, I just didn't want anyone to be left out," I said nicely.

When she finished, I asked her if everything was satisfactory in her room. She looked at me in an odd way.

"Why sure!" she said as she went in and picked up her two suitcases that were already closed. If she had the tree, it had to be in one of them.

They were all anxious to get on the road, so I followed them out to their cars and waved good-bye.

I walked into the house and wondered if I had lost an opportunity to get back Clark's tree. Tina was now gone! I walked back into her room as if there would be a clue for me, but there wasn't. I felt silly, even looking under the bed. My cell phone was now ringing in the kitchen.

"Kate?" the unknown man's voice asked. "Kate Meyr?"

"Yes, this is she," I answered.

"This is your South Haven neighbor John," he explained.

"Oh hello, John. How are you?" I responded in surprise. "Is everything okay?"

"Oh sure, everything's fine," he said with a chuckle in his voice. "The reason I'm calling is that you received a package from FedEx today. When you didn't answer, they asked if I would take it for them. I thought I should, but just wanted you to know."

"Well, that's odd. I'm not expecting anything," I noted.

"It actually has your son's name on it, not yours," he added.

"I think the best thing to do is just drop it off at the condo office," I suggested. "Would you mind doing that?"

"No, not at all," he quickly responded. "That's what neighbors are for."

"How are things at the lake?" I asked to be nice.

"The weather's been great," he bragged. "Nice warm days and cool nights. It's real typical of Michigan in the summertime, or have you forgotten?"

I chuckled. "Well, that's not the case here in Missouri," I complained.

He laughed. "Say Kate, when you return, how about we have dinner on my patio one night and get to know each other a little better," he invited. It took me by surprise.

"Why sure, however I haven't a clue right now when that will be!" I stated.

"Well, if there's anything I can do for you while you're away, just holler," he offered. "Let me give you my phone number."

"Okay, thanks!" I accepted. "May I ask how you got my number?"

"I think the internet. I'm not sure," he said matter of factly.

After he gave me his number, he finally hung up. I couldn't believe this young, handsome guy would even want to be seen with me. He had to be at least 10 to 15 years younger than me.

# CHAPTER 21

Ruth Ann called me the next morning and asked if she could stop by. Susie was here cleaning, but I didn't think that would interfere. I dreaded telling her I suspected one of her students had stolen from me. I could only hope she would keep this incident a secret from Clark. The more I thought about the theft, the more I considered getting a security camera for the downstairs.

When she arrived, I offered her coffee, which we took to the sunporch.

"You certainly have me worried, Kate," she revealed. "Did the girls misbehave?"

I shook my head and smiled.

"They were quite nice, and I especially enjoyed your sister Carole," I noted. "I guess I didn't realize how much quilters enjoy a retreat like this. I have to admit, you could create a whole package of the quilt lessons, historical tour, and a fun trip to the winery."

"I was thinking the same thing, Kate," she said with excitement written on her face.

"I really am hesitant in telling you my reason for this visit and my suspicion, Ruth Ann, but I don't know where else to turn. I do hope you keep this between us."

"Of course," she said with fear on her face.

I tried to tell her how Clark's carved tree was admired by the girls, and the next day it was gone. Her face looked ghostly.

I told her there wasn't anyone else in the house in that period of time. I revealed how Tina's room was the only room which was kept locked, however I didn't examine the other rooms. I also noted that Tina was the one that commented about buying something from Clark and was frustrated that she couldn't.

"This is horrible, but I don't know if there's enough evidence to blame Tina," she defended.

"Well, there is more evidence, but I hesitate to share it with you," I said feeling nervous.

"What on earth could it be?" she demanded. "I think you better tell me."

"Do you have any spirits in your building?" I cautiously asked her.

"You mean like ghosts?" she said wrinkling her face. "My mom always said things would disappear, but I never paid much attention to her."

"Well, without question, I have the spirit of Josephine here in this house," I began to explain as I watched Ruth Ann's face become more puzzled. "She's harmless, but let me show you something on your quilt." I led her to the entry hall.

I tried to simplify the actions of the signatures that appeared on the quilt and the ones that disappeared. I pointed out that Tina's name had not only been removed once, but twice. Her eyes were huge and she listened intently. "Tina also complained about a hovering cloud over her in bed. That's never happened here before in this house. I know you may think this is all nuts, but someone in that group took that carving, Ruth Ann."

She shook her head in disbelief. "Clark will be furious," she finally said.

"You cannot tell him," I demanded. "I will find it somehow. I didn't accuse her, but perhaps I should have. Do you think your sister could shed some light on Tina's history? Perhaps she has a questionable past."

"I suppose I can ask her," Ruth Ann agreed. "I just don't think she would do such a thing. Perhaps you should question Josephine, if she's making things disappear." She had a good point.

"Look, no one likes to accuse anyone, especially not a quilter!" I responded. "I'm just going to have to let this play out, Ruth Ann. I like to believe the best in everyone."

"This is all pretty creepy, no matter who took it," she said as she paced the floor.

"I have a security system, but I suppose I need to get a camera installed here on the first floor," I revealed. "I hate to have guests thinking I'm spying on them while they're here."

"This is such a shame, but I guess I'll have to take some security measures with the banquet hall as well," she admitted. "I've already had people tell me that in a business like mine, the employees are generally the problem. I haven't taken any applications, as yet." I had to agree with her.

Before she left, she reminded me she was the hostess for the next Friendship Circle meeting. She left my place deep in thought. I thanked her for listening and reminded her not to say anything to Clark.

I went back to my kitchen duty of making vegetable soup. I knew Susie may have been listening from the other room, but she didn't say a word. I sent home some soup with her and tried to get my mind on other things. It was Sunday, so I needed to touch base with Jack. Luckily I caught him at home and told him about the package that had arrived for him.

At first he couldn't explain it, but then remembered he had ordered something online and had it sent to the condo. I told him our neighbor would be taking it to the office. He anxiously told me that Jill was going to be arriving for the weekend and that he couldn't wait to show her around New York. I wanted to ask where she would be staying, but remained silent, as a "cool" mother should. I happily responded and knew Maggie would be as thrilled as I was. We would have to figure this out together.

# CHAPTER 22

The next week I had a guest arriving to attend a wedding in Dresden. It was a single woman, which sounded pleasant to me. She said this was a large wedding, so I was hoping to get a few other reservations.

My plan for the day was to have lunch with Ellie. She bragged about a little town that had a small eatery called the Pie Cafe. She said the food was awesome, but that it seated less than twenty people. She said it was located in an old bank building that was built in 1905. I told myself I had to get out more. These were the kinds of places I adored and would not find in Michigan. The country road drive through the small community with tiny buildings was quite interesting. Ellie was a wonderful resource when it came to East Perry County.

When we entered what looked like a little dollhouse, we aimed for the only open table for two in the back corner. Ellie suggested we get the sandwich of the day and choose one of the many pie choices for our dessert. I selected banana cream and Ellie chose apple crumb. The meringue was piled high and the cinnamon crumbs were generous and large. How fun it must be to own a charming place like this! I wondered if the owner ever tired of making some of the same things on a regular basis. I suppose she could wonder the same thing about me and my breakfast muffins. I told myself I may need to bake more pies once in a while instead of muffins.

I finally had a chance to tell Ellie about my quilter guests between bites. Poor Ellie was always the one to hear my grievances. She stopped eating and turned red with anger when I told her about the missing tree.

"I know which girl you're talking about," she stated. "She really came on to Trout the night they were there. She gave Ruth Ann a rough time when she said they had to leave." She said she had a pretty good sense of people's honesty. She definitely encouraged my camera idea.

"I have a guest coming for the Schmidt wedding in Dresden," I shared to change the subject. "I'm hoping I'll have more than one."

"Wonderful! They're having the rehearsal dinner at the winery," Ellie added as she took her last bite of pie.

We chatted another half hour before we left. It was always fun to catch up, despite me complaining. In the car, I told her about my young neighbor in South Haven wanting to have dinner with me when I returned.

"So you're thinking about becoming a cougar now, are you?" she teased, nudging me. We laughed. The thought of me in that role was quite ridiculous.

"I do want to get to know him better," I admitted with a smile. "He loves playing jazz music, and it filters upstairs when I have the deck doors open." She gave me a teasing look of fondness.

When I arrived home in the late afternoon, I had a call on my answering machine from a young man who was bringing his girlfriend to the Schmidt wedding. They had two different last names, but wanted one bedroom. I guess this would be part of the new normal I would have to get used to. I called him back immediately and suggested the attic suite. He was delighted.

The rest of the evening, I sat on the sunporch to make phone calls. I couldn't wait to talk to Maggie, but she wasn't home. I tried to read, watch television, and even quilt on a quilt block, but my mind kept wondering how I was going to solve the crime which had taken place in my own home. I just knew Josephine didn't have anything to do with taking the tree. She would have taken it long before now. I didn't think Saint Anthony would respond since I wasn't Catholic, and it really wasn't lost.

I checked my e-mails and answered two inquiries on room rates. Some of the other e-mails were from the Beach Quilters. One of them reminded me about completing my quilt block for the Blueberry Festival. I had forgotten that the time was slipping away to complete it. I thought about doing some embroidery, which I enjoyed, but I needed a clever design. The raffle quilt was such a profitable fund-raiser. Perhaps I would suggest to our Friendship Circle that we make a Borna quilt for the East Perry Fair next year. I would have to check with Ruth Ann for design ideas when we met at her place.

I went upstairs and succumbed to going to bed early. I tried calling Maggie one more time. I still had many questions in regard to Sandra's suicide, which perhaps she could now answer. It reminded me that I should call James and express my sympathy to him and his children. Sandra must have been so desperate to want to end her life. How would I have responded to Clay's affair had he still been alive? Was I lucky to not have Clay around, as Sandra had declared? Would he have eventually told me about her and left me for her? I would never know.

# CHAPTER 23

Ellie and I went together to Ruth Ann's for our Friendship Circle meeting. It was a pretty warm day, so I took cut-up watermelon and Ellie brought a vegetable tray.

Her workmen were all busy when we walked in the open front door, but there was no sign of Clark. When we got to the top of the stairs, Ellie teased Ruth Ann that she better speed up the completion of the elevator as the many steps were a big challenge. I was pleased to see Emma attending, because I always learned something from her. Every one of the members was present except Esther.

There were lots of compliments from everyone, as Ruth Ann had made many changes since the girls were there last. Ruth Ann had arranged her table setting on her large cutting board. She displayed a long patchwork table runner like the quilters had worked on in class. It was a strawberry print laid on top of her green tablecloth. I told myself I could do that, too.

The smell of the tuna casserole was heavenly. Betsy had brought a colorful salad with fresh blueberries and strawberries. She said her poppy seed salad dressing was a family recipe. Anna brought some of her homemade bread which she called sourdough. Ellen brought a light, heavenly lemon sheet cake that was served with a thin raspberry sauce. The food served in this group certainly was an asset. Very seldom did anyone miss a meeting.

The first order of business, while we were still having dessert, was Ellen's concern on whether our group would have an exhibit at the fair this year. Evidently, this was a traditional practice. She asked if anyone had an idea to bring forth. When no one responded, she said she had been thinking about a fun and unique idea.

"As long as it doesn't take too much time," voiced Ruth Ann. "I am terribly busy!"

"Me too," chimed in Peggy.

"We have a lot of bus tours scheduled, so I don't know how much help I can be," Anna added.

"Well, this can be done quickly, and I will be happy to chair the exhibit, if need be," offered Ellen.

"Sounds good already," Emma teased. "If Ellen is in charge, it'll be a hit for sure!" They all laughed as Ellen blushed.

"How about we have an exhibit called Plants Out of the Pot!" suggested Ellen with excitement.

"What on earth?" asked Charlene in disbelief.

"We all bring a plant for the exhibit, but it has to be planted in something unusual," Ellen described. They all looked at her for more information. "I love to garden, as you know, and I've done some of this kind of planting here and there in my own garden. I went to Oscar's shed and found some things that would hold dirt." They all laughed. "I found a broken lantern, a mailbox, an old tire, and a piece of a broken pipe. You can choose any plant you like, as long as it's not artificial."

"Seriously?" asked Emma in disbelief.

"Clever idea, Ellen," I said. "I have lots of little things in my small barn out back."

"I have a plant already planted in an old shoe I could bring," offered Peggy.

"Perfect!" responded Ellen. "I would like to have a co-chair, if at all possible."

"I think I can handle that," jumped in Charlene. "I'll do anything to get out of working in the cheese stand." They all snickered. Toasted white cheese sandwiches were one of the big sellers at the fair.

We all clapped for the idea and encouraged Ellen and Charlene to move forward. When Ruth Ann walked around filling our coffee cups, I brought up making a Borna quilt for next year's fair. Ruth Ann's eyes were glaring at me like I was giving her a huge project.

"I have been doing this with the Beach Quilters in Michigan, so I'll be happy to gather all the blocks from everyone," I volunteered. "I think it could make us lots of money for a charity or a whole new project, if we want. Each block should represent East Perry County in some way. There are plenty of ideas around. Maybe since I have fresh eyes, I can give you some ideas." Most of their faces lit up with the idea.

"Great, but some of us aren't quilters, Kate," reminded Ellie.

"That's okay," I said, thinking of how to produce more blocks. "You let me worry about that."

"Kate, I have to admit this is a wonderful concept," approved Ellen. Her approval was important, for sure. "I think the church ladies could hand quilt it for us."

"What a great idea!" I said. "It would be a wonderful contribution from our group. Who wouldn't want to own a quilt all about East Perry?"

"We sure have many needs in this county," Peggy noted. "Why don't we all bring back our choice of charity at the next meeting?" They all rejoiced at the idea. Their minds were working, which was great to see.

Everyone had now started to leave, but I got Ruth Ann's attention about needing a design for my Blueberry Festival quilt block. She went to get an apron she had with a teacup on the pocket, filled with blueberries. It was pretty cute, and so I figured out how to outline the design. I knew she'd come up with something, and this was simple enough. My mission was accomplished and I prepared to leave.

I spent the rest of the day and evening working on my quilt block, while I was in the mood. Everything was quiet, and I worked best when I didn't have any interruptions. I was thinking of turning in early for the night, when my cell phone rang. At this late hour, it had to be either Maggie or Jack.

"Still up?" Clark's voice asked.

"Why yes," I answered with surprise. "I don't think you have ever called me on the phone. I wasn't sure it was you." There was a pause. "Is everything all right?"

"Are you up to going for a drink?" Clark asked in a serious tone.

"I suppose," I answered with some hesitation. "Are we celebrating something?" A light snicker of laughter responded.

"How about I pick you up in ten minutes? I'm leaving the winery now."

"Sure, I'll be ready," I said hanging up.

This was truly a surprise, and not like Clark. Maybe he heard about his missing tree and wanted to talk to me about it. At this late hour, it puzzled me. I ran upstairs to freshen up. I was acting again like a schoolgirl with the anticipation of seeing him. I guessed he just wanted to talk about something. Goodness knows, I had many situations I had discussed with him. That's what friends do. I ran downstairs when I saw the headlights turn into my drive.

He knocked at the back door and I let him in. He looked like a troubled man that had a few too many drinks. He looked speechless, as if I were to make the first hello. He didn't look like he needed to be going to another place to have another drink.

"Would you prefer to just stay here instead of going somewhere else?" I asked with concern. He smiled.

"Good idea," he began. "I've had a few drinks, for sure. I went by the winery to bring home dinner, like I always do, but there wasn't anyone at the bar, so I decided to eat there. Well, that was hours ago."

"Do you want another beer or are you ready for some coffee?" I asked with some hesitation.

"I'd like another beer, but only if you'll have one with me," he said. "Let's go sit out on the deck. The fresh air will do me good." I nodded, but knew he didn't need another drink.

I grabbed two beers out of the refrigerator and took them to the steps of the deck where Clark was sitting. He looked deep in thought. Something serious was working on him.

"So what's on your mind?" I finally asked as I joined him.

"You know I never share many of my thoughts, good or bad, with anyone except you, Miss Meyr," he said looking down at the ground.

*So far, so good,* I thought.

"That's what friends are for, right?" I said, comforting him.

"So I guess that's what we have become, right?" he asked still not looking at me. "We're just good friends?"

*Where is he going with this?*

I didn't answer till he said more. I didn't know what answer he was looking for.

"You know, I had this gal come on to me tonight," he

confessed with a slight chuckle. "She tried every trick in the book to get my personal attention, if you know what I mean. Just ask Trout, who was enjoying every minute of it. It was kind of funny, because the more she tried, the more I thought of you."

"Me?" I said with a laugh. "I don't think this is a compliment. I'm sure this is not the first time you've had this experience. Women around here have made it no secret that you're quite the catch."

"Look who's talking," he said, finally looking at me. "You've got some young guy after you in South Haven just waiting for you to return,"

I laughed. "You don't know what you're talking about, plus you've had a little too much to drink, I think," I said dismissing his comment.

"Well, I seem to remember how you were the first to take our friendship out of the box the night you kissed me at my cabin," he accused, slurring his words.

I had to snicker again with embarrassment. "Well, you were being so darn sweet when you fed those deer," I reminded him as I looked directly at him.

"Frankly, Kate, I think we're both in denial about this relationship, but that's okay," he stated boldly, which caught me off guard. He took a deep breath. "Say, what does it take to be able to spend the night here, anyway?"

*Keep calm,* I told myself. *I don't think he meant what he just said.*

"Well, first you have to check in at the front office where I assign you a room, unless you have a preference," I began to explain. "Next, I give you a copy of the house rules before I ask you to sign the guest book and then my guest house quilt on the wall." He leaned back and laughed.

"So I can ask for any bedroom I like?" he asked with a mischievous smile.

"With one exception," I teased back. Now I knew where he was going.

"I think I'm a little too inebriated to go to all that trouble tonight," he said shaking his head. "I'm making you a little uncomfortable, aren't I, Miss Meyr?"

"You might be, but Clark, you know my situation too well," I started to explain. "I don't like playing games, and I don't want to be hurt by anyone again. Look what Ellie just went through with Carson. That smart, independent lady finally succumbed to a business associate's charm after many years of knowing him, and it turned ugly."

"Hey woman, that has nothing to do with us!" he said elevating his voice.

"Oh no?" I came back to say. "Since we're being so honest and open here, I happen to know you feel the same way as I do. Besides, I don't think there's room in your heart and lifestyle for another person!" He stared at me which, penetrated my thought process.

"Well then, how in the world did you get there?" he said in a soft voice.

I couldn't believe what he just said, so I mostly ignored it. I was in his heart as well as his lifestyle?

"How about I fix us some coffee?" I said, changing the subject. "You're letting the alcohol take over tonight, Clark." He stared at me like I said something offensive. He stood up to stretch.

"You know, Trout told me not to drive in my condition, but I told him I wasn't going far," he reported with a slight slur. "I guess he figured where I was headed."

"Really?" I timidly asked. "So is this where I say, 'Clark, since you've had too much to drink tonight, would you like to spend the night here?'" He nodded and I took a deep breath. "Well, the bedroom on the first floor is available and, as a good friend, I won't even charge you for it." I chuckled. "Now that means you do not have access to the other two floors. It's the rule here."

He nodded with a smile. "I'm good with that!" he said looking around. "I've always wondered what a night here would be like!"

Wow, that was a leading statement! I needed to take the conversation away from us.

We chatted for another half hour before I suggested we call it a night. I showed him the bedroom and told him to holler if he needed anything. He thought that was really funny. He truly was ready to pass out somewhere by this time. I turned around and headed upstairs before he could come close to me. This was not a night to turn on the alarm system, plus I was in safe hands, or was I?

I did lock my door. As much as I adored this man, I wasn't going to allow myself to succumb to something I would likely regret later. It felt strange knowing he was just a stairway away from me. I went to sleep repeating in my mind what Clark had said about ignoring the girl at the bar and that I was in his heart. If he were sober, would he have said that?

I woke up into bright daylight, as frequently happens. I looked at the clock and it was only 3:00 a.m. When I looked out my window, there was complete darkness outdoors. Josephine was fooling with me again. Why did she do this?

I got up to get a drink of water and remembered that Clark was sleeping in my house downstairs. The good news was that he was too tired to pursue me in the middle of the night. The bad news was that he didn't pursue me in the middle of the night. I laid down again, wondering if I should check on him. *That probably wouldn't be wise,* I told myself. All of a sudden, I saw headlights leave my driveway. I rushed to the window. What did this mean that he left before morning? A pang of disappointment ran through me, even though I knew it would avoid an awkward moment in the morning.

I finally went downstairs around 4:00 a.m. By now I was totally awake. When I went into the kitchen to make coffee, I turned on the light and saw something written on a napkin. It said, "Let me know what I owe you, Clark." Well, that was hurtful! Was he trying to be cute because I told him he'd have to book a room to stay here? Was he embarrassed and didn't want to face me in the morning? Did he have regrets about even stopping by last night?

While I waited for my coffee, I walked into the bedroom where Clark had crashed. He hadn't even pull back the covers. He must have just crashed when he hit the bed. I went back to the sunporch with a cup of coffee to watch the sun rise. Did Ellie see Clark's car here last night? I should try to call her later, but didn't relish telling her he was here for the night. Would he call me later? No, that wouldn't happen. It took many drinks to get him to call me last night. I needed to stop questioning myself and forget the night ever happened.

As I went to go upstairs to get dressed, my eye as always went to the guest house quilt. Close to the center were the initials CWM. These initials were new and in Josephine's handwriting. Did she take it on herself to include Clark's initials on the quilt? Was his middle initial a W? I continued to stare at it in disbelief. He did indeed sleep here, but not as a paying guest! Carla and Maggie were not paying guests either, but I let them sign the quilt. This was all too weird.

"You're entirely too nosey, Josephine," I called out loud. I stomped up the stairs. Obviously, there were not going to be any secrets or privacy in this house. If word of the mysterious signatures got out in the community, guests may not want to stay here. Maybe the spiritual cloud appeared over Clark in that room, and that's what made him leave. It would certainly make me get out of the house. I always felt safe here and wanted my guests to feel the same. Would this be a problem or an asset?

My morning was occupied outdoors with pulling weeds in the flower gardens and tending to my small kitchen garden. Even without much rain the weeds thrived, and I couldn't leave the manicuring of the flowerbeds up to Cotton. I wanted everything to look perfect for my wedding guests. The heat was rising by the hour, so after I finished watering I cut some mint and went inside the cool air for some iced tea. I was about to open the door when Ruth Ann pulled in the drive.

"Hey there! How about some iced tea?" I asked as she got out of the car.

"Well, that's the best greeting I've had all day," she said wiping her brow. "It's going to be a hot one today." We both went inside to enjoy the air conditioning.

"Thanks Kate," she said anxiously, taking her glass. "The reason I stopped by was to tell you I asked Carole about Tina."

"Oh good!" I said as I offered her a slice of lemon. "Could she tell you anything?" She shook her head.

"She was shocked and concerned when I told her about the missing carving, however she couldn't imagine Tina or any of the girls being a part of such a theft," she reported. "I had a feeling I would get that response."

"Well, I didn't exactly expect anyone to confess, but it has to be one of those girls, as much as I hate to admit it," I said with frustration. "I have nowhere else to turn. I hope you aren't personally offended by my suspicions."

Ruth Ann shook her head.

"Speaking of the famous artist, he didn't show up for work this morning," Ruth Ann shared after she took another swallow of tea. "This is not like him. He had scheduled to meet with Ed, who was going to help him with something this morning. When I called, it went to voice mail. Have you seen or heard from him?"

"Ugh, no," I said in a half lie. "Something must have come up."

"Well, too late now," she shrugged. "Ed left. I guess I'll try calling him later. I gotta run to Harold's before I go home. Thanks for the tea. Say, what did you decide to do for your planter?"

"Thanks for the reminder! I haven't done a thing, but I am nearly finished with my Blueberry block. Thanks so much for that design. It's turning out nicely. What are you doing?"

She gave a hearty laugh. "Well, I don't know if it will work, but there were some old bowling balls left in my building, and one has very large holes," she revealed. "It weighs a ton! I was going to see if I could get some kind of vine plant to take hold on it."

I let out a laugh of surprise. "Now that would be clever, Ruth Ann," I encouraged with a chuckle. "You can tell everyone you had a ball doing it!"

"Funny, Miss Meyr," Ruth Ann teased.

"You will win a prize for most unique, if it works," I remarked. "Now you've challenged me, for sure."

I followed her to her car and waved good-bye. Where was Clark? She knew him well enough to know he wouldn't just be a no-show. She would have fallen over if I had told her he had just spent part of the night here!

I kept walking toward my little barn, that most folks would call a shed. Ruth Ann had my curiosity going now about what kind of container to use for a plant. I opened the door to spider webs and dust. Cotton never seemed to have the time to really clean this up. I would just have to assign this job to myself one day. I supposed it, too, had been built by Doc Paulson for his storage use, but maybe not. I immediately spotted an old rusty watering can, but that was too normal of an idea to use. On one of the shelves, I noticed what looked to be a bird's nest that someone saved. Children may have been living here when they allowed renters, for I couldn't imagine adults saving the nest. I took it out to the daylight where I could see it better. It was amazing how tightly woven it had remained. I wonder how old it really was. I pictured inside of it a cute little plant of some kind, like an African violet which was small and dainty. I shut the crooked door and laid the nest on the deck to consider. It would do nicely if I couldn't find anything else.

Clark continued to be on my mind on and off for the rest of the afternoon, as I went about my business of paying bills and planning menus. Ruth Ann was right on this being odd behavior for Clark. I wondered when I would hear from him again. If he didn't want to talk to Ruth Ann, he sure wouldn't be anxious to talk to me!

# CHAPTER 24

Days flew by with only a short chat with Ellie. She and I had domestic things to tend to with the Schmidt wedding. Ellie had the rehearsal dinner this evening and, tomorrow I would be expecting a nice young couple and a single lady who were going to be my guests during the wedding weekend.

Still no word from Clark, but I wasn't about to call Ruth Ann to see whether she had heard from him. Over and over again, I was trying to convince myself that I had done the right thing by not encouraging anything romantic between the two of us that evening. I was flattered that he cared, for sure, but the timing wasn't there and I wasn't sure it ever would be.

I had Susie cleaning today, so together we had the place looking really nice. She seemed to be more enthusiastic with her cleaning when she knew I was about to receive guests. Ellen called to see whether I was invited to the wedding. I had to remind her I was new to the community and didn't even know the Schmidt family. She invited me to sit at their table if I were going, which was considerate of her.

I didn't disturb Ellie at work, nor did I call Maggie who was in Florida on vacation with Mark. I had just checked in with Carla, and there wasn't anything new with her. My two best friends were busy with their own lives. They couldn't always be at my beck and call, after all, I was keeping some secrets from them.

As Susie and I continued to work, she kept asking about Clark's stolen tree. She thought I should have reported it to the police, but that was the last thing I wanted to do. I had to figure this out on my own and warned her not to tell anyone about it. As I walked back and forth in the entry hall, I was reminded that Josephine may be a concern while my guests were here. I had placed the single lady in The Study. It was the same room where Tina had said she had a spirit hovering over her. I admired once again the beautiful initials that I assumed to be Clark's. His middle name was definitely William, which I had confirmed on his website. I wondered how many guests it would take to fill this entire quilt. It was turning out to be a mystery of its own, but it always made me smile.

I finally ended my day by reaching Maggie on her cell phone. She bragged about getting a nice tan and how they were really enjoying the trip. There were times I was envious of her having a much better marriage than mine. She always loved hearing about my menu choices for the guest house. I planned to serve a breakfast casserole of eggs, cheese, and sausage. Also on the menu was yogurt with fresh blueberries and strawberries, a petite Belgium waffle, and, of course, my signature blueberry muffins.

"I'll try to be there," Maggie teased.

"Oh, I wish you could," I responded with unrealistic thoughts. "I guess you haven't heard anything new in regard to Sandra's suicide, have you?"

"Not really, but I did hear from Jill that her daughter Emily is having a rough time with it all," she noted. "You know they were in the same class together."

"I hate to think what her children are going through," I

sadly added. "I may just have to call her. She's probably still home for the summer. I always liked her, and she was always fond of Jack."

"Well, it sure can't hurt anything, Kate," Maggie encouraged. "Jill hasn't seen her, but her closer friends said she's pretty upset as you can imagine."

"Thanks for telling me," I said picturing what she looked like when I last saw her in the Blueberry Store. "Hey, I'm about to send my Blueberry block, so be looking for it. I hope it's satisfactory. I also convinced my Friendship Circle to make an East Perry County quilt for the fair next year. I may regret it, but it's such a simple and easy fundraiser."

"Aren't you ambitious?" Maggie teased. "What will your block be?"

"Good question, but I'm not sure. I want to represent my guest house in some way, since it's so visible here in Borna. Do you have any ideas?"

"You could embroider the house from a good photo perhaps," she suggested. "You might also find something that represents Josephine, if you have a photo of her."

"Good ideas, Maggie," I complimented as I got comfy on my bed. "There are so many wonderful landmarks in this county. I'll have to think about it for a while."

"I'm surprised you didn't mention that my daughter was in New York last weekend!" Maggie said with a snicker in her voice. "I assume you knew that, right?"

"Oh yes, but to tell you the truth, I'm almost scared to think about it," I joked. "I don't want to jinx anything! It would be so cool if they ended up together, like we hoped."

She agreed, before she said she had to hang up.

"Wait, I forgot to mention that I heard from my Aunt

Mandy in Florida. I think you've met her once or twice. Do you remember? Her name is Amanda, but we always called her Aunt Mandy."

"I'm pretty sure I do," Maggie recalled. "She was there for a Christmas gathering you and Clay had some years ago. A pleasant, southern lady, I recall."

"Yes, I think that was the last time she was here. Her son had cancer for quite some time, and he has passed away. She wrote that she was missing family and thought about coming to visit me some time soon."

"Yes, now that you say that about her son's cancer, I remember having a conversation with her about him. I thought she said he was in remission at the time."

"I know, and I feel bad I haven't kept up any communication with her. She did know about Clay's death, but she didn't know I had moved. I wrote her back and suggested she come Thanksgiving or Christmas. I haven't heard back."

"So does this mean to Borna or South Haven?" Maggie asked, fearing my answer.

"Borna, of course Maggie," I said feeling guilty. "She would love it here, and the weather is so brutal in Michigan that time of year, compared to here."

"So does this mean you will only be a lake girl for the summer season, as they say?" she kidded.

"It might," I said, chuckling. "I'll keep you posted, girlfriend."

I felt so much better after having a conversation with Maggie. What was it about sharing your life with your best friend? It was almost like journaling. Perhaps it keeps one's life in balance to share it with someone.

# CHAPTER 25

I still had to admit that I was nervous about accepting strangers to stay in my home. Having Clark's sculpture stolen reminded me of the risks involved. Perhaps after the weekend, I'd be more used to it. The first of my guests would be Irene Williams. She sounded like she was my age or older. She would be arriving in the early afternoon, and my unmarried young couple would be in the late afternoon. They may know each other, as I learned they were all going to the rehearsal dinner this evening. An early breakfast for them was planned, as the wedding was scheduled for 10:00 in the morning.

I refrigerated the breakfast casserole for the morning and then proceeded to inspect the house for any last minute details. In place of Clark's tree on the mantle, I had placed a nice bouquet of fresh flowers. I couldn't help but wonder if Clark had noticed the empty spot on the mantle when he stayed here for the night. If he did, I'm sure it would have added salt to the wound.

I went upstairs to look presentable for my guests. I gave myself another look in the mirror noticing I had gained some weight, which was no surprise. I also needed a haircut in the worst way. I wasn't ready to settle for a ponytail the rest of my life. I had set aside my personal grooming since Clay's death. He would not be pleased with what I looked like these days. My excuse was I was too busy with the house and no one really cared how I looked. I guess I didn't care whether anyone found me attractive again. Clark never handed out many compliments. I had to give Ellie credit for keeping herself attractive, since she was dealing with the public. I'd have to call Esther, who used to have a beauty shop here in town, and see where I needed to go. It was time.

When I came down the stairs, I saw my first guest approach the front door. I opened it before she had a chance to knock.

"Oh hi, I wasn't sure which door to go to," she said.

"You're fine, it really doesn't matter," I greeted, shaking her hand. "I'm Kate, and welcome to Josephine's Guest House."

She grinned and stepped inside. "I'm Irene Williams," she said as she put down her one suitcase. "I'm so thrilled to finally be here. Your place is beautiful."

She was younger than I expected. I guess it was the name Irene that dated her. I accepted her string of compliments as she walked around the first floor. I then took her to my little office to get her registered. She was particularly impressed when I asked her to sign the quilt as well as our book.

"Oh my goodness, some of these signatures are so elegant," she praised. "I'm not sure I can do this quilt justice, but I'll try."

"Well, as you can see, I haven't been in business for very long, but I'm anxious to fill it up with lots of guests," I noted with enthusiasm.

Irene carefully signed her name and wondered why the hometowns of the guests were not listed. I told her that was what my guest book was for. When I showed her to her room she was very pleased. She then hesitated and said she had a favor to ask.

"I don't know if you allow this, but I have a couple of cousins here in town that I would like to ask to join me for breakfast tomorrow morning," she divulged. "I will be happy to pay any up-charge."

"Well, this is a first request for me, but I don't see why not, as I have plenty of food," I replied with a smile. "Yes, there will be a minor charge."

"That's wonderful. Thank you so much," she beamed. "There isn't a nice place for breakfast in these parts, so thank you again."

She was correct on that observation, I noted.

"So do you know Jim and Candy, who are also going to the dinner tonight?" I asked before she closed her door.

"They are due to arrive here later this afternoon."

"Oh yes, I wasn't sure they could make it," she responded. "Jim is another cousin of mine, but I haven't met his girlfriend, Candy."

I excused myself to answer my cell going off in the kitchen.

"Kate, it's Anna," she stated. "I know you're busy, but I have a favor to ask. I have a wedding next weekend here at the village, and my bride and bridesmaids want a nice place to get ready and change before the wedding. Could we rent your place for the day?"

"I suppose so," I said with some hesitation.

"They would come in the morning and have a light lunch at your place," she added.

"Did you say lunch?" I interrupted.

"Yes, but they are just bringing something light," she explained. "They don't expect you to provide it. If they can just use your dining room, it would make it really special."

"I think it'll be fine, but I'd like to have time to get a price together for you," I added. "I'll call you tomorrow, okay?"

She was fine with that and hung up.

What all was I getting myself into? These requests were certainly another way to provide income for this business, which was good. I had a feeling I could tap into the wedding market very quickly and perhaps work with Anna on her occasional weddings. However, I had to remember this was my home and that I needed to decide how far I wanted to book events ahead of time.

Candy and Jim arrived hand in hand, just an hour before the rehearsal dinner. They were excited and almost giddy about staying here in my guest house. Candy immediately wanted to see the attic suite before going through the registration process. I requested they first sign the guest book and the guest house quilt. Candy thought it would be clever to squeeze both their names into one block, but I requested she stick to my signature plan. She sighed with disappointment, but she drew a tiny heart next to her name. I had to admit the two of them were as cute as could be. When we finally went up the two sets of stairs to the attic, their reaction to the secluded love nest was worth seeing. Their eyes lit up, and Candy rushed to bounce on the bed for approval.

"We will never leave here," Candy gushed as she ran her hands over the linens.

"Look, we can see the whole street from here," Jim noted with excitement. "I was born in Unionville and tried to describe to Candy how charming these little towns are."

"That's what brought me here from Michigan," I added. "You all enjoy the room as well as the party tonight. I know you'll have great food since you're going to the winery."

"That's what I heard," replied Jim.

"Oh, I wish we didn't have to go to that darn dinner," complained Candy as she sat pouncing on the side of the bed. "Honey, can't we just stay here and go to the wedding, tomorrow?"

I didn't want to hear that response. I excused myself, knowing they had other things on their mind. I hoped Josephine's eyes would be closed.

I walked downstairs and poured myself a glass of wine. None of the guests planned to join me since their schedule was so tight. I took my wine outdoors to the lovely evening and sat on the steps where Clark and I had been some days ago. I had to smile inside, knowing I had provided joy to these perfect strangers. They were going to have a great evening at the Red Creek Winery with this perfect weather.

I had to wonder once again what Clark might be doing on this perfect Friday night. I had an inkling he left to go out of town, since no one had seen him. The total darkness of this part of the world made me happy I had installed a dawn -to-dusk light on my property. As I sat alone, I also wondered what I might be doing if I were still living in South Haven. Perhaps Maggie would have dragged me to the country club with her and Mark. Would any divorced or widowed men notice me now that I was available? I was glad I didn't know the answer.

I reluctantly went inside to check my e-mails. Maggie had sent me a photo of her and Mark on the beach. There was an e-mail from Carla describing how Rocky got a nail in his foot and had to be taken to the vet. Poor Rocky! I did miss having regular contact with Carla. She was certainly a good buddy to have when I was dealing with Clay every day. She was good to keep checking on my condo. Perhaps I should make a visit there once the East Perry County Fair was over. I certainly wasn't going to miss what they promoted as the Best Little Fair in the Land!

I put my laptop away, feeling rather nostalgic. When I felt this way, I wanted to express my private thoughts in my journal. Before I left South Haven, Maggie had given me a journal titled *My New Life*. I enjoyed posting in it now and then. I kept it under my chair that sat by the fireplace. Last winter I posted frequently during the long dark nights. In glancing, I noted I had many references to Clark. Perhaps he wouldn't be mentioned much longer if he kept his distance. The fact he stood up Ruth Ann sent a message of Clark wanting some distance. I found myself smiling as I read some of the posts. I was truly happy. There were no regrets about this new chapter in my life. Little did my deceased husband know that he had left me something truly precious.

It was not yet 9:00 p.m. when I heard Candy and Jim enter the back door.

"Back so soon?" I greeted. They giggled.

"Yeah, it was real nice, but we just wanted to hurry back and enjoy our attic," Candy said as she finally let go of Jim's hand.

"We'll see plenty of our family tomorrow," Jim added as they walked past me.

"Well, I'll see you lovebirds in the morning then," I said as they went up the stairs.

"Good night," they said in unison.

I decided my attic must be quite special for them to rush back to. I snickered to myself, remembering what it was like to be so young and in love. Before Clay, I fondly remembered crushes I had on young guys. When I met Clay, he was older and more mature, which impressed me. It also didn't hurt that he was good looking and came from a wealthy family. I was flattered that he found me attractive and before I knew it, I was totally smitten. I let my immaturity and peer pressure decide my future. I was happy to get pregnant and be active with Jack's education as he was growing up. Despite my love for decorating, I didn't think for a moment what I might want for my own future. I now was feeling I was in control of my destiny for the first time in my life. Perhaps that's why I wasn't looking for anything more.

# CHAPTER 26

I didn't see Irene till the next morning when she promptly showed up for breakfast, eager to see her relatives.

"My cousins Beth and Margaret should be here soon," she reminded.

"I look forward to meeting them," I said as I filled the water goblets at the breakfast table. "Coffee is ready if you want some."

"Thanks," she said looking very tired.

"So how was the dinner, if I may ask?"

"Absolutely perfect," Irene bragged. "After the meal, most of us hung out on the deck. It was just so lovely out."

"I thought you all would enjoy that experience," I added. "You certainly look pretty for the wedding."

"Thanks Kate," she said shaking her head. "It just gets harder as I age."

"I was just thinking the same thing, recently." I hated to admit it.

"I met Ellie, the owner of the winery, last night and she shared with me how you came to live in Borna," she revealed. "I have to say I admire your bravery. I think I would go stir crazy in this little town."

I was about to defend my choice when the two cousins arrived at the front door. I hurried to open the door, as they waved hello. One was older than the other, and they were dressed to the nines.

"Thank you so much for letting us crash your breakfast," the older looking lady said. I smiled with approval.

Irene didn't waste any time introducing them to me. They were immediately taken with the beauty of the house and looked amazed at the all the food prepared for them.

"I know you have some time restraints, so please have a seat and enjoy your first course," I encouraged. "Hopefully our other two guests from upstairs will be joining us soon."

The house was filled with delicious smells of a country breakfast. When I brought out the blueberry muffins, Irene was quick to explain how she had read about the muffins in my brochure and couldn't wait to try them. The chatter at the table was lively and happy as they discussed their travel and family members. We were finally joined by Candy and Jim, who looked exhausted but adorable in their church finery. Candy said she was not a breakfast person and would just have coffee. Jim, however, said he would make up for it and admitted he was starving. What was it about men and food? I couldn't help but think about Clark and how food was linked to his happiness. They were about to finish their meal, when Margaret, the older of the two, said she had learned that Clark McFadden lived in this county. She said she had purchased one of his pieces from an art gallery in Springfield, Missouri.

"I would have loved to have met him," she wished. "I told myself I should buy a piece of his work for my boss, who appreciates fine art."

"How did you learn about him living nearby?" I curiously asked.

"It came up in conversation last night with that darling bartender at the winery," she revealed with a big smile. "He said he frequents there often for carry outs. The young man said that you have a carving of his here at the guest house."

I felt like I had seen a ghost and wanted to get away. I just nodded. "Does anyone need more coffee before you leave?" I said quickly changing the subject.

Everyone declined and the subject was dropped.

Irene, Jim, and Candy were all delighted with their stay and hoped to return. The two breakfast guests were thrilled with the visit and admired the guest quilt going out the door. Beth said the next time they would visit Borna, they would book a room and sign the quilt. When I closed the door, I felt the visit was a huge success but was happy they were on their way. I walked into the dining room and saw the breakfast mess, which needed my attention, but for now I was taking personal time and took my coffee to the sunporch.

Susie was due to help me make up the guest rooms at any time. I knew she would enjoy the many leftovers from our breakfast. As I started clearing the table, I thought about Margaret's comment regarding Clark's carving being at my guest house. Thank goodness she didn't ask to see it. What would I have said?

When Susie arrived, she happily accepted my breakfast offer as she complained about Amy Sue's cold. It had kept her up all night. As she helped herself, I told her I would be going to Harold's to pick up some things and then stop by Ruth Ann's place.

"I'm sure I'll be back before you're finished," I said getting my purse off the counter. She nodded between bites, as I watched her enjoy the breakfast delicacies she was not used to.

I jumped in my Mercedes on one of the hottest days of

the summer. As I blasted the air-conditioner, I reminded myself that this car needed to say good-bye to something more practical. I didn't dare complain about the weather to anyone as I hated the winter much, much more. I parked the car and had just slammed the door shut, when I saw Clark coming out of Harold's.

"Good morning, Clark," I suddenly said in surprise.

He hardly looked at me and did not respond. He just nodded and kept walking toward his truck. I wanted to turn around and yell at him for his rudeness, but instead I kept walking toward the entrance to the hardware store. What had just happened?

"Well, good morning, Miss Kate," Harold greeted. "I haven't seen you for a while. I thought maybe you went up north. How have you been?"

"Oh fine, thank you," I responded in a fog of what just happened with Clark. "I desperately need some light bulbs."

"Two aisles over." He pointed as he wiped his apron.

"Thanks," I responded, following his instructions.

I could hardly concentrate on why I was even there. Why was Clark behaving this way? I was feeling sick and needed to quickly grab some light bulbs, dish soap, and batteries so I could leave.

"Saw you had some guests this weekend," Harold noted.

"I had some nice folks here for the Schmidt wedding," I reported as I moved quickly.

"It was quite a shindig from what I heard," he said laughing.

"So you weren't invited?" I quickly asked, without thinking.

"Nah, don't know them that well, but the Schmidt family

goes way back in this county," he added. "I guess you saw Mr. McFadden just left here a minute ago," he said with a tease.

"I saw him pull out," I said, walking toward the door. "Have a good day, Harold."

I sat in my car a moment to think whether I should proceed to visit Ruth Ann. If Clark's truck was parked there, I needed to move on home. I sure didn't want to embarrass myself another time. Thankfully though, when I pulled into Ruth Ann's driveway there were no other cars parked by. I really had to talk to someone about Clark, and she knew him just as well as Ellie did. Perhaps I could learn from her what was going on. Without giving my real reason away, I may have to make up something about needing a piece of her fabric. If I picked up from her that she had personal feelings toward Clark, I would have to remain silent and listen like a good friend.

The front door was open with no one around, so I hiked up the long staircase and rang her door bell.

"Hey, Kate, what a surprise," she greeted with a big smile. "Come on in."

"I think you may have to put a chair on this landing for those who are recovering from the hike on those stairs!" I teased being out of breath. She laughed.

"You can now use the elevator, by golly," she announced. "That's why I had it put in. "There's no way I could keep dragging groceries and stuff up these stairs. The exercise is good for me, so I try to do the stairs when I can. I heard years ago there were some elderly folks living up here. Can you imagine that, with no elevator back then?" We chuckled once more as I entered her lovely home. "So why do I deserve this surprise visit?"

"No special reason really," I said lightly. "I just left Harold's place and thought I'd stop and say hi."

"No one's working here today, so I was going to run some errands myself," she claimed.

"Why isn't anyone working?" I asked with curiosity.

"It's the nature of the beast, I guess you'd say," she said shaking her head. "They all work other jobs, so you get them when you can get them and besides, most of my work is completed."

"That's wonderful!" I added. "So is Clark finished here as well?"

"I'd say he's pretty much on call now," she noted. "He has been a wonderful resource for the entire workforce here. They all really respect his advice. I don't know how I would have gotten through this without his help. He has that eye that can make the average structure look really unique."

I could agree with that.

"Did he ever say why he just didn't show up the other day?" I carefully asked.

Her eyebrows went up. "He just said something came up," she casually said like it was no big deal. "He's a very independent guy and he can afford to be. You ought to know that. Rumor has it that the two of you are pretty close friends."

I paused. "Yes, just friends, but nothing in a romantic way," I explained. "I don't know where folks get that idea. I frankly enjoy having male friends. However, I don't know what to make of his behavior lately."

"What do you mean by that?" she asked with concern.

"Well, I just ran into him as he was coming out of Harold's, and he wouldn't speak to me," I confessed. She looked at me strangely. "I don't understand the sudden change, so I thought I'd ask you about him, since you said he didn't show up for work recently."

"I see," she nodded. "I'm afraid I can't help you there. I never was very good about figuring out men."

We both snickered.

"Please don't say anything about this, Ruth Ann," I pleaded. "This is such a small town and I feel I am always somehow on display."

She nodded. "That's what you get for buying a house in the center of Borna's Main Street," she teased. "Ellie should have warned you about that."

I had to chuckle at myself. "Just remember, Miss Ruth Ann, you are also on Main Street. When you have all those events, we'll be able to see how successful you are and whose cars were there and whose were not."

She doubled over in laughter. "Oh, I never thought about that," she said as she regained her composure. "Say, how about we go to Marv's and have an early lunch? I could go for one of his big, juicy hamburgers and perhaps a beer on tap. It would taste mighty fine on this hot day. What do you say?"

The request took me by surprise.

"You know, that sounds pretty good to me," I said patting her on her back.

"I'll meet you there shortly," she added. "I first have to throw a load of wash into the dryer."

"It's a date," I said, heading toward the long stairs out to my car. I felt so much better after talking to her. It made me feel better that she didn't have romantic ideas about Clark. I liked Ruth Ann and hoped she would keep our conversation confidential.

I parked my car at home so I could tell Susie about my

change of plans. I would just walk to Marv's from there. She was about to finish up cleaning the kitchen floor when I walked in. I told her I was going to Marv's and offered to bring her back some lunch.

"Heavens no," she said, shaking her head. "That wonderful breakfast will keep me full all day," she confessed. "The phone's been ringing, so don't forget to check your messages, Miss Kate!"

"Thanks, I'll get to them later," I said thinking of Ruth Ann waiting for me. "Please take any leftover muffins to Cotton, will you?"

She beamed at the thought.

"I'll see you in a few days then!" I said going out the front door.

It was already crowded at Marv's when I arrived. I found an empty table in the corner for us. Marv's new waitress immediately approached me.

"Hey, Miss Meyr," she greeted. "Is someone joining you today?"

I nodded and smiled. "Yes, my friend should be here shortly," I said as I looked about the room.

"Sure, just give me a nod when you're ready to order," she responded. "I'll go ahead and get you some water."

Ruth Ann came in the door wearing a fresh set of clothes and some makeup which I hadn't seen on her before.

"Well, you cleaned up pretty good," I complimented as she sat down. "I meant to ask you, when is your first booking coming up?"

She snickered. "I don't have one!" she admitted with a sneaky grin.

"Not one?"

"I'm not too upset about it, as Ellie reminded me that my bookings would be arranged far in advance," she said for an excuse. "No one even knows as yet what I look like or what I can even offer."

"I see," I nodded. "That makes perfect sense. So the first thing you need to do is have a big open house for the whole county. The second thing you need to do is invite Ellen and Oscar and promote your services for the lumber company events. Ellen can make things happen for you." She laughed like she knew what I was talking about.

"Yes, I'm planning on the open house right after the fair," she noted. "I thought I could have flyers and materials ready to pass out at the fair like some businesses do."

"Great idea," I said as we started looking at a menu.

"Kate, were you afraid when it was actually time to do what it was that you had planned to do?" she timidly asked. "Does that make sense? You know it sounds great when you talk about something, but then when it's time for it to happen, it gets a bit scary!"

"Sure, that's why I invited my two friends from South Haven to be my first guests. I didn't know what I was doing, so I thought their visit would remind me of what was to happen and what I would need. I think they would be honest with me as well, if I was forgetting something or should be doing it differently."

"I have nightmares just thinking about what all can go wrong with a large hall full of people," she confessed. "What if the air-conditioning goes out or I run out of food?"

I had to laugh, but knew she was serious.

"That's why you see restaurants have dry runs with customers before they officially open," I informed her. "They have to find out how long things take to process and serve, plus how much help that they may need. Do you have anyone hired as yet?"

"Not really, however I have some folks in mind that I may mention it to," she added. "I'm hoping most events will be catered by other businesses."

"Why would you want to do that?" I asked with concern. "You ought to utilize that great kitchen. Plus, that's where your profit will likely be. Remember, we live in a location that doesn't have caterers at your disposal, unless you plan to hire Kelly at the winery."

She nodded and smiled. "I know, but I can't hire a cook if I have no work for them."

We ordered our hamburgers and fries with a couple of glasses of Marv's mellow brew. I could tell Ruth Ann was truly worried about her big new adventure. I didn't blame her. My little enterprise was contained and much simpler. I also had the resource of providing food for my customers. We chatted with many ideas, which boosted her confidence. When our dessert of peach cobbler arrived, our conversation got more personal.

"Do you ever date, Ruth Ann?" I boldly asked.

She looked at me strangely. "You know how tied down I have been with my parents," she reminded. "My life is now completely different living here. The emptiness of them moving into a home was filled with this new business venture. I don't have time to think about it and, for heaven's sake, we live here in Borna. I don't see you running around town with anyone."

We both laughed as I nodded in agreement.

"That's right, you don't," I admitted. "I came to Borna

with a lot of resentment, which perhaps everyone could read all over my face. This lifestyle change has been huge, but very good for me. For the first time in my life I am in control of myself."

"I know that feeling," she agreed. "My friend in Oregon who has a business said I should be cautious about not letting the business run me instead of me running my business."

"That's a very good point," I said as I took my last bite of cobbler. "When Clark suggested I open a guest house, he said it would be perfect for me since I didn't want to be tied down. He had a point there, but you also have to make a commitment to your guests, or you don't really have a business."

"I agree," she nodded. "When you have to make commitments to folks a year or more in advance, it scares me."

I saw her point.

"We're getting pretty negative here, but I have to laugh at myself on how I almost didn't want my house to be finished, because that would mean I'd really have to begin the next step."

"It is such a comfort, Kate, to talk this all out with you," Ruth Ann admitted as she put on her coat.

Our two hour lunch was good for both of us. I really liked Ruth Ann. She was so talented with her quilting and she was undertaking a big business venture.

As I walked back to my house thinking about our conversation, my cell phone rang. A smile came over my face because it was Maggie.

"You sound out of breath. Where are you?" Maggie asked when I answered.

"I'm walking home from having lunch at Marv's," I said as I reached my back steps. "Obviously I need more exercise. I'll have to see if Borna has a gym and spa."

She laughed. "You're funny!" she teased. "I'm calling to pester you into coming back for a visit."

"I was actually thinking about that last week," I noted. "I should probably wait till after the fair is over in September.

"Kate, must I remind you of how short the summers are here in Michigan?" she said. "You live on the lake and you want to come that late in the year? Why can't you come in a week or two? Do you have guests?"

"I do this Saturday," I informed her. "I suppose I could take another look at my calendar. What's going on there anyway?"

"Well, my suggestion on coming home really has to do with Mark's friend, Maxwell Harris," she began to explain. "He just retired and is moving back to South Haven. His wife died about a year ago after a long illness. He retired early to take care of her. He still does a little consultant work I think."

"So, what's that got to do with me?" I rudely interrupted.

"Well, he's looking for a place to live near the lake, of course," she kept describing. "He's staying at the Carriage House right now."

"So?" I asked in confusion.

"Well, Mark thinks you could be helpful to him, having gone through this process. Plus, he thinks the two of you would be perfect for each other."

"Yikes, Maggie," I said loudly. "Don't go there. You know how I feel about another relationship right now. I'm sure he is very nice. Didn't you say he was retired? Why would I want to date an old man if I decided to date, anyway?"

"Kate, he just turned sixty, but he's really good looking and keeps himself in great shape. He's traveled a lot and Mark said he's very intelligent."

This was not convincing, nor tempting.

"That's all nice and maybe we can meet someday, but a blind date is out of the question," I boldly stated.

"Yeah, Max told Mark the same thing," Maggie added. "Don't you need to check on the condo? Carla and I sure thought you'd be back before now. What about that nice neighbor downstairs who wants to take you to dinner?"

"Stop it, Maggie," I warned. "Seeing you and Carla is all the reason I need to visit."

"By the way, Jack told Jill he would be back here soon to see her," she said to entice me further.

"Well, that is interesting," I responded. "So what is Jill telling you about their relationship?"

"Very, very little," she said with a snicker. "That says to me that things are going pretty good. Isn't that amazing?"

"Stranger things have happened, I guess," I happily answered.

"So have you had any interesting guests lately?" Maggie asked, changing the subject.

"I have a wedding party scheduled Saturday," I noted. "They are changing here before they have their outdoor wedding at the Saxon Village."

"That's pretty cool," she added. "Are you going to let them sign that beautiful quilt?"

"I guess so, since they are paying customers, although I think Josephine is deciding who can sign and not sign."

"Oh, Kate, you are always imagining things," Maggie teased before she pleaded one more time for me to visit.

We hung up with another satisfying conversation of true friendship. I hope I hadn't hurt her feelings for trying to have this Max meet me. I had to admit I missed her fun ideas and silliness. I cherished those coffees at the Golden Bakery since I left. Perhaps a trip back to South Haven could be arranged after all. However, if I was going to squeeze in another trip this summer, I had to find a hairdresser to get my hair cut. I had let myself turn into someone I didn't recognize in the mirror. I looked up Esther's phone number on my computer and decided to give her a call for some references.

"Esther, how are you?" I asked, when she answered.

"Hi, Kate," she greeted. "I'm much better with this new medication. So what's going on with you?"

"I need your help in finding me someone that can cut my hair this week," I pleaded. "I can't go back to South Haven wearing a ponytail every day like I do here." She laughed.

"You always look great, Kate, but I think you'd look great in a blunt cut right about your cheek line," she described.

I tried to envision it.

"Do you think so?" I questioned. "It sounds like it would be easy to take care of."

"It is and I'll show you what else you can do with a style like that, to make it look sexier," she said with a chuckle. "No harm in that, right?"

I chuckled to myself. "Oh, Esther, I didn't mean to ask you to do this for me," I said apologetically. "I was hoping you could recommend someone since you don't have your shop anymore."

"Oh, I still do a few family members' hair and many of the children around here whose parents cannot afford to take them to the beauty shop," she explained. "I'll be happy to help you."

"That's wonderful," I responded. "My hair has always been as straight as a board, so if you would agree to give it a try, I'd appreciate it."

"Sure, how about tomorrow afternoon?" she suggested. "I live out a ways, but if you know how to get to Ellie's winery, I'm just three miles down the road. You turn left when you see the yellow mailbox. Our farm is straight ahead."

"Did you say yellow mailbox?" I repeated with a chuckle.

"I know it's strange, but it's the best house number we have," she joked.

"Okay, I'll see you tomorrow," I said feeling relieved.

*Wait till Maggie hears I went to farmhouse with a yellow mailbox to get my hair cut,* I thought.

My next mission was to call Jack and see if we could match up our plans.

"Hey, Mom, is everything all right?" he asked with concern in his voice.

"Sure, why?" I asked.

"Well, it's not Sunday, for one thing," he joked. "What's up?"

"I think I'm going to go to South Haven next week, and I heard through Maggie that you may be going there as well," I explained.

"Yeah, I'm hoping to get there next weekend, but we've got a really big campaign with a client going here, so I won't know till the last minute," he said with frustration. "I hate paying the extra plane fare, but I want to see Jill."

"What about your mother?" I teased. "Would it be okay if I showed up?"

He chuckled. "You're crazy. Of course, it would be a bonus."

"So things are good between the two of you?" I asked, hoping for more information.

"Oh sure," he casually replied. "We really have a lot in common now that we're older!"

"Well, I'll take a chance that you'll be there and I'll probably arrive on Friday night," I reported.

"I'll try to make it work as well," he agreed. "You know we're running out of beach time on the lake."

"I know and that's why Maggie suggested I come soon," I said as we agreed to say good-bye.

Wow, my son was falling in love with the girl that Clay and I had always planned for. The thought of seeing him, Maggie, and Carla was getting me excited. I immediately sent a text to Maggie that my plans were being made.

# CHAPTER 27

I called Ellie the next day to tell her I was coming by the winery to have lunch before I got my hair cut at Esther's house. She was surprised I was willing to risk a small town haircut and teased me about it. She said she'd be there and would be happy to catch up with our happenings. She said she loved the very busy late summer business, but admitted that she needed a break. Surprisingly she told me that Carson had contacted her a couple of times, but that she held her ground about not seeing him. I told her I was proud of her.

The rest of the day I planned for my wedding party's arrival and whipped up a double recipe of German cheesecake. I thought it would be neighborly to take one to Esther tomorrow, for doing me a favor. Baking for me was similar to quilting. The process of assembling my ingredients and slowly combining them for the end result was comforting to me. It was also a time to reflect on issues that I continued to shove in the back of my mind. I certainly hadn't solved the theft that occurred in my own home, and I certainly hadn't figured out how I had lost my friendship with Clark. What was I missing?

I was startled by my cell phone ringing. It was Ellen.

"Hey there, Kate, how are you?" she politely asked.

"I'm just fine, Ellen, how are you?" I responded.

"The same, but the reason I'm calling is since I'm in

charge of our entry in the fair, I need to make a list of what plant items to expect from everyone," she stated. "Have you decided what your entry will be?"

"I think so, if it's still there," I teased. "I found a darling bird nest in my barn that's in great shape, so I thought a little African violet plant might be adorable in it."

"Well, if that isn't the sweetest idea I've ever heard," Ellen gushed. "You'll have to get that rooted soon because we're just weeks away!"

"You are so right," I said. "So what will you be doing? Have you decided?"

"I have several things in mind, but wanted to hear about the sizes of the others before I decide," she noted. "Oscar thinks my ideas are just plain silly, but I told him that we would be sure to win a blue ribbon."

I laughed. "I bet he knows how determined you are, so look out."

We both chuckled.

"So have you decided on your quilt block for next year?" Ellen anxiously asked.

"I want to embroider the guest house, but I can't draw so I don't know if that will happen," I confessed.

"That shouldn't be a problem, Kate," Ellen noted. "I might be able to do that for you with a good photograph. If I can't, Oscar's secretary is quite a good artist."

"Okay! I'll give it a try," I responded. "So what are you thinking about?"

"I think I'll do something that represents the lumber company," she revealed. "I feel it needs to be in the quilt. Their logo is pretty interesting. I haven't embroidered in years, so I hope I'm up to the mission."

"Well, perhaps I can help you there," I offered.

We were thrilled with each other's offer as we hung up. What would this community do without Oscar and Ellen? I reminded myself that I hadn't responded to the dinner invitation they extended to me after church some time ago. I would have to do that soon.

I was ready for bed at an early hour for some reason. When I got comfortable in my bedroom, I made a list for the next day and laid it on the pillow next to me. I reached for my journal and admitted there were moments like this at the end of the day when I felt pangs of loneliness. It would be nice to share my thoughts at the end of the day with someone and, of course, have someone to cuddle up with. As difficult as Clay was as a husband, he never refused my need for affection. I didn't want to second guess what his intentions were, for I would never know.

A light rain was starting to fall when I drove up the hill to the winery the next day. Two couples remained cozy under the umbrellas placed on the deck. I found Ellie behind the bar with Trout. I was embraced with a hug from both of them.

"Kelly has made some great Rueben sandwiches today, served with some yummy potato salad," Ellie enticed. "Does that sound good to you?"

"I haven't had a good Rueben in a long time," I revealed. "That sounds great. Trout, it'll just be iced tea for me today."

He nodded with a smile.

When the food arrived, Ellie and I found a table near the kitchen where we could have some privacy. The first thing she had to tell me was that she had turned a basket wine carrier into a flower pot for our exhibit. She thought ivy would be perfect for the look she wanted.

"Aren't you something?" I praised. "You are so creative. It shows everywhere in your house and here."

"If it turns out well, I might do something like that for the deck," she shared.

As our conversation continued, I gradually broke the news about Clark spending part of the night at my house, because he'd had too much to drink. She nearly fell off the chair and commented how I continued to surprise her with revealing information. When I said he left before I got up in the morning, she thought it quite rude of him.

"It gets worse, Ellie," I said swallowing another sip of tea. "I only ran into him once since that night, and he didn't speak to me. I have no idea why. I was so taken aback, I didn't ask him why."

She listened intently before she responded. "It could be for several reasons, Kate," she suggested. "Did he try to be romantic with you and felt rejected? Did he drink too much to where he felt embarrassed about saying too much? Did he feel terrible about having to stay there and awoke feeling angry?"

I kept nodding. "It may be all of them," I said sadly.

She looked confused with my answer. "Men have much larger egos than women do, in my opinion," Ellie stated. "If his ego was hurt in any way it would explain everything. Men don't like rejection, especially Clark. Artists, I think, are the worst."

How would she know all this?

"I even wondered if he discovered his tree carving was gone while he was there," I said between bites.

"You still haven't solved that situation?" she loudly asked. "How can that be? I thought you knew who took it!"

"I did, but I can't prove anything, Ellie," I whispered back, in hopes no one was listening to us.

"Do you realize that tree may be worth thousands of dollars?" she continued.

I nodded with embarrassment.

"Did you report it stolen?"

"Heavens no," I quickly answered. "Do you think I want the word to get out about what happened? It would be a black eye for the guest house, me, and Clark."

"So I take it you didn't tell Clark, either?" she calmly asked.

"No, I haven't," I admitted with my head down.

Ellie shook her head in disbelief.

I looked at my watch and needed to get to Esther's house, so I went to the bar to say good-bye to Trout.

"Say, how's our friend Clark doing?" Trout asked as he dried a glass with a towel. "I haven't seen him for a while. Is he out of town?"

I shrugged my shoulders. "I can't answer that, Trout," I briefly answered. "Hey, you guys have a good rest of the day."

Out the door I went to my car, realizing the rain had let up. So now Clark was also staying away from the winery. That was interesting. Was it because of my friendship with Ellie? As I came down the hill to turn left, I had to concentrate on Esther's directions to her farm. I had to put any thoughts of Clark out of my mind. Neither of us was good at playing games, so perhaps it was just the end of a nice friendship.

I saw the bright yellow mailbox near a fence of overgrown clematis that was still in bloom. I turned into the gravel road and her white frame farmhouse was straight ahead, as she described. Smaller out buildings and a small red barn with a rusty tin roof were placed about the grounds. I parked my car outside of the fencing surrounding the house. Chickens pranced about the yard like they owned the place.

"Welcome, Kate!" Esther yelled as she came out the back door. "Come in the breezeway, where I keep my hairdressing chair."

Many houses in this county had additions they called breezeways, because the air could enter and escape leaving a nice breeze. Many homes didn't have air-conditioning for some time. The day was quite warm, so I was sure hoping Esther's house was air-conditioned.

"I'm sure glad you had that yellow mailbox," I teased. Esther laughed. "I brought you some cheesecake, for being so nice to take me on as a customer."

"You didn't have to do that," she said as she held the door open. "As soon as we get you trimmed, we'll have some lemonade to go with that."

"Not for me, Esther," I defended. "I just had a big lunch with Ellie at the winery. You and your family enjoy it. It sure feels nice and cool in here."

"Now here's a picture of what I had in mind for you," she said, handing me a magazine. "Do you like it?"

"I love it," I responded with excitement. "You can do this?"

"Sure! That style will look great on you," she assured me. "You can wear this in different ways if you don't like it. I think I best cut this style with your hair dry."

She turned my chair so I couldn't look in the mirror as she began her work. Esther could talk and talk. It must be the nature of this kind of business. I could just imagine her in her own beauty shop.

"You have that beautiful color of blonde that adapts nicely as the gray hair comes in," she complimented. "A lot of women would love to have this color. Have you ever used a color on your hair?"

"No, I haven't, and I don't want to start!" I responded.

"I hope the gray hair doesn't come too quickly. I know it's starting, but it seems to be blending in."

She laughed in agreement.

I finally turned around after a few touches of hair spray. I had to admit, I was very impressed with the more sophisticated change. She told me how to keep a slight bump at the top, which enhanced this hairstyle. No one in South Haven would ever believe this was created in a farmhouse. I gave her a generous payment of cash with a big hug. I went out the door feeling ten pounds lighter as I tried to avoid stepping in any chicken poop. My good mood thought it would be fun to stop at Imy's Antique Shop, since I hadn't been there for some time.

"Well, if you don't look nice," Imy said as soon as she saw me walk in. "You look different."

"Esther just cut my hair," I bragged. "What do you really think?"

"I love it! She is so good," Imy noted. "I sure wish she hadn't closed her shop. You're lucky she agreed to cut your hair since she closed."

"So what's new in here?" I asked looking around.

"I went to the Versaman sale on Saturday and bought some nice things," she said coming out from behind the counter. "Mrs. Versaman died some months back, and she did beautiful handwork. There were stacks of her work at the sale, which must have taken her years and years to do. It was hard on Mr. Versaman as he watched all their treasures get sold off. At one point, I saw tears coming down his face."

"How awful," I said, picturing it in my mind. "All those memories of a lifetime together. He likely felt very guilty. Too bad all of this couldn't have gone to family." Imy nodded.

"I got most of her linens, even though they are hard to sell these days," she revealed. "No one wants all that work, and folks don't entertain like they used to. After I paid up, I went over to him and said the linens were in good hands and that everyone would be told who made them. I could tell it made him feel better."

"That was so nice of you, Imy," I said sadly. "Are these some of his linens?"

"Yes, and look at all the pieces that have hand tatting." She pointed them out. "This tablecloth here is in perfect condition and has ten napkins to go with it. He said his kids didn't want any of the stuff, which makes it really sad. I sure hope my boys don't behave that way when I'm gone. I'm trying to show them the value of antiques. I also purchased a couple of her cake stands. She had a lot of glassware. I have a weakness for cake stands."

"They're beautiful, especially the cut glass one," I said, touching the raw edges. "Is this for sale? I'd like to purchase it."

Imy nodded yes and gave her usual sweet smile of approval.

"I think I want the tablecloth and napkins, too. I have the right size table and the perfect occasion for it."

"Wonderful, I'm glad it's going into Doc's house."

I hadn't thought of it that way.

"You don't see beautiful handwork like this anymore," I noted. "It makes it so special when you know who made it, too."

Imy agreed as she put my choices aside to purchase.

235

# CHAPTER 28

I felt I was prepared for the 10:00 a.m. arrival of the Kassel wedding party. My kitchen island was filled with a variety of drinks and my dining room table was set for a luncheon, as they requested. The bride, Jennifer, and her mother were the first to arrive. I immediately picked up tension between the two of them. I'm sure they had many things on their mind, and the bride had to naturally be nervous. I tried to ignore it. I arranged for the bride to dress in the first floor guest room. From the size of the wedding gown they brought in, it was going to take up most of the room. I tried to make small talk, wishing them a wonderful day, but it fell on deaf ears.

"My daughter is just a little nervous," Mrs. Kassel said for an excuse. "Here are sandwiches and pastries you can place on the table, if the girls should decide to eat something. I want to encourage that, as I know most of them will be drinking, if they haven't already."

"Good idea," I said, taking the boxes from her.

The three bridesmaids arrived a bit later in one car. They carried in dresses in shades of purple and immediately set them down on the couch to help themselves to wine in the kitchen. Mrs. Kassel shook her head in disgust with the way they were treating their gowns. They were quite giddy and cheerful, unlike their bride. Mrs. Kassel told them to have a bite to eat before putting on their bridesmaid dresses. After they nibbled and drank some wine, they scampered all about the house exploring each room before getting dressed.

*Please don't let anything be missing this time,* I thought.

When the mother and bridesmaids gathered back at the dining room table, I noticed the bride had not joined them. I quietly knocked on her door and asked if everything was all right. She slowly opened the door and the face I saw was red and tearful. I went in and quietly closed the door.

"My goodness, Jennifer, this is supposed to be the happiest day of your life," I said to comfort her.

She shook her head in disagreement. "I'm making a big mistake," she whispered between sniffing her nose.

"Why do you say that?" I said pulling her arm to sit next to me on the bed.

"It's a long story, but it's too late now, anyway," she said with frustration.

"I'm sure all the arrangements and fuss are just getting to you," I excused. "Just concentrate on how much you love that future husband of yours."

"I don't love him," she quickly stated as she glared at me.

*Well, that was the wrong thing to say!*

"So how did you end up here, today?" I asked, being in the dark of it all. The girls were now laughing louder in the dining room.

"You won't like the answer. No one does," she said shaking her head and now pacing the floor.

"Try me," I encouraged. She took a deep breath.

"I'm in love with a married man, and now I'm pregnant with his child," she admitted with some sense of freedom in her voice.

I was not expecting an answer such as this.

"Justin, my old boyfriend who's loved me since kindergarten, said he'd marry me. My parents were delighted and insist that this is what should happen if I'm really thinking of this poor baby. So that's how I ended up here, if you must know."

"I see," I whispered in shock. "Does the real father know you're pregnant?"

She nodded, wiping her nose again. "I told him if he didn't get a divorce and marry me, I'd marry Justin. And he said he didn't care," she said, quivering as tears rolled down her face.

"You are in a pickle, Miss Jennifer, but I do know that two wrongs don't make a right," I stated with some anger.

"I'll never love Justin, never," she said emphatically.

This was not good.

"Would you rather raise your child on your own?" I bravely asked.

"Of course I would, but Mother would never let me do that!" she added. "I'd have to be dependent on them with my situation."

"How old are you, Jennifer?" I asked as I handed her another tissue.

"Nineteen," she whispered softly.

"I think at your age you certainly would qualify as an adult," I noted strongly. "You have every right to make an adult decision here. There are social services to help you do this, if your mother defies you. I'm going to leave you with your thoughts, but whichever way you decide, you absolutely must make the best of it. It wouldn't be fair to Justin or you if you don't."

"I know, I know," she said as I gave her a hug.

"I'm sorry I dumped this on you, but you asked," she said as she hugged me back.

I smiled and told myself I had a purpose here in some way. As I joined the others, I noticed that the mother was also now drinking wine. It was no surprise, as it had to be a stressful day for her in every direction.

"Girls, please hurry up changing," Mrs. Kassel instructed. "The flowers will be at the church. Does everyone have their gloves? Look as gorgeous as you can."

Everyone giggled as they headed toward the stairs.

"Miss Meyr, we want to sign this quilt too. Can we please?" one of the girls asked.

"I guess, if you want to," I said, giving in. "Please only use this pen and sign your names in one section of the blocks, so I remember you were a group."

They began to tease one another about what name they would use.

*Bear with them Josephine,* I said in my head.

I began cleaning up the dining room table, feeling terrible about Jennifer's situation. In my opinion, if she went ahead with this marriage it was an accident waiting to happen. One of the girls had spilled a glass of wine on the table without saying a word. I was very glad I hadn't used my new tablecloth from the Versaman family. I kept watching the clock, wondering what was happening in the bride's guest room.

Slowly, one by one, the girls all came down the stairs looking absolutely gorgeous. They were all thin, very young, and so innocent. Mrs. Kassel beamed.

"Will you take some pictures of us with my camera?" one of the girls asked.

I happily responded, but no bride had appeared in the process.

"Where is our bride?" one of the other girls asked. "Is she sick, Miss Meyr?"

I pretended I didn't hear her.

Finally, out of the door came Jennifer, looking quite stunning in her sparkling white gown and her pearl headdress. She had made an amazing transformation. We all admired her beauty and clapped at her entrance as the girls gathered around her. Her red face was altered to look radiant and happy. I gave her a wink and a smile.

"I see the limo just pulled in, girls," I announced looking out the window.

"My husband will be by later to pick up everyone's things, if that's all right," Mrs. Kassel requested.

"No problem, as I'll be here all day," I answered. "Congratulations, all of you." Out the door they went as if everything was wonderful.

It was a warm and beautiful day for an outdoor wedding. I would love to have seen how Anna had prepared the village for such an occasion. Ellie said she always did an amazing job. Deep in thought, I took my own lunch to the porch to relax from all the commotion. I rechecked my watch and realized the ceremony was now in process.

Cotton was now pulling in the drive to cut my lawn. I gave him a wave, remembering that Susie would come tomorrow to help me get the house back into shape after today. I was afraid to look at the bridesmaids' rooms, and I knew Jennifer had lain on the bed and shed tears in the downstairs guest room.

I went to get my cell phone that was ringing in the kitchen. I couldn't believe the call was from Anna.

"I just want to give you heads up, Kate," Anna said in a shaky voice. "The wedding didn't happen. The bride called it off right before she was going to walk down the aisle. The bridesmaids were waiting and waiting, so finally her father came down the aisle by himself and announced the marriage was off. The crowd couldn't believe it. He told everyone to remain, thanked them for coming, and invited them to help themselves to the wonderful refreshments. By the time I realized what was happening, the bride was in the car wanting to leave. The groom and his parents left shortly after. It was the craziest thing I ever saw."

"Wow, I don't know what to say." I reacted with mixed feelings.

"The parents and the bride are on their way to get her things, so be prepared," Anna warned.

"Thanks, Anna," I said letting her get back to the crowd.

Jennifer's parents must be furious and disappointed, but Jennifer had to be relieved that she didn't have to marry Justin. It had to be terrible for all of them.

In just moments, their car pulled in the drive. Only Mr. Kassel came to the door and explained he was there to pick up all of the girls' things.

"Can you guide me to their rooms?" he asked without any explanation as to what had just happened.

"Sure, Mr. Kassel, follow me," I instructed as he complimented me on the guest house.

Jennifer's things were neatly packed in a suitcase by the door, but the other bedrooms had their belongings strung here and there. I helped gather their things and didn't mention the wedding. He graciously thanked me for everything, and he asked if all was paid up, which I assured him Mrs. Kassel had taken care of. I felt so bad for their whole family.

I went back to the sunporch where I would be able to see if someone would get the bridesmaids' car. Observing the girls that were here, they were probably having refreshments and enjoying the crowd left behind at the reception. My feelings were so mixed about what had just happened. I felt somewhat guilty suggesting to Jennifer that she rethink her marriage. Would she have done this without my interference?

The girls did not return for some time. I'm sure they took advantage of the merriment prepared for the wedding. They didn't bother to come in to say anything, as if it didn't matter what I might be thinking. I decided by now it may be safe to call Anna back. The phone rang and rang before she picked up.

"Hey, Kate, we still have some folks here havin' a grand time, so I can't talk long," Anna explained. "Did they come by and get their things?"

"Yes, and the bridesmaids just left in their car," I reported.

"How interesting!"

"This is one for the books, huh Kate?" joked Anna with a laugh. "One of the family members took all the presents with him. That didn't seem quite right, do you think?"

"They should have asked everyone to take back their gift since there was no wedding," I expressed. "I don't know what protocol would have been required under these circumstances."

"The whole darn thing was goofy," she said, laughing again. "Hey, we'll talk later. I need to get them all on their way."

"Sorry, Anna. Good luck," I said, hanging up.

I paced the floor, feeling restless, so I called Ellie to tell her what happened. Bad news traveled quickly in this small town. Ellie said that some of the guests from the wedding came to winery for the rest of the afternoon. From what she was hearing from them, they thought the bride made the right move. This news somehow made me feel better.

I turned on the alarm and decided I needed a hot shower to relax me from the stressful day. I headed toward the stairs, and once again something didn't look right on my guest quilt. What had changed?

I looked closer and noticed that all the bridesmaids' names were totally removed, as if they had never signed it. How does this happen? I guess Josephine or someone was deciding who could qualify to be on this quilt. Whoever that someone was, they knew everything that went on here in the guest house. My pen was a permanent marker, for heaven's sake. I shook my head in wonder. Little did I know having this guest house would become so personal to her. Josephine had removed the names of Carson, Tina, and now the bridesmaids! She was really inserting herself into the business of my guest house.

I showered and fell into my comfy bed, when my cell phone rang. I thought it may be Anna, but it said unknown number. I said hello and there wasn't a response, but I sensed someone on the other end of the line. I asked once again without a response. Who would have my cell number and do this? I guessed it had to be a wrong number and tried not to think of the mystery of it.

My thoughts had to move to more happy things, so I started planning my trip to South Haven. After I talked to Cotton and Susie tomorrow, I would travel to my hometown this week. I had to smile, thinking of putting my feet in the sand and seeing the friendly faces of Maggie, Carla, and even my son. I truly had the best of both worlds and must remember to be thankful.

# CHAPTER 29

I made a quick visit to Ellie's before I headed to Michigan. She had coffee ready and some yummy cinnamon rolls. After we rehashed the runaway bride incident again, she assured me she not only would keep an eye out for my place, but on Clark as well.

"I wish you'd come with me some time, Ellie," I requested. "You need to get away and you would really enjoy the beach along the lake and the red lighthouse I talk about so much. You would want to open a winery there, if you saw the town."

She laughed.

"I know, but it's not realistic right now," Ellie complained. "I can't wait to hear about your visit and that hottie neighbor of yours." We both giggled. "He may not recognize you with this new haircut."

"You think so?" I teased. "I have to admit, he adds a little spark to living at the condo."

We said good-bye with our usual hugs as she walked me to my car. It was so surreal that I was leaving my best friend to meet my other best friend who was waiting for me in South Haven.

It was a clear, hot sunny day when I left Borna. I was certainly looking forward to cooler temperatures up north. I couldn't wait for Maggie's reaction to my haircut. I could only hope Mark had given up on his efforts to hook me up with his friend Maxwell. The thought of such an experience was not anything I was interested in.

The route back to South Haven was now becoming routine. I found myself stopping at the same familiar places. It gave me a sense of security somehow. Like always, I drove onto the drawbridge in South Haven about dusk. The tourists were still walking everywhere. Some were coming back from the beach, and others were on their way to dinner. I had to admit I was hungry for some good seafood, blueberry scones, and putting my toes in the sandy beach.

I pulled into my lit parking lot that now was considered my home of sorts. I followed the sidewalk to my condo carrying my two pieces of luggage. My neighbor's lights were out, so I assumed he was not home. I walked in to my dimly lit condo and started getting familiar again with my surroundings.

My cell phone started ringing, so I fumbled to get to my purse.

"Mom, it's Jack," he said with a somber voice. "It looks like I won't be able to make it. We have a lot of last minute changes to make for this client, so I'll be working. I'm really sorry."

"Oh no, Jack, I hate to hear this," I said with disappointment. "I just walked in the door this very minute."

"I just got off the phone with Jill and she's disappointed as well," he added. "I told her I would work out something soon with my schedule."

"We'll both miss you, but I understand," I sadly conceded. "Call me Sunday, okay?"

"I will, and I love you very much," he said as he ended the call.

That certainly made a difference in my schedule. The only for sure thing I had planned was to have coffee in the morning with Maggie. I was going to work around my personal time with Jack. I probably shouldn't have come. It was hard to shake my disappointment. I unpacked a few things and made up my bed with fresh linens. I knew I had wine, so I poured myself a glass to take to the deck. It was then when I heard a soft knock at my door.

"It's John, your neighbor," he announced.

I couldn't believe it. I slowly opened the door.

"Welcome back!" he said grinning. "I thought I heard someone up here."

"I just got here," I explained. "Forgive me for not inviting you in, but I'm exhausted and have to attend to some things."

He looked a little disappointed. "No problem," he quickly said. "How long will you be staying?"

"I'm not sure, as I've had a change of plans in the last hour," I explained. "How are things with you?" I really didn't care, but I wanted to be polite.

"Couldn't be better," he bragged. "Hey, I'll let you go enjoy your wine!" He was looking at my glass sitting on the counter.

"Thanks, see you later," I said, closing the door.

The last thing I needed here was a nosey neighbor, no matter how attractive and nice he was. I sipped my wine inside as I turned on the news. I got into my sleeping gown for an early night. I did look forward to my morning visit to the Golden Bakery and Maggie.

*Sweet Michigan dreams,* I told myself.

As soon as I awoke, I could feel the cooler temperatures. I put on my robe and opened the double doors to my deck to let in the fresh air. It was a beautiful day. When I showered and dressed, I sent Maggie a text that I was on my way. I was purchasing my desired blueberry scones at the Golden

Bakery when Maggie snuck up behind me to give me a hug. To my surprise, Carla was with her. We did a group hug before going to our table.

"I love your haircut," Maggie was the first to say. "It really becomes you."

"Thanks," I responded. "I have a great story to go with that, by the way."

"You always have great stories, Miss Kate," Carla teased.

I first had to tell them that Jack would not be coming home, which disappointed both of them. Obviously Jill had not shared that news with her mother. I had so many questions for them and them for me as well.

"I just want you to know I have made plans for us for dinner!" Maggie announced.

"Super, what restaurant is that?" I asked with excitement.

"Hawk's Head," she revealed, smiling.

"Terrific!" I nodded. "I haven't been there since Clay passed away."

They both were now looking guilty, like they had a secret.

"We've asked Maxwell Harris to join us," Maggie meekly reported. "Don't yell. We're in a public place."

They both laughed.

I stared at her. I had to admit I felt betrayed. I was not ready for anything like this.

"What if I refused?" I said with a tease.

"You won't, because it will be a fun evening," Maggie promised. "You both have nothing to lose. Don't take this gesture so seriously! It's just a fun dinner. Remember the great salmon they serve? Hey, Max is feeling like you, if that makes you feel any better. He's agreed to come as a favor to us. You should do the same."

"Can you believe Maggie wants to fix me up with an old guy that's retired?" I asked Carla. She laughed. "What does that tell you? I could have kept my old haircut." Now they knew I was teasing.

"Maggie told me all about him, and he sounds perfect for you," Carla described. "She's not asking you to marry him. She just wants you to share a meal with them. How many times since Clay died have you had dinner with anyone but the girls?"

I thought about Clark and our budding friendship.

"Of course I'll go, Maggie, but this is risky business," I warned. "You may lose one or more friends after this."

She waved her hand to dismiss my comment. "We'll come by around 6:00," she stated. "Max is going to meet us there."

I nodded. "Now that we got the bad news out of the way, tell me about the Blueberry Festival." I looked at each of them.

"The quilt brought in about $2,500," Maggie reported. "We did better last year, but this is still good. It rained off and on throughout the festival, which I think made a difference. I think a blueberry torte won this year for best baked item, but I don't know who the maker was."

"I would have liked to have seen that." I pictured it all in my head.

"Now back to the subject of Max. He said the breakfasts at the Carriage House are amazing," Maggie noted. "He loves that prime location by the lake and isn't in any hurry to move, so I guess he can afford it. See why I thought you two could discuss this topic?"

I shook my head in disbelief at her determination. "Yeah, I've heard all about their great breakfast menu," I added.

"Maybe he can manage to get me one of their cookbooks, if they have one."

"I just bet he can, if you treat him nicely," teased Maggie. After a long visit, we said good-bye. I was anxious to get back to my place to give it some attention. Carla informed me she had tidied up before I came, which was nice. I had shopping on my mind, as well as a few errands, but wasn't quite sure where to go first. Eventually, I decided to swing by Cornelia's Quilt Shop, not only to see her but to find a pattern for a lighthouse quilt to make for Jack.

"I love your hair," Cornelia said first thing, giving me a hug.

"Thanks, so what's new here?" I responded. "Is there any earthshaking news from the Beach Quilters?"

"None, other than deciding how we share the charity proceeds," she noted. "Their next meeting is here at the shop, if you're still in town."

"No, I'll be gone. But can you show me the lighthouse pattern I saw on your website?" I requested to speed up my visit.

"Sure, this has six different houses on it, and I think the red one is very close to what we have here in South Haven, don't you?" she said pulling it off the rack to show me.

I could visualize it in a bigger bed-size quilt. I could make them all into a sampler quilt or a medallion design, featuring the South Haven lighthouse in the center. I hated appliqué, but knew if I had any problems Ruth Ann could help me with it.

"I can see it combined with another pattern like Ocean's Wave, if you really want to get fancy," Cornelia suggested.

"That sounds too hard, but I will take this pattern and several yards of this white background fabric," I instructed.

"This will get me started."

I left Cornelia's feeling ambitious. I needed to challenge myself once again with my quilting. I had plenty of scrap fabric for the lighthouses and a border. I then remembered the great stash Ruth Ann had at her studio.

As the day went along, I looked forward to visiting Hawk's Head once again. It was located on a popular golf course, and the dining was upscale, yet casual in atmosphere. It was quiet for conversation and always exposed a great view from wherever you sat. I thought I'd wear a simple black dress that I brought with me and take my red paisley shawl, for when it got cooler this evening. My new haircut would give me a confidence boost. I only wanted to look good for myself, not for anyone else.

When I heard a knock at the door, my nerves appeared out of nowhere. I said a little prayer to help get me through the evening. Why did I agree to go?

"Wow," Mark said when he saw me at the door. "The country has been good to you, Miss Meyr." He gave me a little squeeze before we went down to the car to join Maggie.

Mark and Maggie tried to pump my ego as we made the pleasant drive out to Hawk's Head. I was glad to hear Max was as hesitant about this visit as I was.

When we entered the bar area, a distinguished gentleman turned around on his barstool. He quickly stood for Mark's introduction. He was sharply dressed in a navy blue blazer, white shirt, and khaki pants. His salt and pepper hair was perfectly groomed and matched his healthy tan. He sure didn't look sixty.

"Nice to finally meet you, Kate," he said shaking my hand. "Mark has told me so much about you, and from what I see he was entirely correct."

We all nervously chuckled. I just nodded, not really knowing what to say.

"Our table is ready anytime, but why don't we have a drink here in the bar before we go in the dining room," Mark suggested.

Everyone agreed, as I just kept smiling.

Mark and Maggie did most of the talking as we enjoyed our drinks. It was a strange feeling to be seen here in South Haven with a different man other than Clay. Having Maggie and Mark with the two of us made it even more surreal.

"I understand you arrived yesterday," Max commented politely.

"Yes, it's an easy drive," I said taking a bigger swallow of my red wine.

"I've been to Missouri several times through the years, and I have always been impressed with its beautiful landscapes," he revealed. "It must be quite a change for you coming from the north."

I ignored his comment, but it was the perfect lead in for me to brag about East Perry County. He seemed to listen intently, which I appreciated.

When we went into the dining room, he shared that he was looking for a condo near the lake and asked me if I liked my new purchase.

I told him it was perfect for my son and me for when we visit. I was hoping he wouldn't ask to see it.

"I guess what I love most about staying at the Carriage House is that each and every day I meet people from all over the world," he acknowledged. "They have so many repeat guests that have wonderful stories."

That opening, led me to tell him a little about my own

guest house experiences. So far, so good, as Mark and Maggie were very careful about not interrupting our conversation.

We actually talked nonstop through the very delicious meal. I was glad he seemed easy to talk to. The salmon was as good as I remembered. Max and I were doing all the talking. Mark and Maggie just kept nodding with smiles on their faces. When Mark insisted we have dessert, Maggie asked if I would come with her to the restroom.

"What did I tell you, Miss know-it-all," Maggie teased. "I knew you guys would hit it off. So what do you think?"

"He's a very nice man, that's all," I admitted. "All your friends are nice. You're right though, he's not stuffy and he doesn't look his age."

"I can tell you right now that he is very impressed with you," Maggie noted as she put on fresh lipstick.

"Hey, you know I am a friendly person who doesn't have a problem talking to strangers, so don't go reading too much into this," I warned her.

Maggie shook her head like she didn't believe me.

After a round of strawberry and chocolate soufflé, the four of us went back to the bar to have an after dinner drink. When I ordered amaretto on the rocks, Max joined me in the selection.

"Max, I think Maggie and I will be on our way. So if you don't mind, will you be kind enough to see Miss Meyr home?" He asked so politely.

*This is not the game plan I agreed to,* I thought.

"That's not necessary, Mark," I quickly responded.

"I would enjoy a few more moments with you, if you would agree to do so," Max said looking into my eyes. "I really want to hear more about this little town of Borna."

He said the magic word of Borna, so that seemed harmless enough.

"Very well," I said nodding. What else could I do? "Mark, thank you for this lovely meal."

"Our pleasure," he responded. "You all have a good rest of the evening."

Maggie gave me a wink as I stared into her conniving face.

"Did I put you in a difficult spot, Kate?" Max nicely asked.

"Why were they so insistent about us meeting?" I bravely asked. "I think we both like where our lives are right now."

He nodded with a smile. "You know, after being tied down so many years with my dear wife's illness, I was just ready for any kind of freedom," he shared. "I know that sounds somewhat cruel, but I too like where I am right now in life. I find myself not planning too far ahead, which I really enjoy. If I feel like doing something or going somewhere, I just do it. I came back to South Haven for many reasons. I've even thought of buying a sailboat at my age, how about that?"

I smiled with approval. "I can imagine how you must feel," I said, feeling his emotions. "We all have that bucket list, I suppose."

We talked for another hour before I suggested we head home. We walked to his new, black BMW that the valet boy brought to him. My main observation about Max at this point was that he was a very sensitive, caring person. I was surprised how our age wasn't obvious as we discussed things. I felt like the older, inexperienced one as he described his many activities and interests. Max walked me to the door like a perfect gentleman. He asked if he could take me to lunch the next day, which caught me by surprise.

"I really shouldn't," I responded. "I have a lot to accomplish while I'm here."

"Is there anything I can help you with?" he quickly offered.

"No thanks, and I'll have to let you know about lunch," I said with hesitation. I felt we had already talked about everything under the sun, and that wasn't why I was here for my visit.

He kissed me on the cheek and said he'd call me in the morning. I politely thanked him for a pleasant evening. I went inside with a lot of questions about him. As personable as he was, why didn't he have a lady friend?

# CHAPTER 30

I was up most of the night, replaying the conversation that Max and I had shared. I was moving slowly as I took my coffee to the deck. I couldn't decide if I really wanted to go to lunch with Max. I needed to be doing other things and didn't want him to think I was interested. One of the items on my to-do list was to call Emily Meyr, my niece. I decided I would do it this morning.

I finally went in to shower and change. I loved my new shower, compared to the one I had in Borna. It had better water pressure, which was always important to me. I would have to check into that when I got home. My cell was ringing, so I quickly wrapped in my robe to answer. It was Max, who was wasting no time to hear my answer for lunch. I reluctantly agreed to meet him at Tello's for some pizza, which I had a weakness for. I warned him it would be a quick lunch.

Before I left to meet him, I made the call to Emily. There was no answer, and the call went to voice mail, which was James' voice. How would he feel about me contacting her? I felt I owed Sandra something. I didn't think she would mind. I still didn't know the whole story regarding her suicide. Perhaps I never would.

I dressed casually for lunch and, to my surprise, so did Mr. Harris. He looked dapper in his snug jeans and black shirt with a handsome belt. He surely didn't look like the typical retired dude.

"Katy, I'm so glad you could fit me in," he greeted so warmly.

*Why did he call me Katy?*

"I'm not going to turn down one of Tello's pizzas when I'm in South Haven," I joked.

He laughed. "I know, it's the first place I come to have a meal," he admitted. "It's the best, so what kind should we order?"

"I'm hooked on thin crust pepperoni with onion, extra sauce, and cheese," I described. "I'll be happy with whatever you choose."

"Good choice," he cried out. "We'll get an extra large. Do you want a salad?"

"No thanks," I said, shaking my head.

"What are we drinking today?" he asked with a teasing voice.

"Well, it'll just be iced tea for me," I answered. "I had enough wine last night."

He nodded and grinned. He told me he had plans to play golf later in the afternoon, and I shared with him my shopping plans.

"Hey, I happen to know there's a famous sunset this town is known for," Max revealed with a smile on his face. "It still happens around 8:00 in the evening. I don't like to miss it. How about I pick you up and we park at the beach to check it out? We can walk out on the pier to the lighthouse, if you'd rather watch it from there."

I couldn't believe how much this was sounding like my high school days. It was the very thing we did on Friday nights. I had to laugh at his suggestion, because it was really on my to-do list on this visit.

"I have no plans for this evening, and I haven't done that in quite some time." I once again was giving in.

"Great. I'll come by around 7:45, so we don't miss it," he said with excitement.

After enjoying a delicious pizza, we parted ways with a friendly wave. I got in my car and headed to Country House Furniture where I had selected some things online to look at further. I found a smile on my face. Was I having fun? The last twenty-four hours had been interesting, for sure. Max was certainly fit, active, and very handsome. He would really be a good catch for someone, but not me. I frankly didn't think I could keep up with him. When I got to my parking lot at home, I called Maggie.

"Good afternoon," she greeted. "How did the rest of your evening go?"

"Pretty good, and you'll be happy to know I just met Max at Tello's for lunch," I said knowing it would shock and please her at the same time.

"Really?" she replied. "That's awesome. I told you you'd like him."

"He's all those things you described, Maggie, but don't jump to conclusions," I said to calm her down. "I think he needs a job or a life of some kind, don't you?" She roared with laughter. "I don't want a needy man that requires me for his social life. Perhaps that was a bit harsh, but in this stage of life he lacks a purpose."

"Mark said Max was very impressed with you," she revealed. "Don't be so hasty to judge him. Just enjoy his company."

"That's very nice, but I have no intention of spending my whole visit with this guy," I admitted. "He's hard to say no to, that's for sure. I'm going to see the sunset with him tonight at 8:00."

"Yahoo! That's what I want to hear. What a nice romantic touch."

"Nothing romantic going on here, girlfriend," I confessed. "I had planned to do this before someone introduced me to this guy. I appreciate what you and Mark are doing here, but it's not going to work. I'm sorry!"

"Whatever, Kate. I know you so well," she said more seriously. "Just enjoy the moment, okay?"

"I wanted to tell you that I called to talk to Emily Meyr and had to leave a message," I updated. "She still hasn't returned my call. What else can I do?"

"Nothing, leave it be," she advised.

I took a deep breath.

"Any sighting of your young neighbor downstairs?" she asked to change the subject.

"Oh yes, the very first night I got here," I informed her. "He knocked at my door to welcome me back!"

She laughed like she was amused. "Well, you've got your pick now," she teased. "What's it gonna be, the young or the old?"

We had a good laugh. Before we hung up, we agreed to lunch the next day, and I told her to invite Jill.

Max and I took our shoes off after we parked the car along the shoreline. It felt so good to feel the sand between my toes. We giggled like little children as we found an empty bench facing directly into the sunset. It brought back so many memories!

"I think we need some ice cream, or would you prefer a soft drink?" Max politely asked. The concession stand near us had been there since I could remember. I knew exactly what I wanted.

"Yes, I'll have the vanilla, single-dipped cone," I stated with a big grin. "I hope they make them like they used to."

Max gave a chuckle. "I have always loved their root beer float, but that is a bit much for me to handle tonight," he revealed. "I think I'll have what you're having." Why did he always copy me?

"They're big," I warned. "Do you need some help?"

"Nah, you stay here and keep an eye on that sun," he teased. "I'll be right back!"

I watched him walk away in his bare feet, with a slight bounce in his step. He certainly had a zest for life, like catching this sunset. He returned with dripping cones, as we quickly ate and laughed at the same time. They were just as yummy as I had remembered.

"Do you want to walk the pier to watch, or stay here on the bench?" he offered.

"I like it better here," I nodded. "We can walk out after the sun has completely gone into the water."

He smiled and agreed.

We joined the gathering crowd, and we watched in silence as the sun very slowly disappeared before our very eyes. Some were clapping at the finale. It was such a ritual of peace. Everyone on the beach seemed to be reflecting as the sun sank into the water. Moments like this I considered a gift from my maker. Nature was God's special gift to us. Max softly put his arm around me as he also felt the spirit of the moment. I didn't mind at all.

We put on our shoes and headed toward the big red icon of South Haven. The long walk out to the edge of the pier was part of the process which made the lighthouse bigger and bigger. This was where zillions of photos were taken with couples kissing and families happily posing with their loved ones. When we reached the giant lighthouse, we watched the many beautiful boats go by. Max once again put his arm around me as we captured the moment. It felt weird and comforting at the same time.

"You want a photo?" an young man asked.

"Sure, why not?" as Max handed him his cell phone. "Thank you!"

We smiled, and then I handed him my phone as well, without a second thought. It was just the thing to do. We turned around and headed back to the car. It was great people watching, as we passed folks from all over the world. Both of us were probably wondering what this friendship was all about.

"Are you up for going for a drink somewhere?" he asked as we got closer to my condo.

"Thanks, Max, but I need to get home," I answered as nicely as I could. "This has been such a fun evening and pretty clever on your part to suggest it."

He smiled, but I knew he was disappointed.

When we arrived at the parking lot, I knew he expected to walk me to the door. But I didn't want to put us in that situation again, and I certainly didn't want to ask him in.

"I'll just say good-bye here, Max," I said as I opened the car door.

"I'd like to see you again before you leave, if you can fit me in your busy schedule," Max pleaded.

"I can't tell you much at this point, but I thank you so much for lunch and a perfect evening," I said most earnestly.

"I had a great time today, Katy," Max said sincerely. "It's the most fun I've had for some time. I look forward to having more time with you."

Where was this name Katy coming from? He was too nice for me to correct him. I closed the door and left him behind as I walked to my condo. I sensed Max was very lonely, but that sure wasn't the way Maggie and Mark had described him. They said he was happy to finally be independent and alone! Max would be a nice man to stay in touch with, but not as he would like. I couldn't help but wonder what Clark was up to. Could I ever share this visit with him?

# CHAPTER 31

I stayed home for the morning to receive a delivery of things I had purchased yesterday. I picked out two modern tables, two lamps, a bookcase, and several decorator pillows. I was pleased how the whole look of the condo was coming together.

I had plans to meet Maggie for lunch in hopes Jill would come with her. While I enjoyed my second cup of coffee on the deck, I called Ellie to see if everything was okay in Borna.

"Good morning," she greeted. "How are things at the lake?"

"Wonderful," I responded. "Last night I got to put my feet in the sand and watched the sunset, which was incredible! It's seventy degrees here, which is right up my alley."

"We got to the nineties yesterday which hurt business, I'm afraid," she complained. "It really makes a difference if they can't sit on the deck."

"Well darn," I came back to say. "So is my house still standing?"

"Oh sure, all is well, but no sign of Clark, which is now starting to bother me," she stated. "I can't understand why he isn't coming in anymore to pick up food. I don't think he's out of town. Trout thinks he saw his truck parked at the bank."

"You can probably thank me for that," I admitted. "It's obvious he's angry with me, so when I get back I've decided to confront him. This is ridiculous! If he doesn't pick up my call, I'll drive out to his place, if I can remember how to find it."

"That may be a good idea, Kate," Ellie agreed. "Everyone's

getting ready for the fair, so you better hurry back, soon. I had a guy here at the bar yesterday who wants to come back for the fair he asked me where he and his wife could stay. I told him about Josephine's, so you better check your messages. I think he said he has family here."

"Thanks, I'll be sure to do that," I assured her. The thought of being needed somehow felt good.

I was glad I called Ellie. She had a way of lifting me up, just like Maggie. Thoughts of my Borna home were always comforting.

"Hey, good morning," a voice yelled up from below my deck. "How's your visit going?"

"Well, good morning to you, too," I responded as I leaned over the rail to see him better. "I'm really liking these temperatures compared to my home in Missouri."

"I'm cooking some halibut on the grill tonight about 7:00 or so if you'd like to come down and join me. I'm a pretty good cook, and I bet that refrigerator of yours is pretty bare."

"You've got that right," I said laughing. "It does sound pretty nice. Can I bring something?"

"What do you drink?" he asked cocking his head to the side to avoid the sun.

"It sounds like a good white wine would go nicely with halibut, and I have some cooling. I can bring a bottle with me, if you like?" I suggested.

"Love it, sounds great," he said with a big grin. Darn, he was handsome. "Say it looks like the delivery guys may be looking for your place!"

"Oh yes, send them up," I instructed. Two guys were headed my way and I anxiously opened my door to greet them. As soon as they left, I had to hurry and get ready for my lunch plans.

Unfortunately, Jill did not come with Maggie because she had other plans. Maggie said Jill was terribly disappointed and really did want to join us. We were at the new restaurant downtown called Taste.

"So please give me the entire scoop," Maggie begged.

"Max and I had a pleasant evening, for sure," I began. "Here, I have a photo someone took of us out on the pier."

She loved it and gave me a wink of approval. It was flattering the way she wanted me to enjoy more of life.

"So did you agree to see him again?" she asked with excitement.

"I don't know, Maggie," I said to discourage her. "I don't want to lead him on into thinking I am really interested in him. I still have things to do here, and I need to get back to Borna. Tonight I'm joining my downstairs neighbor for a cookout. It sounds really relaxing to me, and I do want to get to know him better."

"What? Are you kidding me?" she asked loudly enough so that the other people were looking at us.

"Don't get so excited Maggie," I whispered smiling. "It's pretty innocent. He's grilling halibut and I'm bringing the wine!"

"And please tell me what is so innocent about that?" she said with some concern. "First, I can't get you to hardly look at any man, and now you have two age ranges of men who want your attention."

I laughed at her reaction. "Don't worry, I'm headed back to Borna and will leave them both behind," I joked as we started eating. "It feels rather good to have a little fun with no commitment. I have no intention of getting serious with anyone at this point in my life, if ever!"

She shook her head like she didn't believe me.

I stopped in at Murphy's Antique Mall before I went home. It was on my way, and it just had to be a part of my home visit. I quickly ran through the two floors of booths, only finding a couple of things to purchase. I fell in love with a set of "days of the week" towels which had wonderful small hand appliqué on them. Each towel showed the chore of the day and I wondered if women actually followed the folklore. I also found a lovely blue Dresden china rolling pin to take back to Ellie. I could just see it in her charming kitchen.

I got home and crashed, hoping to get in a quick nap, when my cell phone rang. It was Max's name showing up. I really didn't want to talk to him and explain why I couldn't see him another time, so I let it go to voice mail.

When I awoke, I realized I had little time to get dressed for my first neighborhood cookout. I decided to wear jeans and a cream knit sweater for the cooler evening. I could now hear John's lovely music playing when I opened my door to the deck. I waited till I heard his voice outdoors before I decided to go down the stairs.

"Hey, neighbor," he greeted with his hands carrying our wine glasses. "Do you mind pouring the wine while I get organized here?"

"I'll be glad to," I said, feeling a little nervous. "Do you entertain often, John?"

"I enjoy it when I have a chance to," he explained. "I don't have family here, but I enjoy a dinner club with some friends where we take turns cooking a gourmet dinner." That sounded so cool to me.

"I really enjoy your taste in music, if I haven't told you before," I admitted. "I am surprised you're not listening to rock or hip hop."

He looked at me funny, and laughed. He finally sat down to join me with his wine.

"These pleasant nights on the deck are numbered, I'm afraid," I said sadly.

"I know, but I'm one of those creatures that still walks along the beach in the winter," he admitted. "I bundle up and there's nothing more invigorating."

"Wow, good for you," I encouraged. "John, I never asked what you do for a living."

"I'm a writer," he simply answered as he checked the grill.

"Oh, so you work out of your home?" I asked with much interest. "I always thought that had to be the perfect job."

"I write here some of the time, but I mostly write when I'm on the road," he described. "I'm a travel writer, but I enjoy writing about other things as well."

"That sounds like a wonderful life and career," I said with admiration. I thought about Mary Catherine back in Borna who was a freelance writer.

"I'm a contributor to the magazine called Scenic America, if you've ever heard of that," he added. "I've written a travel series of books as well. I hope to try writing fiction at some point. I think I have a pretty good imagination, and it's so different than writing research material."

"Yes, I can imagine," I agreed. "You would love East Perry County. It is so beautiful and about as Americana as you can get. Missouri is very diverse, but I don't think people appreciate it. We have beautiful lakes, you may know of the Missouri Ozark Mountains. Personally, I'm partial to the rolling hillsides where I live now."

"It is beautiful, like you described," John admitted. "I've been to the Lake of the Ozarks, and I've covered the wine country around there. Missouri was one of the leading wine producers during prohibition, and they continue to win awards nationwide. It's not a bad subject matter to write about."

I laughed in agreement. "Yes, my good friend and neighbor in Borna owns a winery," I shared with pride. "She just purchased land to grow her own grapes, but now she carries wine from the local producers. I know she does well with California wines, too."

"I googled your name, by the way," he announced out of the blue. "I hope you don't take offense, but I've been curious about you. I should have known you were wired into the Meyr Lumber Company here. I also picked up that you are the owner of a guest house called Josephine's. If I may ask, why the name Josephine? Is she a relative of yours?"

"No," I stated with a smile, "my house was built by a Doctor Paulson, and his wife's name was Josephine. He not only lived there, but had his practice on one side of the first floor." He nodded with approval as I explained. "I am fascinated with exploring more of Josephine's life. I wanted to honor her with this guest house."

He smiled, as if he approved.

Our very pleasant conversation continued as we ate by candlelight under his umbrella table. To my surprise, he used fine china, silver, and crystal as if we were in his formal dining room. Besides the halibut, he fixed twice-baked potatoes and a wonderful spinach salad. I don't know which I enjoyed more, the conversation or the food. His career was fascinating. I wanted to ask his age, but assumed he was in his forties.

When the chill got the best of us, he invited me into his condo. I didn't hesitate for a moment, as I helped carry in our dinner dishes. I loved his eclectic décor which he said was from all over the world. I couldn't help but think that he and Clark would be great friends if they met. It was obvious this guy had been most everywhere and at such a young age.

John made some flavored coffee to warm us up and brought out some Kilwin's ice cream, which Michigan was known for. I forgot how yummy it was. Going to Kilwin's on a Sunday afternoon was a wonderful memory from my childhood. He garnished the scoop of vanilla ice cream with a dash of raspberry sauce and some shavings of dark chocolate. He topped it off by serving us a small wine glass of red wine. My kind of dessert! This guy was unreal. How come he was still single?

"I wished you lived here year round," John said on a serious note, laying his head back on the couch.

"I couldn't possibly do that, John," I sadly remarked. "I had to run away from here after my husband was killed in a car accident. I learned some things about him later that hurt and embarrassed me. I needed a new life, and I found it in Borna. Ironically, it was a piece of property that he had left to me."

"That's pretty cool," he said, nodding. "You are so easy to talk to Kate. I feel as if I have known you a long time."

"I have to admit I feel the same, but you are so much younger than me," I said letting the wine get to me. Why did I bring up our age gap?

"That, my dear neighbor, has nothing to do with anything," he strongly stated. He poured me more wine. I knew I had struck a nerve.

I was speechless, as he turned on his gas fireplace. "Have you ever been married, John?" I was feeling brave enough to ask.

"No, but I came close at one point," he admitted. "I'm not

good marriage material with what I do for a living. I love to travel and meet new, interesting people like you, for instance."

I blushed. "Me?" I said with a laugh. "I can't imagine, with all the people you have met, that I would be referred to as interesting."

"Independent women like you are fascinating to me," he said moving closer to me. "You are certainly not the norm, I can attest to that. It sounds like you have the same interest in people, or you wouldn't have opened a guest house."

He may have been right

"You are sweet to say these things, John. But really, you don't know me," I said in defense.

"I'd like to know you better," he said sweetly. "It's why I wanted to spend this evening with you. I feel you would be a great friend."

By using the word friend,he put me more at ease.

"I want to be your 'friend,' John, if you don't think I ask too many questions," I teased with a wink.

It was 1:30 a.m. when I said good-bye and went up the steps to my place. I couldn't believe I stayed there so late! I shut the door and felt as if I had stepped back in time twenty years. I had met a man that was so fascinating to me. Why hadn't I met a man like him before Clay came along? Just hearing him talk about his writing and traveling career was fascinating. I could have listened to him all night. I would love for him to visit Borna so he could have the experience I had. What a great guest he would make, in more ways than one.

I slept late the next day and lay in my bed to decide what was likely to be my last day in South Haven. I hated to admit I was having a wonderful visit without my son. Meeting Max was fun and truly to be admired, but John was a total surprise to me.

I wouldn't mind spending more time with either one of them, but I certainly could relate more to John. Why was Clark so private with his life?

When I came out of the shower, Jack called to see how my visit was going. If he only knew! I told him I had invited Jill to lunch, but she wasn't able to come. He was frustrated with how things were going with his project, so he didn't know when he could get away. Hearing his voice was such a comfort to me, despite his stress.

In my robe, I walked room to room to see what else I may need. Every room was looking good except my loft. I wanted to make it an office/sewing room. I need a laptop for this location and some furniture to put it on. I would ask Cornelia to keep an eye out for a used sewing machine, in case I would need one here. I had it all pictured in my mind.

Maggie called and said Mark wanted to barbecue for dinner, so she thought she would invite me and the Beach Quilters, if I could come. It was a last minute invite, but I told her to proceed. I think she thought I might be with Max tonight, but I fooled her. I had to admit, after two great nights with men, I was ready to see my girlfriends again.

With the evening to look forward to, I rushed downtown to a new computer store to buy a laptop like the one I had at 6229 Main Street. I decided I could wait to have it hooked up on my next visit here. The cabinetry I picked out came in boxes with small pieces. The good news was that it fit in my car. The bad news was how to assemble it. Where was Jack when I needed him? My next challenge would be for me to get it up my stairs.

When I got home, I did fine with all the boxes but one. It was quite heavy, especially for one person. I thought of John and knocked on his door. No one answered, so I left the box in my car. There was still no sign of John when I left for Maggie's barbecue. I felt like a nosey neighbor.

I couldn't wait to get to Maggie's to see everyone. Mark had on a cute chef's hat when I arrived and assured everyone he was going to disappear, as soon as the food was ready. All the girls were there but one. I immediately told Cornelia about needing a sewing machine, and she said I should consider the task to be done. Maggie was in a great mood. She said she had her share of wine as she was preparing our side dishes. The conversation was wild and getting noisier. Maggie wasted no time teasing me in front of the girls about my old and young boyfriends. I blushed and responded with just enough information to keep them all guessing. I shared with them some of my guest house stories. They were all ears, especially about the runaway bride story. I didn't share the bad story about my missing tree, and that I suspected a quilter to be the thief. They would never believe that one.

A couple of the girls brought their small wall quilts which they were going to enter in a fiber arts show. I was continually amazed at the talent in this group. I couldn't help but compare this group to my Friendship Circle. I explained to my friends how diverse they were, but that most were not quilters. I also bragged about Ellie and how close we were, but saw the somber look on Maggie's face. I knew I needed to stop talking.

When they all agreed they liked my haircut, Maggie insisted I tell them about my experience. They were hysterical when I told them I had gone to a farmhouse with a yellow mailbox to get my hair cut. They encouraged me to write a book about all my experiences, which made me once again think of John.

# CHAPTER 32

I came back to my condo as happy as a lark. John was out on his patio, listening to his usual music and reading a book. Feeling carefree from a few glasses of wine, I greeted him in a friendly manner.

"Had a good night, did you?" he asked with a huge grin.

"I did, John," I happily responded. "I have the best friends ever. By the way, I needed you this afternoon. You were nowhere around."

"I'm sorry to hear that, but someone around here has to work for a living!" he teased. "What did you need, a cup of sugar?" We laughed.

"Funny, John," I responded. "I bought some furniture for my computer room, and I managed to get all the boxes up the stairs but one, which was too heavy."

"So what did you do?" he asked with concern.

"Not a thing!" I flippantly answered. "It's still in my car."

"Well, let's take care of that right now," he offered as we both walked toward the parking lot.

"Oh, I can do this alone!" he said picking it up. "This will be no problem. You get the door."

Up the stairs we went. I couldn't believe how easy it looked for him.

"Where to now?" he asked, looking about the room.

"This is fine. Just put it here," I instructed. "It will eventually go up to the loft."

"Well, then that's where it should go," he said as he lifted it to attempt the curved staircase.

"Thanks so much, John. In Borna I have someone that helps me with things like this."

"Anytime," he said walking back down the stairs. "How about a glass of that delicious wine you had last night, or did you drink it all?" he asked with a grin.

"Ask and you shall receive," I happily answered. "Of course there's some of it left!" We laughed as I went to get the wine. "You don't know how much I appreciate you doing this for me. Have a seat."

"You've got your place looking pretty cool," John observed. "Somehow I didn't figure you to be the contemporary type."

"I know, I'm surprising myself," I admitted. "I have all antiques at the guest house, so I thought it would be refreshing to have a different look here that reflected the lake."

We both sat on the couch with our wine, as if we were longtime friends.

"So when did you decide to leave for Missouri?" he asked with some hesitation.

"I'm going home tomorrow," I quietly said.

"Tomorrow?" he repeated in a louder voice.

I nodded. "I need to get back to get ready for the East Perry Fair," I stated. "I have guests coming and the fair is next weekend."

"So you're rushing home for the county fair," he said in a teasing manner.

"It's a big deal, John," I said as if it were a joke.

"I know all about fairs. I'm just teasing," he admitted. "I have even covered a few. I get it. It's nice you are getting some business from it."

"I know!" I acknowledged proudly.

"You know I had such a great time last night," he said brushing his hair out of his face, "I thought perhaps tomorrow I would be brave enough to ask you out to dinner."

"Oh, that's very sweet, but unnecessary," I politely said. "I actually owe you a meal after such a pleasant dinner last night. Perhaps, when I return."

"When will you return, by the way?" he asked so sincerely.

"It may not be till Thanksgiving or Christmas, depending on when my son decides to make it back here. I really would like it if he came to Borna, since he has yet to visit me there. He has a girlfriend living here in South Haven, so I hope that is going to encourage him to come here for sure."

"I can't wait to meet him," John said as he filled his wine glass. "He's a handsome fella, from what I remember."

"I'd love for you to visit Borna some time," I said catching him by surprise.

"I just may do that if I can stay at Josephine's," he teased.

"Of course, and I will give you the royal treatment," I promised. "I may try to replicate that wonderful meal I owe you." I think I was flirting with him.

"I bet you would like me to leave so you can get ready for your trip, don't you?" he asked, looking deep into my eyes.

I wasn't sure how to answer.

"Well, I know I can't handle another night like last night and get up early," I confessed. "I'm not used to drinking this much wine for days in a row."

He laughed and got up from his seat as if he were leaving. "So, Kate, do you have a boyfriend in Borna?" he asked, catching me off guard.

"No, I really don't," I claimed. "I do have a good male

friend, but that's a long story. I'm just not there to handle much more than that, right now."

He stared at me, crinkling his face. "I guess I understand," he said slowly as if he were digesting my words. "So I can't persuade you to stay just one more night?"

"I'm sorry, John, it would be nice, but I need to stick to my game plan," I explained. "I am finding you extremely attractive and very interesting, which is not a good thing." Oh dear, what had I said?

He chuckled a bit. "So what's wrong with that?" he said, as he looked straight through me. "I feel the same way about you." I smiled and got up out of my chair to pace the floor. "There certainly isn't anything wrong about those kinds of feelings."

"I have to keep reminding myself who I am and who you are," I tried to explain.

He chuckled. "I don't know what that means, but I'll do as you want and tell you goodnight," he said as he put the wine glasses on the counter. "Holler at me in the morning if you need help with anything, okay?"

I nodded. "I'll be fine," I said following him to the door.

Without words, John pulled me close and kissed me. It was delightfully innocent and pleasant, and I encouraged another. I couldn't believe my reflexes. I actually didn't want to let him go.

"You are very special, Kate," he whispered in my ear. "I want to get to know you better."

"I think you are special, too," I whispered, backing away. "You are one delicious trap that I have no business falling into. We must remember we are just good neighbors."

He snickered. "It's really hard for some reason to say

good-bye to you," he admitted like a little boy. "I'll e-mail, text, call, or whatever, okay?"

"I would love that," I said, feeling liberated somehow. "Thank you so much for helping me tonight."

"That's what good neighbors are for!" he said walking out the door.

I closed the door and felt myself shaking inside. I didn't want him to leave! I really enjoyed his company. This was shocking to me. It scared me to think what might have happened here tonight. It was as if my body had been awakened from years of being dormant. I could have listened to him talk all night. He was not just a pretty face, as some would say. I stayed up late packing and planning for the next day, so I wouldn't think about John. Who was that person that flirted and kissed her neighbor? When I got into bed, I couldn't erase my contented smile. Surely I would have pleasant dreams.

Thankfully there was no sign of John when I went to the car the next morning. I took a deep breath and started my car to head back to Borna.

When I stopped for gas, I checked my phone for messages. It was as if I already missed those I was leaving behind. The first text to pop up was Max. He simply said to hurry back soon. I smiled, thinking of him, but he really needed to find someone local that he could enjoy the rest of his retirement years with. That was not going to be me!

I sent Ellie a text telling her I was on my way home. Shortly after that, I was very pleased to see a text from John appear. I was glad to see it, as I had neglected to get contact information from him. His message was brief.

> Good morning beautiful. Have a safe trip.

I smiled, picturing him all ruffled at the early hour.

My trip slowed down with rain near Chicago. It was stressing me out, so I stopped at a Cracker Barrel to have lunch and wait out the heavy rain. I wanted to text John, but searched for the right words.

> I'm halfway home, driving in heavy rain. Thanks again for a fun visit!

> East Perry County, where agriculture and industry meet! Sounds like a road trip!

*Cute,* I thought. I texted him back.

> Just let me know.

Was this a good thing or a passing fancy? Clark didn't text or even use his cell phone. The differences between Clark, Max, and John were amazing.

When the rain stoppped, I got back on the road. So John

was considering a road to trip to Borna. That would prove to be interesting, in more ways than one. I hoped Max didn't decide to do a road trip.

I loved arriving in this sweet little town. I felt like I had never left! Walking into my guest house was extra special with no one else here. For now, it was just mine to enjoy. I checked my messages and the Brueckners confirmed they wanted Josephine's Attic Suite and were arriving on the first day of the fair. I knew nothing about them, other than they had relatives in the area.

After I unpacked, I checked my phone once more for messages from John. I couldn't believe I was responding to this guy who was only my neighbor. I needed to put my Michigan visit aside and concentrate on my life here.

Before the total darkness came that evening, I went outdoors to get my bird's nest so I could plant my smallest violet. I scooped up dirt from my flower bed and the nest appeared to hold the soil nicely. I watered it to see how rapidly the water would escape. I was pleasantly surprise to see that most of it had been absorbed. It turned out very well. I needed to get a photo and e-mail it to Maggie. I may not have the most original pot in the exhibit, but I would have the cutest entry for sure.

Ellie called as I was about to shower. She said she'd be by in the morning to have coffee and retrieve the blueberry scones and wine I always brought her. I thought about suggesting we include Ruth Ann, but decided against it. I only felt comfortable telling Ellie about Max and John. She would not believe how I had gone astray. I had to chuckle to myself.

I checked my phone once more before crawling under

the sheets. No text. Without a second thought I texted him.

> Arrived safely with my blueberry scones. I bet our building is quiet now that your chatty neighbor is gone.

*I clicked on a smiley face. Why did I click on a smiley face?* I fluffed my pillow and got pretty comfy when I heard a text arrive.

> The lake and the condo are very quiet. I am missing my neighbor!

*Very sweet,* I thought, so I simply returned another smiley face. Maybe I should google him before this goes much further.

His travel, non-fiction series appeared immediately. The titles were Know Before You Go, Ask The Locals, and Eat, Drink and Stay. They all sounded great. There was a photo, but no mention of his age. He had received a US Travel Writer's Award for an article he wrote called Traveling Alone.

*I definitely should read that,* I thought.

As I read on, I realized he was a perfect catch for some beautiful, successful, young woman and not a middle-aged widow like me.

*Forget him,* I advised myself.

# CHAPTER 33

I happily embraced Ellie when she walked in the door the next morning. Her eyes went directly to the dining room table, looking for the platter of scones. They were still fresh, so once we poured our coffee, we bit into the delightful texture with moans of delight.

Before I decided to tell her about Max and John, I told her I would be calling Clark today. She said she passed him as she was coming home from work yesterday.

"I know he saw me, but he didn't even honk or wave," Ellie said.

"Very strange! Something is going on, and I am no longer afraid to ask," I said as I poured more coffee.

I slowly introduced the report of my two male friends in South Haven, starting with Max. She was shaking her head in disbelief as I described him. When I told her about John and our dinner, her eyes began to enlarge and she listened more intently. To her credit, she didn't interrupt as I gave all the details.

"You let him kiss you?" she asked as if she didn't hear me correctly.

I nodded and blushed. "I kissed him back!" I bragged as I watched her reaction. "Ellie, this guy could charm anyone, if they let him. I could listen to him talk all night! Please don't make me feel guilty."

"So Miss Meyr is human after all," she said, grinning.

"The way you've been rejecting Clark, I was beginning to wonder. Of course, I'm the last one to make you feel guilty. You won't get into trouble with anyone, but just don't get too carried away with your emotions. You are probably realizing that you have missed out on a lot of living these past years."

"What?" I asked harshly, "I'm not looking for a man, first of all, but what I'm discovering is that I'm not as old as I make myself out to be. I feel young and feminine again. It's such a treat for me to have a man truly listen to me. It's nice to have men appreciate what I have become. I checked John out on Google, and he's got an impressive resume."

"So does the Mr. McFadden that you know," she teased. "Do you think John will really visit here like he said?"

I smiled and liked the thought. "I do!" I answered without hesitation. "He's very curious about East Perry County and, as a travel writer, I think he would have a lot to say about Borna. It would be good exposure for the town."

"Well, the proof is in the pudding, as they say," Ellie said shaking her head. "Before you know it, you'll have a whole guest house of men suitors."

We laughed.

Before Ellie left, we went outside so I could show her my bird's nest. She loved it.

"I saw Anna at the bank, and she's using an old work shoe she found in the barn," she revealed. "She's still talking about the runaway bride from last week."

We laughed and acknowledged the whole town knew about that wedding.

"I just have one couple staying here for the fair," I shared with Ellie.

"You know, it's not a very good weekend for us at the

winery when the fair is going on," Ellie complained with her hands on her hips. "Most everyone stays at the fair pretty late in the evening, but that's okay. Say, let me know what Clark has to say when you talk to him."

I nodded. "Oh, I will, if I can track him down," I assured her. "I really would like to talk to him face to face instead of over the phone. He wouldn't pick it up anyway if I called."

"Well, if you're not busy today, why don't you drive out to his place and confront him?" Ellie suggested.

"You think if I bring him blueberry scones and wine he'd turn me away?" I teased.

She laughed.

When Ellie left, I decided I wasn't going to call Clark ahead of time. If he wasn't home, I would just leave him a little basket of my goodies on the front porch. I would include my business card with maybe a lipstick impression and say "Love from South Haven." On the drive out, I asked God for some help. I think having been with Max and John recently helped me become more confident with relationships. I felt I needed to be more aggressive with Clark. If it turned him off, so be it.

I was beginning to think I was lost when I recognized a barn along the side of the road from my previous visit. When I turned on his gravel road, the only vehicle of Clark's at home was his SUV.

As I was about to get out of the car, a sudden crackle of thunder erupted and rain started pouring down. I was hoping to make a dash to the porch without getting my basket wet. I knocked at the door, with no response. I waited a bit, in case he was asleep. I tried again, and it became obvious he wasn't at home. With the storm increasing, I placed the basket close to the door so it wouldn't get wet. I started to make a quick dash to my car, and Clark pulled in next to me. I stood still in the rain, making sure it was really him.

"That's not a good place to stand if you don't want to get hit by lightning," he yelled out his window.

I ran back to the porch, but my clothes were already soaked. Clark got out of the truck and shook his head in disgust. I grabbed my basket and eagerly followed him inside his cabin. I stood on the braided rug, as water dripped from my body.

"This storm came up so suddenly," I said trying to wipe the rain from my face. "I brought you a peace offering of scones and wine, since you've been ignoring me for some reason." In silence, he handed me a towel to dry myself off.

"Thanks, but why drive out here, for heaven's sake?" he asked as he turned on his tea kettle.

"Look, I don't know what I did to offend you, but you left my bed in the middle of the night without saying anything, and then you continued to ignore me, like that night didn't happen."

"Look lady, first of all I wasn't in your bed, and thank God I wasn't," he harshly responded. "Drink some of this tea!" He handed me a mug to drink from.

I reluctantly sat down and put the towel around my shoulder to take away my chill. This was not going well.

"Look, I admit I had too much to drink that night, so forget anything I might have said."

"Nothing was said that you have to be sorry for," I meekly replied. It was then I looked past Clark and saw his carved tree sitting on his fireplace mantle. I got out of my chair to examine it further. "What is this doing here?" I said accusingly.

"You may want to tell me about that, Miss Meyr!" he said with a raised tone and dagger eyes.

"How did you get this?" I was now shaking.

"If you really want to know, I purchased it off of eBay! I guess you could say I had to buy my own work back!"

"That's impossible," I shouted back

"Thankfully a good friend of mine spotted it going up for sale and told me about it," he said in a huff. "So it's back where it should have stayed in the first place."

"That's pretty harsh," I accused. "That tree was stolen from my guest house when I had the quilters staying with me. I knew exactly which person took it, but I couldn't prove it. I even asked for Ruth Ann's help, because she knew the girls pretty well. She didn't have any luck solving the mystery either!"

He seemed amused, and he twisted his chin. "Did you think to even tell me about what happened?" he asked in anger. "I may have wanted to know about this crime that involved my work."

"I couldn't, I wouldn't," I said in confusion. "It was your work, but my property."

"So did you report it stolen to the authorities?"

I shook my head. "No, I couldn't do that!"

He glared at my answer. "

"That would mean telling you, and I didn't want a rumor flying about things being stolen at my guest house. I really took it on myself to solve the crime."

"That didn't go so well, did it?" he said in a calmer voice. "When I was at your house last, I thought maybe you sold it or gave it away when I didn't see it on your mantle."

"Why would I do that?" My voice was now shaking. "This

one quilter, by the name of Tina, had admired it and was frustrated because she wanted to purchase some of your work when she was here. I just know it was her. I am so, so sorry." My head was now between my hands looking down at the table.

"I have no reason to doubt your story, Kate, but you were sending me strong signals that night on the deck that you weren't ready for any relationship, so I figured I wasn't the same friend to you that I thought I was. You really didn't handle this very well."

"No, I may not have, but neither did you," I defended, as I got up from my chair. "You don't handle friendships very well at all. You're even ignoring friends like Ellie and Trout, who did nothing to you."

He looked at me strangely. "Well, I just haven't been in the mood for small talk lately, and I knew if I saw them, your name would come up in conversation," he explained. "I'm sorry they took offense. I have a lot on my mind."

"Aren't you sorry I took offense?" I asked in a sharp tone. "I am sorry about you having to buy back your darn tree. I'll pay you back, if you like."

He was stunned.

I walked toward the door to leave. There wasn't more I could say. We had misjudged each other, and at least now we cleared the air between us.

"See you around, I guess," I said in a low voice, as I opened the door to hard rain. I kept going and he did nothing to stop me. I knew our stubborn personalities were a match. I slammed the car door very hard and drove away. I didn't know if the water on my face was from my tears or the pouring rain.

# CHAPTER 34

The next couple of days, I prepared food for my guests and studied the schedule for the upcoming fair. I didn't want to miss a thing. I told Ellie I felt relieved the tree was back in Clark's hands, but reminded her that the thief was still at large. I could tell she also felt bad for Clark, so I thought best to drop the subject.

The Friendship Circle had a quick meeting at Ellen's house to firm up our display for the fair. We all brought our planters so Ellen could now apply her magic touch for some kind of display. We met on the lovely patio behind her house and enjoyed lemonade and a variety of fancy cookies. I carefully carried my bird nest on a platter, so I wouldn't ruin it. Everyone was very creative with their planters. Of course, Ellie brought her wine bottle planter, but there was also an old shoe, a tractor seat, a blue tin tea kettle, a bowling ball, a 1950s jewelry box, a lunch box, a pair of red mittens, and a crock-pot. Each one was sillier than the next. We were all laughing.

"Ellen, where is yours?" asked Mary Catherine as she looked around.

Ellen grinned. "I'm afraid it's a little bigger than what you all have," she began to explain. "I asked Oscar to build me a wooden cradle so I could fill it with baby's breath." She opened the garage door and there it was. It was adorable as we all imagined. It would make the grand centerpiece for sure!

We all clapped at our approval.

I left before everyone enjoyed the refreshments, as I needed to get home in time to meet the Brueckners. As I returned home, I could already see an increase in traffic due to the fair. I was somewhat disappointed my house wasn't full to capacity for the weekend. I guess there were still some folks that didn't know a guest house in Borna even existed. Yards along Main Street were immaculately trimmed and fences were freshly painted for passersby.

Around 3:00 p.m. the Brueckners arrived. They appeared to be in their fifties and casually dressed for the weekend. Before they stepped in the front door, they admired what all I had done to the property since they were in Borna. I offered them some refreshments after I checked them in and explained the guest book and signature guest quilt. Mr. and Mrs. Brueckner had both grown up in East Perry and dated through high school. Mrs. Brueckner was a Meisner growing up in Eggersville before she married. It was a popular German name in the county.

"So tell me, what was it like going to the fair as you both grew up?" I asked after they accepted a cup of coffee.

"It was really more exciting for me than Christmas," Mr. Brueckner confessed with enthusiasm. "I grew up on a farm, so I always had a calf or pig to enter for competition. If I didn't win a ribbon, one of my brothers did for sure!" He chuckled with pride.

"My family just baked," she bragged. "We baked all kinds of things and we still do today. I can't wait to see what will all be there. My Aunt Wilma always entered one of her quilts. She still quilts with the church ladies and always wins some kind of ribbon. My whole family quilts, but she was the only one that would ever agree to enter the fair. I take it you've not been to the fair before?"

"No, I haven't," I admitted. "I can't wait."

"Well, Pop, we'd better get settled and changed to make it to Aunt Wilma's for supper," Mrs. Brueckner warned.

I thought it was cute the way she called him Pop.

"Your place is sure nice! Say, Pop, we need to sign the quilt before we go up."

We all walked to the guest quilt.

"I think I may have made this pattern years ago," Mrs. Brueckner said viewing it closer. "This is a lovely idea. It's like the quilt wants to speak to you with all those names staring at you."

We laughed, but if she only knew how true that was.

The parade was scheduled for 10:00, so after I served the Brueckners their breakfast, I would be on my way. Hopefully they would enjoy my muffins, despite their family's reputation for baking.

The next morning, Mr. Brueckner was up at the crack of dawn, helping himself to some coffee. He and his wife both had heavy German accents, which was endearing to me. When his wife joined us, she was all excited about seeing some of her relatives in the parade. She bragged that one year her father was the Grand Marshal.

"Being the Grand Marshal is a pretty big deal," claimed Mr. Brueckner. "Last year Sharla Lee from the museum was the Grand Marshal. She's really done a lot for this community. You know she's not a native of the area. I don't know some of the newer people to the community, and I haven't heard who the GM will be this year. They try to keep it a secret."

*Wow, it was a big deal,* I assessed.

"This breakfast is mighty good, Kate, especially these muffins," Mrs. Brueckner bragged. "I'd love to have the recipe. Do you have a guest house cookbook?"

I smiled and shook my head. Another idea, I supposed.

"They are just as good as yours, Mom," Mr. Brueckner teased.

I couldn't believe he called her Mom. That was another generational habit I noticed from older couples here.

They excused themselves from the table, and I began clearing the dishes. I needed to check in with Ellie before I left.

"Good morning, are you going to the parade?" I asked when Ellie answered.

"I can't afford to be stuck in the traffic, Kate," she explained. "If we get busy here that would be a problem, so I'm not even sure I'll get to the fair at all. I would love to see our display, so please take some photos."

"I will, but I surely was hoping we could go together," I responded. "Promise me next year you'll make plans ahead for us to go, okay?"

She humored my request.

"Okay, I better get going," I said, looking out the window. "The traffic is already slow outside my door. Talk to you later."

I locked the house and got on my way. I certainly wasn't going to miss "The best little fair in the land," as they advertised. The traffic was bumper to bumper as we got closer to Dresden. Ellie said most folks parked in the surrounding fields. As luck would have it, I managed to steal a spot alongside the road when a car pulled out. I knew it would be a good hike to the fairgrounds on foot, but that was okay.

The yards were packed with relatives and friends who were cooking outdoors and drinking beer out of their coolers. I walked along with the crowd, heading to the center of the fair. Most of them were carrying lawn chairs. I supposed it was for watching the parade or visiting with their friends.

When I finally got to the fairgrounds, the parade had not yet started, so I made my rounds visiting the many booths and outside buildings. It wasn't just food, crafts, and beverage vendors, it was companies which represented the farming community. They mostly drew clusters of men who visited outside the tents.

I knew Peggy and Betsy were working in the cheese stand, so I made sure to try one of the popular white cheese sandwiches. They were thrilled to see me, and the sandwich they presented was delicious. What a unique food offering that would go great with the beer and catfish booths. I wanted to try all the food like everyone around me.

In the distance, I heard the parade coming so I managed to squeeze between a little girl and a lady with a cane sitting on a long bench. They were grinning ear to ear as they awaited the excitement. Children were running in the street with excitement as they looked anxiously down the road. The nice, heavy set lady said she had sat in the same spot for many years.

The Grand Marshal led the parade in a carriage, but I didn't know him, of course. The lady said his name, which I didn't recognize, but I clapped out loud as he passed. She said he was most deserving. The little girl was kept busy looking for the first morsel of candy to be thrown her way. What fun this had to be for her. Between floats, tractors passed of every size and color. I didn't know they made so many different kinds. Two large, local school bands marched by, which was my favorite part of the parade. Candy was thrown from floats, cars, and walkers in the parade. Needless to say, the little girl was out in the street most of the time, picking up candy which she proudly showed us when she returned to her seat. The parade went on and on it seemed. I think there were as many folks in the parade as there were bystanders.

When it was finally over, I joined the others to head to the exhibit hall. It was shoulder to shoulder as we went down the stairs to see the exhibits. It was just like in the old time movies. There were shelves and shelves of canned food ranging from pickles to jellies. Hand crocheted and knitted items lay on tables. Many of them had ribbons attached. A variety of artwork was also shown on shelves and tables. Quilts of every size and color lined the walls of the hall. My idea of providing a Borna quilt raffle once again popped in my head as such a good idea. The volunteers sitting at the door would be the perfect folks to sell the tickets and the quilt could be displayed behind them.

Unsurprisingly, Ruth Ann's quilt titled Sunrise had a blue ribbon hanging on its border. What a talent she had! I started taking many photos. Plants and flowers of different varieties were displayed on the stage. Everyone was posing for photographs with their ribbon achievements. It was a happy place. I was happy.

All of a sudden there it was, a sign that read: Plants Out of Their Pots by the Borna Friendship Circle. Underneath the title was a list of all our names. I couldn't believe I had an entry in a fair for the very first time. I was so proud.

"Did you see it?" Ellen's voiced yelled from behind me with excitement. "We got a blue ribbon!"

"How wonderful!" I responded with delight. "This would not have been possible without you, Ellen. This was a lot of work, and you brought it together. It all looks great."

She beamed with pride. "It was such fun and your little nest is just the cutest thing I ever saw," she complimented back.

"I have to admit, it says cute all over it!" I bragged, wanting to touch it.

I took some pictures and admitted I was proud of my little part. I stood there for a while listening to everyone's reaction. Each person had their favorite, so it truly was a conversation piece in the exhibit hall. What could we do to top this for next year?

I left the fairgrounds feeling I really belonged. I loved seeing many friendly, familiar faces and how folks enjoyed each other's company on benches and groups of lawn chairs. I loved that children ran freely among the fairgrounds, enjoying their friends and ice cream cones. I knew one of the popular highlights of the fair was the mule jumping contest. It generated the most publicity for the fair. As amusing and unique as it sounded, I kept walking to my car to get on my way. I could also imagine that as the night went along, the fair would become even merrier.

When I finally got back to my car, I remembered Ellie saying how her place could sometimes be slow during the fair, so I decided to stop at the winery on the way home to say hello. She was right. There were very few cars around, even though happy hour was approaching. She and Trout were both surprised to see me.

"Don't tell me you got bored at the fair and decided to come here instead," Ellie teased.

Trout chuckled.

"It would have been so much more fun if you had come with me." I teased with a big smile.

I filled Ellie in on every detail and followed it up with my phone photos. I could tell I was bringing back past memories of the fair she had often enjoyed. She loved the photos of our plant display and beamed at the news of our blue ribbon.

"Did you see the Brueckners?" she curiously asked.

"No, but I'm sure I saw all of their relatives!" She laughed.

"So who was the Grand Marshal this year?" Trout asked.

"You may know him I suppose, but the name on the sign was Pastor Dr. Paul Winningham, Winniferd, or Willmington," I tried to recall. They both laughed. "The lady next to me said he was the pastor from Unionville and that everyone loved him."

"Oh sure, now I know who you mean," jumped in Ellie. "He's done a lot for East Perry. I met him and his wife at the museum where they sometimes volunteer. He's quite the runner too, I understand. That was a good choice, don't you think, Trout?"

He nodded as he continued to wash wine glasses.

Ellie and I went to a table for two as Trout brought us glasses of wine. He said we had to celebrate our blue ribbon and me, for surviving my first fair. I agreed.

"The drinks are on me," added Ellie. "It's likely the only time you and I will win a ribbon for anything, anywhere." We laughed and clanked our glasses.

Just then a text message rang on my phone. It was from John. I turned my stool around to read it.

> Giving you plenty of notice, dear neighbor. I've cleared my schedule to visit Borna Thanksgiving weekend. I'm missing you and I want to write a story about Borna for the magazine. Will you be there and do you have a room to spare?

I wanted to fall off my chair. Ellie looked at me for a response.

John was calling my bluff about a visit. Now what? Ellie was watching me closely.

"Is everything okay?" she asked as she helped herself to some cheese and crackers.

"John is coming for Thanksgiving," I said slowly like I couldn't believe it.

"Well, how about those apples," Ellie teased with a big grin. "This guy does have a thing for you, and it's going to be real interesting, girlfriend."

I took a deep breath. "He's coming to write a story about East Perry County for his magazine," I explained. "Here, read this." I handed her my phone.

"I'm just seeing the part that says he misses you," she teased. "East Perry is just benefiting from it. That's pretty cool, really. I hope he includes my winery!"

"It's less than two months away, so we'll see if he changes his mind," I said to make light of the news.

"Aren't you going to respond?" Ellie asked with a suggestive grin on her face. "You want to see him, don't you? If you really want him out of your life, now is the time to send that message. If you don't, tell him you have booked his room! It's as simple as that!"

Ellie was right. Now would be the time to send a message. I had to admit I liked him a lot, despite our age difference. The publicity for East Perry would be wonderful. I liked the idea that I would have been a part of that. John would be fun to have around and possibly dangerous. Ellie watched as I sent him a welcoming text that I had booked his room!

After a couple of hours with Ellie, I had to get home and prepare tomorrow's breakfast for the Brueckners. My mood was quite happy from the fair, the wine, and hearing from John.

It was 10:00 p.m. when the Brueckners arrived back at the guest house. I was in my bedroom answering my e-mails, when they passed my room to go up to the attic. I'm sure they were exhausted from a full day and wanted their privacy. I was about to turn off the lights when I got a text from Jack. He said he was going to spend next weekend at the condo in South Haven. It was the only time he and Jill could get together. I promptly let him know how pleased I was, even though I knew it was likely planned so they would have the condo to themselves. I couldn't wait to tell Maggie. Perhaps I should tell John to keep an eye out for them. What would Jack say if he knew John and I had become close friends? That little condo of mine may become its own little Peyton Place.

# CHAPTER 35

After serving the Brueckners a hearty breakfast, I fixed up a basket of my muffins for them to take home with them. Mr. Brueckner was elated and said they wanted to book a room next year for the fair. Repeat business was what I was looking for. I wished all my guests would be this courteous and appreciative.

As soon as they left, Susie arrived to do some cleaning and start the laundry. I had planned to get ready for church, so I left her a long list of chores to complete. She once again commented on the missing carving and what a crime it was. It was likely a frequent topic of conversation between her and Cotton on any given day. I didn't respond, nor did I want to share the news that the tree was back where it belonged. They would find out soon enough. I hated the thought of adding cameras to the downstairs, but I was determined this incident would never happen again.

"We had so much fun at the fair," reported Susie as she got out her cleaning supplies. "I just loved the plant display, and your little bird nest was my very favorite. I just couldn't believe what you all thought of."

"Thanks, it was fun," I said remembering. "I got to see most everything except the mule jumping contest."

"Oh, it's Cotton's favorite part of the fair," Susie said with a chuckle in her voice. "The animal rights folks don't always appreciate that, you know."

I wondered about that, but stayed silent.

"Say, Kate, were you still there when the ambulance showed up for Harold?"

"No! Do you mean our Harold from the hardware store?" I quickly asked with concern.

"Yeah, he had a heart attack, I think," Susie said while she kept cleaning. "I don't know much else, but he collapsed in front of the fish stand."

"Oh, that's awful," I sadly responded. "I'll have to call the store tomorrow to find out how he's doing. I bet his wife, Milly, is most upset."

I left for church, hoping I would hear more about Harold. I was also hoping to see Ellen and Oscar, so I could invite them to dinner one night.

When I walked in the church, I immediately saw Emma, so I sat next to her. She was always so happy to see me. We briefly chatted about the fair, and then she told me that Harold was in stable condition. That was good news, and I was thankful. The sermon was on second chances. The message was to become a better person, even though we may have made poor choices in our past. It was positive and right to the point, which was what I liked about Pastor Hermann's sermons. In his closing he said a prayer for Harold. It was special touches like this that made living in a small community so uplifting. Everyone was pulling for one another. Everyone loved Harold, and there were many folks with tears in their eyes.

I didn't see Oscar or Ellen, so they must have gone to an earlier service. Emma and I went into the fellowship hall to have a cup of coffee when the service ended. Ruth Ann suddenly showed up to join us.

"Congratulations ladies on your blue ribbon," she gushed.

"Look who's talking!" I teased. "Congrats to you also on your spectacular quilt."

"Thanks, Kate," she blushed. "Another blue ribbon never gets old. Say, Kate, I have a word with you before you leave today?"

"No problem, Ruth Ann," I said.

"I have to get going to my son's for dinner, so you girls go right ahead and visit," Emma encouraged.

We both wished Emma a good day, and Ruth Ann sat down in her chair in silence. I looked at her to respond. What now?

"I heard from Carole yesterday," she began. "She was beside herself in telling me that her friend Tina had been arrested for shoplifting in a St. Louis department store." I was stunned. "I thought of you right away, Kate. Carole said she was reselling stolen items on eBay. She's in big trouble, I'm afraid. I didn't say anything to the others about the missing carving, but now I realize it was likely her. I am so, so sorry. I feel somewhat responsible. I just can't believe she would do such a thing."

It was horrible and yet a relief that Tina was caught. It would have taken me forever to solve that crime. I guess it's true that what goes around comes around. Eventually the truth would have surfaced. I told Ruth Ann about Clark getting his tree back. She was devastated that he had to buy it. We both felt justice would be done to Tina. Since I now knew the whole story, I would have to tell Clark about it all at some point. Right now, I didn't care to talk to him.

"So how could Clark ever think that you would sell his piece?" Ruth Ann asked, shaking her head.

"There's a little more going on here than you realize," I vaguely indicated. "It's hard to explain when you have two independent people like Clark and me. We're stubborn about our feelings and just trying to protect ourselves. It drives me crazy."

"I see," she simply said. "Thinking about how the quilting retreat all went down, I'm not sure I want to try that again."

"I sure hope you do!" I encouraged. "It's a grand idea for both of us. They loved you and your class. I enjoyed having them here. It was just unfortunate there was one bad apple!"

She nodded. "Say, on a more positive note, I keep meaning to tell you that I have my first wedding reception booked," she bragged. "I also have dates on my calendar for my smaller meeting room. I think that is probably going to be my bread and butter." She beamed with pride.

"That's wonderful! I will try to remember that space as well, and our Friendship Circle should be a good resource for you." She nodded and smiled at the thought.

"I also have an open house scheduled in a couple of weeks, which will showcase the place for future dates. I may pick up some holiday business from that."

"Awesome," I said, getting ready to leave. "Let me know if you need some help."

I had happy thoughts for Ruth Ann as I drove home. She was a smart businesswoman and I knew this banquet facility would be a big hit in Borna.

On my way home, I decided to pick up Marv's fried chicken for my lunch. The parking lot was full from the after church crowd, but I was no longer intimidated to walk in the place as I had been I arrived here in Borna. Luckily I grabbed a stool at the end of the bar, as an older gentleman was just leaving.

Marv came right over to greet me with his usual smile.

"Nice to see you, Miss Meyr," he said with his usual big grin. "What can I do for you today?"

"When are you going to start calling me Kate?" He blushed and I smiled. "Of course I'm here to get your Sunday special of fried chicken and the usual sides. No one makes fried chicken and chili like you do, Marv."

"You are way too kind, Kate. You want that to go?" he asked as his eyes looked above me.

I nodded. "Say, what do you hear about Harold these days?" I asked, figuring if anyone knew the latest, Marv would.

"Oh, he's home and doin' pretty good," he reported as he looked distracted. "Milly said it'll be hard to keep him out of the store."

"Oh, that is good news," I said taking a sip of the water Marv had put in front of me.

"We have got to quit meeting like this," Clark's voice said from behind me.

I jumped and turned around in total confusion.

"Marv, the special sounds good to me, too. You may as well make mine to go but, I don't like eating alone." He had a smirk on his face as he looked at me. "I hope you don't mind of I join you somewhere. I promise to mind my manners his time."

I couldn't help but smile. I knew he was referring to his leaving my house in the middle of the night. "So you decided to make nice, huh?" I said not completely turning around.

"I think I'm capable, and when I saw your car here, I thought you'd be a real nice lady to have Sunday dinner with." He teased with that sexy grin of his. This guy was so unpredictable.

"I guess there's nothing wrong with a man who's offered to buy you a meal more than once from this place," I confessed as Marv handed Clark our food order. "Thank you."

He nodded in acceptance.

"I'll meet you at your house," Clark ordered.

*He can sure be bossy at times,* I thought. He had a charming way of getting by with that.

I rushed home to place two settings at the table, and poured us two glasses of water before letting him in the door. This was going to be interesting, and somehow I had lost my appetite. Without knocking, he walked on in the house and handed me the dinners. I remained silent as I placed them on the table.

"Oh, I forgot something in the car," he noted as he turned around to go back to his SUV.

I was placing some napkins on our placemats when Clark walked in with a huge box.

"What in the world is that?" I asked, getting closer to look.

Without a word, he unpacked the tree carving and sat it back on the mantle where it had been. I didn't know what to say at first. Still silent, he took the empty box and placed it in the sunporch.

"Clark, I can't let you do this. It's not right," I stated with a heavy tone.

"What's not right is our relationship, and I want to make it right," he said coming close to me. "We have something special going on here, and I've been really bad about communicating with you. It's not my strong point, as you know. You're important to me, so I need to share some things with you."

I was puzzled. "What do you mean by that?" I asked as I sat down.

"I tracked you down today, not only to give you this tree back, but to ask you a favor," he said pulling up a chair. Now it was getting interesting.

"I've been dealing with something that's not been easy to share with anyone, especially you," he began. I stared at him for more information. "I want to make this explanation as simple as possible, so don't ask a lot of questions, okay?"

I nodded my head without saying a word.

"Some time back, I was diagnosed with prostate cancer." He now stood up, and I wasn't sure if I heard him correctly. "Mine is a more aggressive cancer, so they want me to start treatment in St. Louis next week. I've been putting it off. I'll be gone for a while, and the favor I'm asking is that you keep this to yourself. This means from people you are close to, like Ellie." He paused while I was feeling faint with fear.

"You know what a private person I am, so if you really want to be helpful to me, you'll keep this close." He paused as he took a deep breath. "I should be able to beat this, but the bad news is my father wasn't that lucky. The hereditary factor is rather important here, the Doc said." I wasn't sure I could speak and questions were zooming around in my head. "Okay, I'll try to answer any questions you might have, if I can."

I swallowed before I spoke. "So this is what's been bothering you?" I shyly asked. "How long have you been dealing with this?"

"Well, it's certainly been on my mind, and I haven't exactly felt very sociable," he said as he paced the floor. "My early symptoms had me seein' a local doctor, but then he sent me to St. Louis to pursue it further. I haven't seen a doctor since I sprained my ankle, ten years ago or so. I've been pretty healthy."

"What kind of treatment will you have, and how long will you be gone?" I asked as my anxiety rose.

"Good questions," he replied as he touched his chin to think. "They are trying radiation first. Most folks do well, some require more. I'm not sure I can say how long I'll be gone. I would guess at least two months. I promise I will be in communication with you, Kate. I don't want you to be checking on me. I'll be in touch and, actually, I'll be able to do some work where I'll be stayin'. I'm in good hands but would rather not share that information." I swallowed deeply, not knowing what to say. Why was he so secretive about all this? "Most folks around here are used to me being gone, so I'm counting on you to tell them I'm out of town on business if they ask. As you have mentioned many times, this is a small town and I don't want them counting me dead until I am."

I wanted to break down and cry, but I knew that wouldn't be a very good idea right now.

"Of course, I'll do whatever you like, Clark," I sadly responded. "I'm so sorry you have to go through this. Please remember everyone is different, and just because your dad died from cancer doesn't mean you will."

He smiled, knowing he had revealed pretty heavy information for me to digest. "I understand, but it's a fact I can't ignore," he noted. "I was hoping this would be a slower growing cancer than I had read about. My biggest concern is that it will metastasize."

Now I was feeling sick and excused myself to go to the bathroom. When I finally returned, Clark knew he had truly upset me. He took my hand and pulled me over to his lap.

"If I didn't think you could handle this, I wouldn't have told you," he said in a soft voice. "I'm in good physical shape and I can beat this. I don't want you to worry. I'm sorry I've not made more advances in regard to our relationship, but this was hanging over my head. You go about your business, and I will take care of mine. We will always be friends, and if we can take it further, that's a bonus, right?" He smiled and kissed me on the cheek. I turned his face and kissed him on the lips. I wanted him to know I really cared, and that it wasn't a sign of sympathy. He pulled away with a big smile.

"You are something, Kate Meyr," he said as he held me close. "I hope I won't regret sharing this with you. The last thing I want from you is sympathy. I should have been more open about my feelings, but I knew you weren't ready and frankly I wasn't sure about myself. I knew the first moment we met that you weren't going to disappear out of my head. We'll see what happens when I come home, okay?"

I nodded with my watery eyes. My feelings were all too jumbled inside to respond.

"The chicken's getting cold, we better chow down," he said avoiding any more sweet nothings. This was truly Clark.

I smiled and got up from his lap. "Good idea," I said taking a deep breath. "Is there anything I can do for you at the cabin while you're gone?"

He smiled. "You mean like feeding the deer family that shows up each day?"

I laughed, remembering the scene. "Yeah, what are they going to do without you?" I joked.

"Let me think about that offer and get back to you, okay?" he said as he took his first bite off of a chicken leg. "Man, this is good, even cold!"

"Men can eat under almost any circumstances, can't they?" I teased.

He laughed, taking another bite.

We actually enjoyed our meal, as we both felt like a large stone had been removed from our relationship. It was not a pretty story to hear about, but I felt privileged Clark had shared a very private part of his life with me. I could tell his spirits were raised, as he continued to tease me about various things in our conversation.

When Clark left two hours later, he told me again he would be in touch before he left. This news was going to take me a while to adjust to, and he knew it. He blew me a kiss as he pulled out of the driveway. This was not the Clark I knew before. I suppose when one faces a scary moment like he was facing, one evaluates what's really important and what is not. I prayed to God for a complete and quick recovery for Clark.

As I now replayed our conversation in my head, I was relieved that Clark left our relationship open. Who would know how he would still feel about me after his treatment and time away from Borna? I was relieved I had time to digest things as well. Clark was special to me, but how special and what would that require? I walked back into the house and stared at Clark's tree on the mantle. Wait till Ellie hears the tree was returned. How would I be able to keep Clark's secret? Could my two best friends accept my explanation about Clark being gone?

I was pleased with Clark opening the door to his inner feelings about me. I was grateful he didn't tell me he loved me, or I would have been lost for words. This was not a time to say things to each other we may regret, because we were caught up in the moment of this horrific challenge. We seemed to be in different places in this relationship and yet bonded. I was just feeling open to responding to my feminine desires since I was back from South Haven, so where was I heading? Time would tell, I supposed.

I was mentally exhausted and just wanted to lie down. As I headed toward the stairs, I glanced fondly at my guest quilt. I was so lucky to be grounded with my guest house and East Perry County friends. I was happy how the names were slowly filling in on the quilt blocks. I sat on the bottom step to admire it and wondered if Josephine was with me in my sadness. Perhaps she would guide me through this in some way. She certainly had no problem letting her feelings be known

I walked over to caress its precisely pieced blocks, when I noticed that Clark's initials were missing from the quilt. I double-checked to make sure. I couldn't believe she would choose to remove his initials, when she knew I was so fond of him. I kept staring and looking where his initials were, like I had to be mistaken. Josephine had to know how important Clark was to this house. He worked long hours here and loved this house almost as much as I did. What was going on? Was his absence on the quilt telling me he would not be around anymore? Could Josephine's activity on my quilt actually reveal the past and predict my future?

# RECIPIES FROM EAST PERRY

## Home Made Wheat Bread

- 2 cups all-purpose flour
- 3 tablespoons vegetable oil
- 1 package rapid rise yeast
- 1 teaspoon salt
- 1 cup whole wheat flour
- 3 tablespoons sugar
- 1 cup hot milk

Combine 1 cup all-purpose flour, yeast, sugar and salt. Add the hot milk and oil. Mix. Add the whole wheat flour and mix. Gradually add the second cup of all-purpose flour, mixing to create stiff dough that pulls away from the mixing bowl. On a floured surface, knead the dough for 2-4 minutes. Rest for 10 minutes, then roll into a rectangle. Roll up jellyroll fashion, pinching ends together. Fold in half and place into a well-greased bread pot. Cover pot with a piece of oiled plastic wrap and tea towel. Let rise for 30-40 minutes. Place in cold oven. Set temperature to 350 degrees and bake for 25-35 minutes or until golden brown. Enjoy!

## Egg Custard Pie

- 3 eggs
- 4 tablespoon sugar
- 1½ cups milk
- ½ teaspoon vanilla

Heat the milk. Beat the eggs and sugar together. Pour hot milk slowly into egg mixture. Add vanilla. Pour into unbaked pie shell and bake 375 degrees until custard is set and crust is brown. It makes a large pie. Enjoy!

# Blueberry Muffins

- 2 eggs
- 1 cup milk
- ½ cup cooking oil
- 3 cups flour
- 1 cup sugar
- 4 teaspoon baking powder
- 1 teaspoon salt
- 2 cups of the larger fresh or frozen blueberries
- Crumb topping or light icing is optional

To prepare batter, combine eggs, milk, and oil in a bowl. In a separate bowl, combine flour, sugar, baking powder, and salt. Stir wet ingredients until just moistened. Fold in blueberries. Spoon generous amounts of batter into paper-lined muffin cups. Add any topping at this time. Bake at 400 degrees for 20-30 minutes.

# Blueberry Scones

- 2 cups sifted flour
- 3 teaspoons baking powder
- 1 teaspoon salt
- 2 tablespoons sugar
- ⅓ cup butter or margarine
- ⅓ cup buttermilk
- 1 egg
- 1 cup fresh or dry-packed frozen blueberries

Sift dry ingredients and cut in butter with knives or pastry blender. Add buttermilk to egg (reserving 1 Tbsp. unbeaten egg white.) Beat until blended. Pour into dry ingredients all at once, stirring quickly. Lightly fold in blueberries. Turn out on slightly floured board. Pat into ¼ or ½ inch thickness. Cut into squares, triangles or diamonds with floured knife. Brush with egg white diluted with one teaspoon of water. Sprinkle with granulated sugar. Bake on cookie sheet in hot oven at 425 degree's for 10-15 minutes. Makes 15 to 20 medium scones. When cooled, ice with a light, white icing. (optional.)

# EAST PERRY COUNTY SERIES

Journey to East Perry County in this dynamic series
about love, friendship, and staying strong.

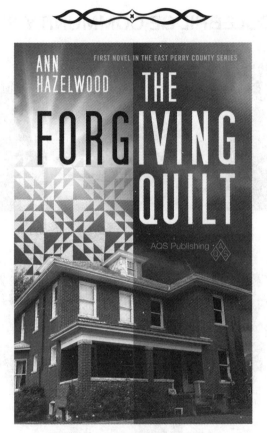

**PRINT AND E-BOOK EDITIONS AVAILABLE**

"East Perry County is the perfect fictional setting for Ann's new series. There is no
place with more authentic German-American culture, beautiful landscapes, and
memorable characters. I cannot wait to begin her journey."
—Carla Jordan,
Director of Lutheran Heritage Center and Cape County History Center
Cape Girardeau, Missouri

"I have really enjoyed reading Ann Hazelwood's Colebridge Series. I found it
uplifting and charming. I'm looking forward to reading more of her work."
— Jacalyn Ryberg
Las Cruces, New Mexico

# More Books from AQS

# Ann Hazelwood

*American Quilter's Society* Bestselling Author

## THE COLEBRIDGE COMMUNITY SERIES

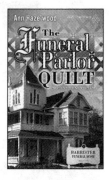

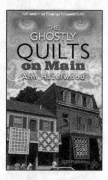
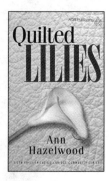

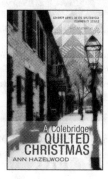